ON THE EDGE

TONY ASHMAN

For Lis
This would not
have been possible
without you

TONY ASHMAN

ON THE

EDGE

ON THE EDGE

First published in Great Britain in paperback, October 2018
by Paul Dickson, 8 Bridge Court, Fishergate, Norwich NR3 1UE
T. 01603 666011, paul@pauldicksonbooks.co.uk
www.pauldicksonbooks.co.uk

ISBN Paperback 9780995618770
ISBN e-book 9780995618787

A CIP catalogue record from this book is available from the British Library.

Designed by Brendan Rallison
Printed in Norwich by InterPrint

PROLOGUE

The prisoner teetered on the very edge of the roof, peering down at the spiked iron railings sixty feet below. Blood trickled from his trembling wounds, tracking across his skin, soaking into his cotton convict shirt. A few drops escaped, drifting through the air towards freedom. A light summer shower of ruby rain.

He twisted to gaze behind him at the evening sun. For the last time. Its rays were reflected by the oozing blood. He studied the flow. It was strangely pretty.

He allowed himself precious seconds to experience the sublime spectacle of heather-coated fells. On the nearby river sunbeams sparkled across rafts of dancing ripples. A kestrel was making the most of the breeze, hovering above the riverbank at the same height as the roof.

The prisoner winced. The glass cuts on his wrists and face were painful, intensely painful. But it would soon be over. His heart had been pounding against the wall of his chest just minutes ago. Now it slowed. He was gaining control. He was ready.

He turned back to face the edge to discover that he didn't know whether to dive or jump. Surely, he thought, head first is the best way to go. He bent his knees a little and held his hands out in front.

Sounds of movement on the roof. They're coming! He bent his knees a bit more, his centre of gravity tipping forward. He took a deep breath. Ready.

A distraction. A glint of light from a distant house. He squinted at an open window from which a motionless figure stared back at him. A female figure.

Noises behind him, coming closer. It's now or never.

The figure in the window remained perfectly still, definitely looking straight at him. For a few moments he was in a dream.

Back to reality as he was jerked backwards by an arm around his neck. He writhed in his struggle for freedom but was wrestled into submission. His chance had gone.

He screamed out, in a tortured voice: "Please, help me, I'm sinking! I don't want to die!"

PART ONE

CHAPTER 1

The heatwave was well into its third week. Alice pulled into the Lakeside Clinic car park at 8.35am on a cloudless Friday morning. As she reversed her scarlet Mini into a space, she was singing a duet with Tom Jones.

"The neighbours might think." ("Baby, it's bad out there.")
"Say, what's in this drink?" ("No cabs to be had out there.")
"I wish I knew how…" ("Your eyes are like starlight now.")
"…to break this spell." ("I'll take your hat, your hair looks-")

Alice pulled the key from the ignition, cutting Tom off in full flow. She glanced into the rear-view mirror to check if her blue-grey eyes were still red. Not too bad.

As she approached the building her gaze was drawn to the magnificent fellside climbing to the heavens from the western edge of Watertown. The early morning sun warmed the magenta heather. Bracken swayed to and fro in the breeze. A song thrush repeated a sweet melody especially for Alice. It should've been wonderful to be alive.

As she entered the clinic Alice scanned the notice board in the foyer. At the top was a photograph of a serious-looking lady in her fifties, along with the words 'Miss Diana Foster, Manager'. Below that was a group of smiling faces, including one belonging to 'Alice Alexander, Psychologist'. Every time she passed her picture Alice remembered how proud Dad had been when she was appointed. That was eighteen months ago. Her world had been turned upside down since then.

Alice entered the main office to be met by welcoming faces. "It smells like a tart's boudoir in here!" she announced. "One of you's bought some interesting perfume."

"You don't think any of us would wear that stuff," responded a voice from the other end of the room.

"Well, I did wonder," replied Alice with a sniff and a grimace.

"The words mutton and lamb spring to mind," added another voice.

Alice lifted the hem of her skirt to her mid thighs and took some steps on tiptoe, having acquired a pair of imaginary high heels. Everyone laughed. At that moment the mutton entered. Alice fell off her heels. Everyone tried to look busy.

"Miss Alexander," whined the mutton, "I want to see you in my room in five minutes, if you don't mind."

"Of course," replied Alice, straightening her blouse. She surveyed her boss, and without thinking added: "That's a stunning dress, Miss Foster. Anyone would think you were years younger than you are." Alice put a hand over her mouth.

A stifled giggle from somewhere, then silence.

Diana Foster's eyes narrowed, then pierced Alice with a sharp glare, forcing her to take a step back.

"No, Miss Foster, I didn't mean…"

From the corner of her eye Alice caught sight of one of the office girls shaking her head, eyebrows raised, mouthing the word "No!"

"…I just meant that you look…great."

A wave of exasperation swept across Diana Foster's face. "Five minutes!" She strode out of the office.

There were giggles all round.

"Oh, Alice," said a voice, "it would be so boring working here without you."

"How," said another, "did you ever manage to qualify as a psychologist when you're so good at putting your foot in it?"

Alice screwed her face up a little, tilting her head to one side. "I really do try not to do it. There's a voice in my head telling me not to say those things. It's just not very loud."

"At least you didn't dig too deep this time."

One of the girls reached under her desk. "Before you go into the dragon's den, we've got a little something for you."

Everyone stood up as Alice accepted the bouquet of pink, yellow and lilac flowers. She lowered her nose and breathed in the heady scent of freesias. A tear ran down her cheek. "I don't know what to say."

"You don't have to say anything, sweetie. We just wanted to tell you that we know how tough the last year has been. The way you've stayed positive is amazing."

"Thank you all so much." Alice wiped away the tear. "What time is my first appointment?"

"You've got Bonny Mason at nine."

Alice took the flowers through to her consulting room and closed the door. She stood in front of the wall mirror, stroking the mole in the centre of her forehead. "Keep going," she advised herself, "one day at a time."

Five minutes later Alice was contemplating the ornate beauty of her manager's desk. The interesting perfume made her nose twitch.

Diana Foster was also wearing a look of disdain which aged her. "This will only take a minute!" she snapped. "I've had a call from the new client you saw yesterday. She doesn't wish to make a formal complaint, but she was rather shocked when you were so free with your opinion about her hair colour."

"Yes, I remember...it was a stunning deep pink." Alice pictured the rose-coloured locks in her mind's eye.

"Do you really think it's appropriate to be so blunt about a client's appearance within thirty seconds of meeting them for the first time?"

Alice lifted a hand to cover her mouth. "Yes, of course, Miss Foster. I mean...no, you're right."

"You agree that your behaviour was inappropriate?"

"Yes. That's the word, inappropriate."

Diana Foster hesitated, half closing one eye. "Very well, I accept your apology." One corner of her mouth lifted a fraction, then dropped back to its more comfortable position. "I persuaded her to give you another chance."

"Thanks, Miss Foster. Thank you very much." Alice started to rise.

"One more thing!"

Alice sat back down.

"You have a new client starting on Monday. He's an ex-policeman with a criminal record." Miss Foster examined a sheet of paper on her desk. "He has always denied his guilt but is now apparently ready to work through what really happened."

"But you know I can hardly find the time to deal with my current caseload. And I think I'm reaching a breakthrough with Bonny Mason, so I'll definitely need more sessions with her in the next few weeks."

"I'm sorry, but there it is."

"Please, Miss Foster. It's a year this weekend since Dad and Jamie died." Alice swallowed hard. "And you do understand how much Mum needs me, don't you?"

"Yes, yes, I know all that. But I think I've been more than patient, don't you? I have a business to run! You were taken on full-time, yet I've allowed you to work part-time for a whole year. There has to be a limit. You will start seeing your new client on Monday."

Alice groaned.

"It wasn't my decision," her manager continued. "You can blame your old friend Esther Williamson. She's responsible for the referral, and she requested that the client be allocated to you personally."

What on earth is Esther up to, thought Alice? I'll have to speak to her about it over the weekend. Right now, my only ambition is to get out of this room.

Miss Foster rose from her chair, putting both hands on the desk. "You do realise that this is your last chance, don't you? You've already put the reputation of this practice at risk. Do you know how bad it looks when a client commits suicide a few hours after seeing a psychologist?"

"Come on," replied Alice, "we've been through this. The inquest found that I wasn't at fault, not in any way at all."

"That's all very well. But people talk, don't they? Once a reputation is damaged it's hard to recover. I'm giving you one more chance. I want to see successful outcomes with all of your current clients, including this crooked cop." She waved the sheet of paper at Alice.

Alice stood up. "What if I don't want one more chance?"

"It's your choice." The corner of Miss Foster's mouth twitched. "Now, it's nearly nine o'clock. I don't think we should be keeping our clients waiting, do you?"

Alice hurried out without another word. She ran straight to her consulting room, collected the bouquet of flowers, and left the building.

She sat in her Mini, holding the key in the ignition. "It's just not fair," she told her eyes in the rear-view mirror. "It's not bloody fair!"

She flipped over the card attached to the bouquet and read the message.

> To our brave Alice,
> Keep smiling.
> Love, the Office Girls.

Alice got out of the car, walked back in past her photograph, entered the waiting-room and called, "Mrs Mason, please."

CHAPTER 2

Alice sat down at her desk. She turned with a smile of encouragement to find Bonny hesitating halfway between herself and the door, hands trembling.

Bonny's face was even paler than usual. Her sunken eyes peered at Alice, at the door, back at Alice. "I'm sorry, I have to go."

"Please, Bonny, sit with me for a few minutes. I know how difficult it is for you to talk about what happened. You don't have to tell me any more today if you don't want to."

Alice got up, put an arm around Bonny, and ushered her away from the door. Bonny sat down in slow motion, her eyes on the floor.

Alice retook her seat. She gazed with a touch of envy at Bonny's short golden hair. She remembered the time, in her teens, when she'd shocked her parents by dyeing her hair blonde. It hadn't suited her.

"How's Tom?" asked Alice.

Bonny raised her head with a grateful smile. "He's ever so excited. It's his tenth birthday next weekend and I've arranged a party. He talks about it all the time."

"That's wonderful. I hope the weather stays fine." Alice paused. "Bonny, why don't we run through what you've remembered so far? Then you can say if you'd still like to go home early."

"Okay, thank you."

"It's just, I had a feeling last time that you might be ready to tell me a bit more."

Bonny ran one hand over the other. Alice thought they were more cracked and red than the last time they'd met.

"Please understand," implored Bonny, "it's not that I don't trust you, or anything like that. I don't think I've ever met anyone like you. I know you'd never let me down."

Alice wanted to hug Bonny. Maybe this is it, she thought.

"Only, the more I tell you about what happened, the worse I feel. And the nightmares are coming more often."

"Would you like to describe your nightmares to me?"

"Will it help?"

"Possibly."

"There's only two really. They keep coming back, again and again. The first one's strange. I'm standing at the side of a road, and my home's on the other side. If I try to cross, a train appears from nowhere, blocking my way. There are no tracks. The train runs along the middle of the road without tracks. It goes on and on and on. Hundreds of carriages, thousands. After it's gone I try to cross the road, but another train always comes, so I can't get home."

"Do you ever get across?" asked Alice.

"No, never. What do you think it means?"

"I'm not sure. I'll give it some thought. What about the other one?"

"It's horrible," shivered Bonny. "I'm lying on my back on the grass. There's nothing there, just grass, and the sky. I'm watching the clouds, looking at the shapes. Then the trees come. They're all around me, moving closer and closer. I want to get away but I'm paralysed. The trees bend over me. They push down on me, on my chest, squashing me. I can't breathe. Then I wake up."

"That must be very frightening."

"It's awful. And it's happening more and more since I've been seeing you. I know it's not your fault, but maybe I should stop coming. I've been thinking, wouldn't it be better to forget about the past, concentrate on…"

Alice had an urge to say something but fought to control herself. She waited for Bonny to continue.

"Trying to forget the past hasn't worked," admitted Bonny, "and it's not going to work, is it?"

"No, Bonny, it's not going to work."

Bonny sat up. "Okay, I'm ready."

A wave of relief lifted Alice. "Good girl. Right, you've told me about your happy childhood, growing up in the circus. From sixteen you had your own act which you loved very much. Ten years ago something happened. Since then your nerves have been a problem for you, feeling anxious all the time. This has got worse over the last few months. You're losing weight. Every day's a struggle now."

Bonny nodded, eyes closed.

"Are you ready to talk more about what happened?"

Bonny slid a hand into her floral cloth bag. It reappeared, grasping a folded sheet of paper. "I knew I wouldn't be able to say it, so…" She placed the paper on the desk, sliding it towards Alice with her fingertips.

Alice touched one edge with her own fingers and waited.

Bonny lifted her hand. "Don't read it out loud, I don't want to hear it."

Alice unfolded the paper. It was covered with tiny but perfectly-formed handwriting. Some of the words had been distorted by tear splashes, but all were legible.

Bonny leaned forward, elbows on knees, hands covering her eyes.

Alice started to read.

> 'We arrived in Watertown on the Monday for two weeks of shows. The first night was great, nearly a full house. Sparky had a sore paw so Flash and I went on without her. Next day I took them for a walk. Someone was there in the trees. It was the same the next day, and the next. I didn't tell the others, they were so busy. I thought I was safe with the girls. It happened on Friday. Flash ran off and Sparky went after her. He came from nowhere. He put a bag over my head and everything went black. I couldn't breathe, it was so tight. He said if I made a sound he'd kill me and the dogs. He pushed me down on the ground then tied my arms behind my back. It happened so fast. He lifted me up. He was so strong, there was nothing I could do. He carried me to the car and put me in the boot. My arms hurt a lot. I wanted to say but I was too frightened. When we got there he carried me again. He dropped me on my back and tied my legs to the ground, not together. He kneeled on my shoulders and tied my hands down as well. Then he pulled the bag off. All I could see was the trees. One had big nests in it. I just stared at the nests.'

Alice folded the paper and touched Bonny's arm.

"That's all I remember," sobbed Bonny. She slid her hands down onto her cheeks, uncovering her wet eyes, and stared into space. "Except that...afterwards he didn't put me in the boot. I sat in the front. He kept touching my hair."

Alice shuddered. "How did you get back to the circus?"

"He let me out of the car and pointed the way. It wasn't far. He asked if he could see me again. I didn't say anything. He said he would definitely see me again."

"Did you go to the police?"

"I told my parents I'd lost the dogs and spent ages searching for them. Of course they got back before me, clever things. But Mum knew something was wrong. She wouldn't stop until I told her the truth. Mum and Dad took me to the police."

"Is that when you met your husband?"

"Not right away. Leo took over my case a few days later, on the Monday."

"Was it love at first sight?" Alice put a hand over her mouth. "I'm so sorry, that was a stupid thing to say. You must've been so traumatised."

"No, it's okay. You can say anything you like, I don't mind."

What a darling, thought Alice.

"Leo sorted out a bed and breakfast for me when the others left town."

"What? The circus went without you?"

"He said it was important that I waited," explained Bonny, "in case they arrested someone, though they never did. Mum and Dad didn't want me to stay, but I had to."

"I think maybe there was another reason he wanted you around, don't you?"

"I suppose so."

"A pretty girl like you." Alice tried to imagine Bonny as she would've looked ten years ago. "And talented."

"Leo always said he wished he could've seen one of my shows."

"You never performed again?"

Bonny shook her head.

"Do you have any photos of you at the circus?" asked Alice. "I'd love to see what your costume was like."

"No, sorry. Leo said I shouldn't keep anything that would remind me. Bad memories. But I kept my knives. No one's taking my knives!"

Alice was taken aback by the sudden determination in Bonny's voice.

"I polish them every day. I think I'll do them when I get home. What time is it?"

"Just a few more minutes," promised Alice, "if you feel okay to continue."

Bonny was shivering. She gave several tiny nods of her head.

"There's one more thing I'd like to ask you. Why do you think your anxiety is so much worse recently?"

Bonny's response startled Alice. "It's happening again!" she cried, thumping her thighs with clenched fists. "I'm being stalked."

Alice rode a rush of adrenaline. Stay cool, she told herself. "I'm sorry, who is stalking you?"

"If I tell you, you have to promise you'll say nothing to Leo, or anyone else, nothing at all. Do you promise?"

"Everything you say to me is in complete confidence, Bonny. I can't discuss it with anyone without your permission, not even your family." Alice waited for Bonny to take this on board. "Who is stalking you?"

"His name is Paul Ireland. He's a policeman...was a policeman. He was a dog handler in the drugs team. Leo worked with him, they were friends. I used to walk Paul's German Shepherds sometimes. Lucky and Scamp. They're lovely." Bonny gazed into the distance.

Alice waited a few moments. "Go on," she nodded.

"He ended up in prison. Leo was shocked. He never knew Paul was keeping drugs for himself, and selling them."

"When did he start stalking you?"

"He got out six months ago. It started after that. I thought it was my imagination, but then I saw his face. It's definitely him, I promise."

"I believe you, Bonny." Alice squeezed her hand.

"At first he tried to hide, but now he stands under the blossom tree across the road, as if he wants me to know he's there. I keep telling myself he can't get to me. I never go out without Leo, and the doors are always locked. But he could break a window, couldn't he?"

"Why on earth haven't you told Leo about this?"

"You don't understand, I can't. When Paul Ireland was in prison he tried to hang himself. He nearly died. If he gets into more trouble he might do it again, and that would be my fault."

"He's not your responsibility, Bonny. I think you should go to the police. Or I can speak to them on your behalf, if you like."

"You promised not to say anything, to anybody!" Bonny jumped to her feet.

"Yes, of course. I won't let you down." Alice recalled how she'd felt when a client had killed himself after seeing her. "I think it's time to stop for today. I know how difficult it must be for you to talk about these things. You've been very brave."

"Thank you," whispered Bonny.

Alice got up. "How would you feel if I was to chat to your husband about what happened? You know, to get another perspective?"

Bonny screwed up her face. "I suppose so," she murmured, glancing at the door. "Why don't you ask him? He's waiting outside."

A minute later Alice was gazing upwards into a pair of dark brown eyes which she guessed were about forty years old. A perfect age, she thought. She tried not to appear impressed. "Hello, Mr Mason, it's nice to meet you."

The dark brown eyes looked deep into hers without blinking.

A tingling sensation started in Alice's stomach, passed through her chest, and settled in her throat. She gulped.

"It's my pleasure, I assure you," said Leo, in a deep voice which resonated straight into the pleasure centre of Alice's brain.

Alice involuntarily lifted her heels from the floor. She examined the scar on Leo's left cheek. It was fascinating, in the shape of a crucifix. She realised she was staring at it and forced her gaze back to his eyes. Be professional, she thought, stay cool. She found herself saying out loud: "Stay cool."

Leo smiled without batting an eyelid. "You wanted to speak to me?"

A second wave of tingling. "Would it be possible to arrange an appointment for you to give me…" Alice was now sure that her face must be cherry-red. "…your perspective…on your wife's condition."

"I'd be delighted. I'll do anything to help, naturally. Anything."

At last Leo blinked, slowly. Alice sighed.

"Work is hectic," he continued, "so getting away could be a problem. However,

I'll be at the school fete tomorrow afternoon between two and four. We could meet there, perhaps find a quiet spot to talk. How about three o'clock?"

"That'll be perfect," breathed Alice.

"You have an interesting accent," he suggested. "There's some Scots in there, I think."

Alice blushed. "Dad came from Inverness. Mum's from Piraeus."

"A perfect combination, obviously."

As Leo walked away Alice's heels touched back down.

CHAPTER 3

"I can get the strings you need by next week," said the assistant behind the counter of Mellow Music.

"I rang yesterday," replied Angus, "and was told you had them in stock. The fellow I spoke to promised he would put them to one side. I wouldn't have come into Inverness otherwise."

"Sorry," said the assistant, "that was Malcolm. He's new."

"What d'you mean he's bloody new? All he had to do was-"

"I'm sorry, Sir. Would you like me to order the strings for you?"

Angus threw his arms up. "You're taking the piss."

The assistant shrugged.

"Bollocks!" Angus stormed out of the shop, thumping the door, and charged along the pavement. He was on a collision course with a man holding a bunch of leaflets. The man was wearing a T-shirt bearing the words 'If Lost Please Return To Jesus'.

Angus veered to one side. The leaflet man mirrored his change of direction. At the last moment Angus made an extra lurch sideways to avoid a head-on collision. A glancing blow sent the leaflets to the ground.

Angus held his arms out, fists clenched, as if he was gripping a pair of ski poles. He threw his head back and roared at the sky: "I don't need this!" He glared at the man who was collecting the leaflets from around his ankles.

The man stood up and beamed at Angus. "Jesus loves you," he said, holding out a leaflet.

Angus ignored the offer, glowered at the man, and brushed past him.

"Is Jesus in your heart, Brother?"

Angus didn't look round. "I'm not your brother, and this isn't a good time."

"Now is always the best time to find Jesus, Brother."

Angus stopped in his tracks. He spun around. "Which were you first, Brother?! Religious? Or a nutter?"

"I don't understand," said the man, still holding out the leaflet.

"That figures." Angus snatched the leaflet, screwed it up, and tossed it at a nearby bin, into the section marked General Waste.

"Open up your heart before it's too late," pleaded the man.

"It's already too late," growled Angus.

"I sincerely hope not, Brother."

Angus flushed the colour of his shaggy flaming hair. "Human beings have been on this planet for half a million years. Your mate Jesus only just turned up. People were doing fine without him, thank you very much."

"And you?" asked the man. "Are you doing fine without Jesus?"

"Who the hell d'you think you are? What gives you the right to-"

"You're in grave danger, Brother."

"You're in grave danger of getting my fist in your face, you prat!" Angus waved his fist momentarily, then snatched the rest of the leaflets and threw them into the section of the bin labelled Recycling.

"Excuse me, Sir!" boomed a voice. "That's not very nice, is it?"

Angus turned to find a police officer standing behind him, arms crossed. A pair of handcuffs hung from one side of his belt, a truncheon from the other.

"Please retrieve the papers from the bin and return them to the gentleman."

Angus reluctantly followed the policeman's instructions.

"Now move along please."

"Why don't you ask him to move along?" moaned Angus, jabbing a finger towards the leaflet man. "If he hadn't been hassling me-"

"I said move along please! This gentleman has not committed any offence."

"That's a matter of opinion. Most of the evils of this world are carried out in the name of religion."

The policeman wrapped his hand around the truncheon handle. The handcuffs glinted in the sunlight.

"Excuse me, Officer," said a female voice, "can I help?"

Angus turned to look into a face he knew well. "Jess!"

"Do you know this gentleman, Miss?"

"Yes, Officer, he's a...friend of mine."

"Would you be so kind as to escort your friend away from here?"

"Yes, of course." Jess took Angus by the arm.

"Thank you, Miss."

"Lord be praised!" cried the leaflet man.

Angus scowled at the man as Jess led him away along the pavement.

"What was that all about?" she asked.

"Nothing. Just another bad day, that's all."

"You've lost weight, Angus. You're too thin. The designer stubble suits you though."

"It's not designer stubble. My shaver broke."

"There's a chemist around the corner. We can buy you a new one."

"I can manage, thanks. I'm not your problem any more, remember?"

"Don't, Angus, please."

He laid a hand on her shoulder to slow her to a stop. They stood facing each other.

"Why did you have to leave, Jess?"

"Let's not go through that again. It's time to move on."

"Simple as that, is it? Just move on."

She turned her face away, a tear in her eye.

"I don't believe it!" blurted Angus. "You've found someone else, haven't you?"

"It's been six months, Angus."

"Who is he?"

"His name is Colin...and we're engaged."

The news hit Angus like an uppercut.

"I'm glad we met today," she continued. "I wanted you to know."

Angus struggled to recover from the blow. "Do you love him?"

Her eyes pleaded with him to stop.

"Do you love him, damn it?!"

"Yes, Angus, I do."

His throat tightened. "As much as you love me?"

"I have to go." She turned towards the kerb.

He gripped her arm. "Give me another chance, Jess. Please, just one more chance."

"No, Angus. I can't go back to being the second most important thing in your life."

"I treated you badly, Jess. I was a fool. But I've learnt my lesson."

"It doesn't matter what you say. Your music will always come first, we both know that."

"Then wait for me! The band won't last forever. Then it'll be you and me, for the rest of our lives."

"Goodbye, Angus." She pulled away and ran across the road.

Angus watched as the most important person in his world walked out of it...again.

CHAPTER 4

For the majority of his forty-nine years Sammy Rice had dreamt that he would learn to fly one day. He never actually believed the day would come, but here he was, butterflies in his chest, preparing for his maiden flight.

It had been a struggle heaving his hefty frame to the topmost branches of this monster of an oak tree. But he'd made it.

Sammy had passed a few squirrels on the way up. Most of them ignored his puffing and groaning, but one curious squirrel had followed him upward. There it now sat, on a branch no more than ten feet from his, watching and waiting for Sammy to make his next move.

Sammy was self-conscious having an audience for his first flight. Oh well, he thought, I'm the outsider here, so I can't exactly ask it to leave.

Sammy winked at the squirrel. It winked back.

Encouraged, Sammy stood as tall as his aching back would allow, and raised both arms high into the air. Out of the blue a swirling gust of wind lifted him from the tree. He performed a slow-motion pirouette until he was clear of the uppermost leaves, and came to a halt. The gust of wind had passed, leaving Sammy hovering in mid-air.

The squirrel's jaw dropped.

Sammy tilted forward, assumed the Superman position, and soared effortlessly into the sky. Wearing the broadest of smiles, he arched his back and performed a perfect backward loop-the-loop before zooming into the heavens.

The trees, now far below, appeared no larger than a group of bushes. He singled out his take-off oak and plunged back down towards it. As he approached the tree he heard a shrieking voice emanating from its branches.

"I don't believe it!" screeched the squirrel. "You're going to kill yourself, don't you understand that? Haven't you got any sense in that thick skull of yours?"

The squirrel's cries reminded Sammy of Suzie on a bad day. Suzie was the perfect secretary, but had been hard work since she became his girlfriend a few months ago.

Swooping closer to the squirrel, Sammy saw that it had now acquired Suzie's eyes and mouth. He panicked. Staring at the ground, he flapped his arms as fast as he could. It was no good. He went into a tight downward spiral and crashed headlong into an open skip bin.

Sammy screwed up his face as the stench of stale booze and vomit entered his nostrils. His mouth tasted like crap. He spat.

"That's disgusting, you revolting creature!"

Sammy tried to open his eyes but the lids were stuck. He winced as his ear was pinched roughly and stretched outwards.

"Wake up, you stupid sod!"

A finger pushed against his eye and jerked the lid upwards. Sammy tried to focus. A few inches from his face he could make out the shape of a whisky bottle. He hauled an arm from his side and fumbled at the bottle.

"Don't bother, it's empty."

Sammy managed to get both arms onto his desk. He groaned as he pushed down against it. A pair of hands grabbed his collar and helped him achieve an almost upright position in his chair.

Suzie walked around to the front of the desk. She slapped both palms onto its surface and leaned towards him. "You're going to die if you keep this up, you do realise that."

Sammy gave Suzie the best puppy dog face he could manage.

"It's no use giving me the Jake Blues eyes," she snapped, "it's not going to work this time!"

Sammy's expression turned to a grimace as he dropped both hands onto his belly and moaned.

"I warned you this would happen, didn't I? Your ulcer's come back. Don't expect me to clean up the mess when you start throwing up blood again."

"I'm fine," groaned Sammy.

"I bet you haven't made an appointment to see the doctor, have you? You never do anything I say. Oh, what's the point!" She thumped the desk and moved away to open the window.

"I've learnt my lesson this time, Babe. I'll never touch another drop, I promise."

"Hah!" Suzie took a carton of milk from a plastic bag she'd brought with her. She returned to the desk and poured some milk into Sammy's empty whisky tumbler. A drop plopped over the rim of the glass and soaked into the sheet of blotting paper underneath. "Drink it."

Sammy took a mouthful of milk.

"Why didn't you come home last night?" grilled Suzie. "That's the third time this month. You've been out on the town again, haven't you?"

"No, Babe."

"You've been out with some tart, haven't you, you cheating swine."

"I've been here in the office all night, Babe. I've been busy."

"You've been busy all right!" she screamed. "I never should've trusted you."

"I only have eyes for you, you know that."

"Don't you lie to me. You must be seeing someone. You haven't been able to perform with me for weeks. Who is she? What's her name?"

"There's no one else, I promise."

Suzie scrutinized Sammy's face through half-closed eyes. "If it's not another woman, then it's the booze that's making you useless. And you're never gonna end your love affair with Tullamore Dew, are you?"

"I'll get some Viagra, Babe."

"What? You wouldn't need Viagra if you still fancied me."

"I can't stop thinking about you. I'm crazy about you, you know I am."

Suzie put her hands on her hips.

"You're right," pleaded Sammy. "I'll stop drinking. I'll never touch another drop as long as I live."

"And look at the state of you. You've put on at least two stones since we first met. Even if it did get hard you'd never find it under all that blubber."

"I can't help it, Babe. It's your delicious cooking."

"It's too much beer and whisky, that's what it is."

"I'll make it up to you," promised Sammy. "How about a holiday? I'll take you away, anywhere you like."

"What a joke. You haven't got two pennies to rub together. When's the last time you charged a customer the going rate for your services?"

"Most people can't afford-"

"Other private investigators charge ten times as much as you do. There's a good living to be made, if you weren't such a…"

Sammy gave the puppy dog face one more try.

"…such a…such a great big softy. I hate you, d'you know that? I hate you!" She kissed him on the cheek and poured some more milk. "Drink up, then we can get you home and into the bath."

There was a knock on the open office door. Sammy and Suzie turned their heads in unison to find a young woman standing in the doorway.

"Shall I come back later?" she asked.

"Yes," said Suzie.

"No," said Sammy at the very same moment.

Suzie flushed. "I'm going home," she snorted. "If you're not back in one hour, I won't be there waiting!" She forced a smile at the young woman as she stormed past her and down the stairs.

The young woman began to weep.

Sammy tried to get up without success. "How can I help you?" he asked, pointing to a chair at the side of the desk.

She sat down, tears trickling down her cheeks.

"I'd offer you a tissue," said Sammy, surveying his bare office, "if I had one."

"That's okay." She took a hanky from her bag and dabbed her eyes.

Sammy took the opportunity to run his hand across his scalp to smooth the few strands of hair that remained. "How can I help, Miss…"

"Guest," she whimpered. "My name's Zoe Guest."

"How can I help you, Zoe?"

"It's my brother," she howled, "he's disappeared!"

Sammy took a pencil and notepad from a half-open drawer. "Tell me about your brother, Zoe."

"His name's Robbie," she sobbed. "Robbie Johnson. He's my half-brother."

"When did you last see Robbie?"

"A few months ago."

"Months? Why didn't you come to me earlier?"

"You're not the first investigator I've tried. You're the third. Sorry."

"I'm not offended," smiled Sammy.

"The others didn't get anywhere. They took my money though."

Sammy shrugged.

"I don't have much, Mr Rice. I can't afford to-"

"Let's worry about that after we've found Robbie, shall we?"

"Thank you, Mr Rice, thank you."

"Call me Sammy."

"Thank you, Sammy."

Sammy was already taken by Zoe. Her hazel eyes and dimpled cheeks reminded him of his daughter Emily. "Tell me about your brother," he said. "How old is he?"

"Fifteen. He's five years younger than me."

"Did you say he's your half-brother?"

"My dad died after an accident. Six months later Mum got remarried to...Jimmy Johnson."

Sammy could tell from Zoe's face that even saying the name disturbed her. "Robbie's father?" he asked.

"Yes," whispered Zoe.

"Six months. Did you think that was a bit soon after your dad died?"

"Jimmy was Dad's business partner, so he and Mum already knew each other. Dad had three operations, but it was no good. Jimmy took Mum to the hospital every day. After Dad died, he kept coming round."

"Then he became your stepfather."

Zoe nodded.

"Did he treat you badly?"

"Not at first. He was strict, but we got used to that. Then last year the arguments started. He was really horrible to Mum, but he started being nice to me. He kept giving me presents. I thought he was just trying to be, you know, a proper dad."

"Yes, I see," said Sammy, picturing his own daughter.

"Then it started. At first I thought I was imagining it. He'd accidentally brush his hand against my bum, that sort of thing. One day he insisted on doing my seat belt up for me. He put his hand on my chest. I knew it wasn't an accident. Then he kissed me, on the mouth." Zoe screwed up her eyes. "It was horrible."

"Did you tell your mum?"

"I couldn't. She was always complaining that I had to be nice to Jimmy. She said if it wasn't for him we wouldn't have anything, we'd be on the streets. What was I supposed to do?"

"I understand."

"So I tried to forget what happened. Then he said he was going to give me driving lessons. I didn't want to, but Mum talked me into it. She didn't do it on purpose. I mean, she didn't realise..."

"Of course not."

"It was an automatic so it was easy. One day he made me stop the car in the middle of nowhere." Zoe's face turned scarlet. She stared into space.

"What happened?"

"He got his...his thing out," she sobbed. "Said it was time for me to learn how to handle a gear stick."

"I'm sorry, Zoe."

She wiped her eyes with her hanky. "After it was over he gave me a present. I don't mean a cheap present. It was a mobile phone, covered in stones. He said they were diamonds."

"Yes, I've heard of phones like that. The diamonds are usually fake."

"He said they were real. He promised to give me lots of presents like that if I was a good girl. I shouldn't have taken it, I know."

"You were in a difficult position."

"I thought, what if the diamonds are real? I could sell the phone and find somewhere else to live. I didn't want to leave Robbie, but I had to get away, didn't I?"

"Of course."

"I left during the night. I woke Robbie to tell him I was going, to say goodbye. He begged me not to go, asked me why I had to leave. I couldn't tell him the reason, so I gave him the mobile to calm him down. He loves gadgets. I made him take the sim out."

"The what?"

"The sim."

Sammy gave her a blank look.

"You do know what a sim is?"

"Sorry, I'm still using real phones." He pointed at the mustard-coloured relic on his desk.

"Without the sim the phone doesn't belong to anyone," she explained.

Sammy shrugged.

"Anyway, if Jimmy ever finds out that I gave the phone to Robbie he'll go ballistic, so I told Robbie he mustn't use it whatever happens. I didn't tell him where I got the phone, I just said it was stolen and worth a lot of money. I told him any calls would be traced back to him, then he'd lose the phone and be in big trouble."

"Do you think he still has it?"

"I hope so."

"Then why don't you try ringing him?"

Zoe tilted her head. "Because it hasn't got a sim. And if it did have, the call could be traced. Haven't you been listening?"

"Sorry, rough night. Tell me more about Robbie, what's he like?"

"He's lovely." She held up her hands. "I don't mean he's perfect. He's no angel, if you know what I mean."

"A bit of a rascal?" suggested Sammy.

"I suppose so. He's always getting into scrapes. Nothing serious though. He's been in court once or twice, but never gone to prison. That's why I was so happy when he told me he'd found a job."

Sammy made a note on his pad. "What sort of job?"

"I'm not sure. Robbie said it was a secret, that he wasn't allowed to tell anyone. He joked he was working for MI5!"

"Hmm. Is there anything else you can tell me?"

"I don't think so. Except, last time I saw Robbie he'd got himself a tattoo. On the side of his face."

"What sort of tattoo?"

"A footprint."

"A what?" choked Sammy.

"An animal footprint."

"You mean a paw print?"

"Yes, with claws."

Subtle, thought Sammy.

"It's quite big, you can't miss it." Zoe placed her hands on the desk. "You will help me, Mr Rice, won't you?"

"There's not much to go on, to be honest. The tattoo should help, assuming it's a permanent one, but-"

"Only, I heard your lady friend saying you've got to charge more for your work. I don't want to get you into trouble." She started to get up. "It's no use. I haven't got any money, and even if I did have, I'll never see Robbie again!" Her tears returned. "I'm sorry, I've wasted your time."

"Don't worry about Suzie, she's not as hard as she seems. I'll find Robbie for you."

"Will you? Are you sure?"

"To tell you the truth, I'd like to help you. You remind me of someone special."

"Who's that?"

"My daughter Emily, from my first marriage."

"How many times have you been married?"

"Too many." Sammy glanced at his watch. "I'll contact you as soon as I get any news."

Zoe came around the desk to give Sammy a hug.

"Here's my mobile number," she said, taking the pencil from Sammy's hand and scribbling the number on his pad.

"One more thing before you go," said Sammy. "Would you mind giving me a hand to get out of this chair?"

CHAPTER 5

Alice finished work at noon, as she'd done on every Monday, Wednesday and Friday for the past year. These were the days she could spend more time with Mum. And these were her running days!

Before leaving the clinic, Alice changed into her lime green jogging outfit and slipped on a pair of burnt orange trainers which almost matched her hair colour. She used a polka dot scrunchie to tie her shoulder length hair into a ponytail, and was ready for action. She skipped past her Mini, through a gap in the car park hedge, and into paradise.

Alice was soon speeding along the lakeside path, her ponytail tap-tap-tapping against the back of her neck, keeping time. A couple ambled towards her hand-in-hand. As she passed them her smile met theirs.

A flash of blue caught her eye as a jay swooped into the berry-laden branches of a mountain ash. She glanced across to the tiny island in the middle of the lake, where a silver birch had managed to get a foothold. Its leaves rustled in the breeze.

Alice checked her watch. Concentrate, she thought. You'll never beat your personal best if you don't concentrate!

A few minutes later she left the lakeside path and veered off into the woods. Much cooler now, out of the sun. She jogged over and between the hundreds of tree roots which lay across her path. Concentrate. She recalled her last fall, which had taken the skin off her elbow.

Alice scanned the ground ahead as she started a downhill stretch strewn with rocks and stones of all sizes. She made an effort not to slow down.

The woodland became more dense. No track now, but Alice knew the terrain like the back of her hand. She landed her foot on a boulder which gave a wobble to remind her to be careful. She didn't heed the warning. Her toe caught the top of a gnarled root and she spun round as she hit the earth, rolling into a cushion of stinging nettles. Well, she thought, that was lucky.

Alice got up and examined her arms and legs for scratches. Her skin prickled. She glimpsed at her watch, groaned, and set off again.

After another half mile she decided she was too far behind schedule and paused to examine an orange-brown bracket fungus protruding from the trunk of a dead oak. She leaned closer to sniff the combined odours of mushroom and rotting wood. Life and death in harmony, she thought.

Off again, Alice ducked under one branch and leapt over another. Five minutes later she escaped from the woods and rejoined the lakeside path for the home stretch. She dashed past the couple she'd seen earlier. They were skimming stones on the surface of the lake. Enjoy yourselves, she thought, make the most of every day.

Alice drove home to find a grey-haired figure dressed in black sitting at the window, watching out for her arrival. She found this pleasing and irritating at the same time. Surely, she thought, not all Greek mothers worry this much.

"Are you feeling any better?" she asked, giving Sofia a hug.

"I cannot walk straight, all my bones hurt, and I see two of everything. Apart from that I am fine." Sofia signed the cross on her chest. "I will feel better when you put some dry clothes on," she added, pointing at Alice's damp running top. "And I wish you would not run on your own. It is not safe for a young girl."

"Mum, I'll be thirty in two years."

"To your mother you are still a girl." Sofia threw up her arms. "If you must run, then find yourself a tall rich man to run with you."

"Do me a favour, Mum."

"I know, Aliki, I know," shrugged Sofia. "But we have both been grieving for one year, and for you that is enough. I will soon be gone. While you are single, what hope do I have of seeing my grandchildren before I die?"

"Don't talk like that, Mum. The radiotherapy hasn't had a chance to kick in yet. You're going to get better, just wait and see."

"Wait and see!" squawked a voice from the budgie cage in the corner of the room.

"Thank you, Petros," responded Sofia, picking up her crochet and getting to work.

Alice had a shower and prepared dinner. They sat quietly at the table, neither with much of an appetite for their lamb chops. Sofia found it difficult to grip her knife.

"Shall I cut it up for you?" asked Alice, stroking the prominent veins on the back of her mother's hand.

Sofia tutted. "I am not a child." She took a forkful of sweet potato.

"Mum, I've been thinking."

"You think too much, darling."

"I really should be with you all the time, and I've decided-"

"Aliki! We have been over this a hundred times."

"I know. But I had words with Diana Foster this morning. She wants me to increase my hours. She's booked me a new client, and I told her I can't do it. She thinks that after a year I should be getting over losing Jamie and Dad. What does she know, stupid cow?" Alice put down her knife and fork. "You won't consider having carers, so I have to give up my job. I'm going to quit."

"You must be strong, darling, like my old Aliki. You must go to work, and help your new client. We cannot live without your money."

Sofia took an envelope from her pocket and handed it to Alice.

Alice read the letter from Watertown prison.

> Dear Mrs Alexander,
>
> I hope you are keeping well. Everyone at Watertown prison sends you their warmest regards.
>
> I am sure you know how much we all miss Richard. For thirty years he was one of the finest officers this prison has ever had. He will never be replaced. Neither will your delicious cakes.
>
> This is a difficult letter for me to write, even though the information it contains will not be a surprise to you. After Richard's death you requested, not unreasonably, to be allowed to continue living indefinitely in your prison officer's house. Under normal circumstances a three-month notice period would apply, but in view of Richard's

long and excellent service, and in view of your health problems, the Board agreed to extend this period to one year.

We are now approaching the latter part of this notice period. I have been instructed to inform you that you should arrange to vacate the property within three months of the date of this letter. I am sure that you have already made appropriate plans, but you will understand that it is necessary to send you this letter formalising the position.

I do hope that your treatment is going well and your health improving.

Yours sincerely,
Brian Stevenson
Deputy Warden.

"Mum, this is dated two months ago!"

"I know." Sofia wrung her hands. "I kept forgetting to show it to you."

"I realise how much you love this house, but you can't bury your head in the sand."

"I am sorry, darling. I thought I would be gone before another three months had passed. Thirty years, Aliki. Thirty years! You grew up in this house. So many memories." Sofia gazed upward. "I thought I would be in Heaven now, with Richard." She smiled as if she knew he was watching. "God wanted your father and Jamie by his side. He gave his blessing for me to stay here and look after you." She squeezed Alice's hand. "Now we have to leave our home. So you cannot give up your job, can you?"

"What if you have another stroke while I'm at work?"

"And what would your father say? It would break his heart. He was so proud of you, the first in the family to go to university." Sofia reached across the table and pinched Alice's cheeks. "You have your father's brains, you know that?"

Alice winced. "Yes, Mum, I know. And I do love my job, it's just…" She began to weep. "Why did they have to die? It's all my fault. I should've been there."

"No, you must not blame yourself, Aliki. It is my fault. If I did not have this stupid tumour…" Sofia slapped the side of her head. "…they would both be here with us now."

Alice threw her arms around Sofia's neck. They cried together.

Later that afternoon Alice entered the living room to find Sofia snoozing on her reclining chair. On her lap was an edition of the Watertown Press from the previous summer. Alice realised immediately which edition it was. She froze, her heart thumping. It was the one with the article about Jamie and Dad. Mum had studied it again and again, but Alice couldn't bear to read it. Her face started to burn. She turned to leave the room, but stopped after a couple of paces. She glanced again at the newspaper, and was shocked when she realised that her anxiety had turned suddenly to intense anger, the like of which she had never before experienced.

Alice Alexander, she thought, are you going to spend the rest of your life trying to hide from the truth? It's not good enough! Dad must be turning in his grave. He never ran away from anybody or anything, and he brought you up to be the same. You're a disgrace.

Alice realised that she'd been mouthing these words, an audible angry whisper emanating from her lips. Her whole body was shaking, her fists clenched.

Sofia moaned but didn't wake.

Alice held her breath until Sofia had settled, then with trembling fingers lifted the paper from her lap. She sat down on the carpet and turned the pages. When she got to page six she found the two most important men of her life beaming at her.

The headline read, 'Drowning at Moston-on-Sea'. Beneath that was a photograph of Jamie and Dad at the beach, wearing black wetsuits and yellow swimming caps, standing with arms around each other's shoulders. Alice smiled back at them and pressed the paper twice to her lips.

She started to read.

> Tragedy struck off the coast of Moston yesterday as two swimmers got into difficulties while taking part in a fundraising event. Richard Alexander, a prison officer aged 58, and Jamie Carpenter, a farmer aged 42, were raising money to pay for a potentially life-saving operation for Richard's wife Sofia, who is suffering from a brain tumour.
>
> The two men were rescued by lifeguards who performed resuscitation at the scene. Both were rushed by ambulance to Carlisle General Hospital where Mr Alexander was pronounced dead on arrival. Mr Carpenter was transferred to the Intensive Care Unit where his condition was described as critical. He sadly died six hours later.

The men, both experienced swimmers, had been sponsored to swim out to the tiny island of Tern Rock, no more than 100 metres from Moston, and then swim around the island as many times as possible before returning to shore. Conditions were perfect.

The cause of the tragedy is unknown. Witnesses report seeing one of the men swimming away from the island in the direction of the open sea. The other man reportedly followed, and the two appeared to have an argument. The witnesses heard shouting as the two men struggled in the deep water. Two lifeguards sprang into action, heroically returning the men to shore, but the outcome was disastrous.

Richard Alexander was an insulin-dependent diabetic. Our medical expert has suggested a possible explanation for the tragedy. Richard may have developed hypoglycaemia (dangerously low blood sugar level), a condition known to cause confusion, erratic behaviour, and even aggression, followed by coma if appropriate treatment is delayed for any reason.

Richard leaves behind his wife Sofia, 55, and daughter Alice, 27. Alice and Jamie were engaged to be married next year. Alice, a psychologist, was at her fiance's bedside as he lost his fight for life.

Alice folded the paper and placed it back on her mother's lap. Sofia opened her eyes.

"Nice nap?" enquired Alice.

"Yes, darling. But I think I will go to bed early."

Alice helped Sofia get ready for bed, then withdrew to her own room.

She searched her iPod. Cardigans, Catatonia, Charlatans, Chemical Brothers, Chopin. She found 'Favourite Piano Pieces' and pressed play. She sighed, thinking of Jamie, remembering the day they'd discovered Chopin together. They'd been wandering aimlessly through town and discovered some people queueing for a piano recital. It was love at first hearing for both of them. They'd planned to have Tristesse played at their wedding.

Alice half-opened her bedroom window. The sun warmed her face as she took in the familiar view across the treetops. Its rays were scattered by a faint cloud of dust hovering over Pilston quarry. Before that was the familiar red-brick structure of the prison. How many times as a child, she thought, did I look towards that building, wondering what Daddy was doing, and what time he'd get home?

She sat on the edge of her bed, facing the window, spinning her engagement ring around its finger. "Hi, Jamie. I've had an interesting day, there's lots to tell you about. The girls gave me some flowers, I had a row with the boss, then I fell over in the woods. Ooh, I saw an amazing bracket fungus, you'd have loved that. And I've got a bit of a confession to make. I met someone today who reminded me so much of you. Same height, same age, same smile...same eyes. We always said that if anything happened to either of us..." Alice grinned. "Don't worry, there's no need to get jealous. He's married...to a client!"

The opening bars of Tristesse played. Alice's smile faded away. She stared into her lap. "Everyone says it gets easier after the first year. There must be something wrong with me, Jamie. I don't think I've got the strength to-"

Alice was stopped by the faint but definite sound of breaking glass. Puzzled, she got up and stepped over to the window. To her amazement she could see the figure of a man on the roof of the prison. She watched, mesmerised, as he walked in her direction towards the edge of the roof. He was standing at the very edge. He was going to jump!

Alice's head was spinning. She thought of phoning the prison, but knew that the man would surely jump before anyone could reach him. There was nothing she could do. Nothing. She pushed the window wide open, ready to shout an appeal across the treetops. She took a deep breath, but the air stuck in her lungs. Because the figure had stopped moving and was looking directly at her.

They stood motionless, staring at each other across the void.

Two other figures appeared on the roof. Alice's jaw dropped as they wrestled with the man and pulled him away from the edge. He screamed, in a tortured voice: "Please, help me, I'm sinking! I don't want to die!"

Alice watched in horror as the man was dragged across the rooftop and back into the building. She took a step back, her knees buckling. She sat on her bed, trying to make sense of what she'd seen. Tiredness prevailed, and her head dropped onto the pillow.

Alice slept fitfully. Nightmares woke her again and again.

In one, she was up there on the roof, not far from the prisoner, knowing that he would leap at any moment. She tried to approach him, but an invisible barrier held her back. She wanted to call to him, but no sound came from her lips. In desperation she tried to wave her arms, but they were so heavy that she couldn't lift them. Suddenly two other men, both faceless, appeared out of thin air and grabbed the prisoner. As he was being dragged across the roof, he called out to Alice: "Please help me! Please help me!"

Alice woke in a sweat, heart pounding, and sat bolt upright.

Eventually she settled back to sleep. The next nightmare was exactly the same until the two men appeared and grabbed the prisoner. This time, before dragging him away, they both turned to Alice and smiled. Jamie and Dad...they're alive!

Alice jumped out of bed to tell Mum the news. "They're alive!" she screamed. She froze with her hands against the bedroom door, collapsed to the floor, and sobbed.

After that Alice didn't want to go back to sleep. But she was exhausted and was soon back on the roof. The prisoner was there, same as before. She was desperate to do something to help him but was powerless. The two men appeared and grabbed him. Again they became Jamie and Dad. They were so pleased to see Alice that they forgot about the prisoner. He escaped their grasp and, in slow motion, made for the roof's edge. Alice looked on in horror as Jamie and Dad ran after the prisoner, caught him just in time, and wrestled with him. The three became one mass, arms flailing in all directions. In a flash they were gone, over the edge, towards certain doom.

Alice woke, face screwed up, fists clenched tight. She realised where she was, and her anguish turned to relief as she grasped that Jamie and Dad hadn't died in the fall.

Nor had the prisoner.

CHAPTER 6

At 11am the doorbell chimed. Alice opened up to find a smile and a hug dressed in a tweed suit.

"You look exhausted," observed Esther.

"Absolutely knackered," mumbled Alice.

"After I've said hello to Sofia, I'm taking you out for a strong coffee. I can't think of a better way to kickstart the weekend."

Ten minutes later they were driving down a narrow hillside lane, a grey stone wall holding back the trees on one side, the river rippling twenty feet below them on the other. The sunlight found sufficient gaps through the trees to make pretty dappled patterns on the road. Alice's hair was ruffled by the balmy breeze as she tuned in to the music of the gurgling river. Sometimes the world was a perfect place, and for a few moments Alice soaked up its magic.

She didn't mean to break the spell, but a question jumped out of her subconscious and took a shortcut to her lips. "Who on earth is this client you've lumbered me with?"

"Am I to infer that you're not delighted at the prospect of seeing him?"

"I don't see how I'll find the time. Miss Foster knows I'm really pushed, but her attitude is that I should get on with the job and stop whingeing." In a caricature of Diana Foster's voice, Alice continued, "I'm giving you one more chance!"

"Oh dear. I hope you didn't do your usual thing of-"

"No, I managed to control myself quite well, under the circumstances."

"I am sorry."

Alice turned to her companion. "You don't have to apologise, Esther. You know I'd do anything for you. You've been the best mentor anyone could ever wish for. But I'm on a final warning, so I've got to come up with the goods, and soon. Tell me about this ex-policeman."

"I started my forensic psychology post at the prison a few days before he was convicted. He was one of my first clients there, and my only failure." Esther paused as they rumbled over a cattle-grid. "As you know compulsive lying is one of my research interests, and he's a fascinating case. He totally believes the web of lies he's fabricated. He was convicted for drugs offences but steadfastly denies his guilt despite overwhelming evidence, including damning testimony from one of his police colleagues."

"Oh God! Is his name Paul Ireland?"

"That's right. Didn't Diana Foster tell you his name?"

"No, she got sidetracked. A client called Bonny Mason mentioned him. The colleague who gave evidence against him wasn't...Leo Mason?"

"Yes indeed," nodded Esther. "The plot thickens."

"Bonny informed me that Ireland is stalking her. He stands across the street while her husband Leo's at work. She has severe anxiety which has been worse since Ireland started bothering her. Are you sure I should be taking him on as a client? Surely there'll be a conflict of interest."

"Perhaps. Why don't we discuss that after his appointment? I expect he'll deny the whole thing."

"Careful!" cried Alice as they approached a family of ducklings wading in a puddle of spring water at the edge of the road.

"I've spotted them," responded Esther. "I did a lot of work with Paul Ireland, trying to help him gain insight into his lying, but his belief in his story is unshakable. He insists that Leo Mason set him up by planting drugs on him. Having lost everything, he has to believe that someone else is to blame rather than risk being destroyed by his own guilt. He became a bit of an obsession of mine, but I'd made no progress by the time he was released. I offered to keep seeing him, but he refused. Then last week, out of the blue, he rang me. He said he's prepared to do some further work on his condition. I agreed instantly, but he surprised me by insisting that he wants a different psychologist, one with no prior involvement in his case, no prejudices. He was adamant, so I agreed. He asked me who I'd recommend. I gave him a couple of names and he chose you. Actually, I was pleased. It'll be good experience for you, and I know you'll keep me in the loop."

"Of course," agreed Alice.

"I didn't mean to cause you problems."

"It's okay. This might work out for the best. If I can get somewhere with Ireland it should help to relieve Bonny Mason's anxiety, assuming that he recognises the impact of his behaviour and leaves her alone".

"Here we are," said Esther as they reached Teggins Farm tearoom, purveyors of the finest teas, coffees and cakes in the county.

They chose a quiet corner table covered with a red gingham cloth. They admired the ceramic brown cow creamer jug and its two companions, black sheep called Salt and Pepper. The aroma of freshly baked cinnamon cake filled the air. They asked for two slices and a large pot of coffee.

"How's Mum?" asked Esther. "Are there any signs of improvement?"

"The good news is that her fits have stopped since the radiotherapy. But she's had two more mini-strokes. She gets confused and can't talk properly for an hour or two, then gradually picks up. Her GP warned me that she's at risk of having a big one. She should have someone with her all the time but she absolutely refuses to accept anyone other than me. Then she insists I carry on with my life as if nothing's wrong!"

"She loves you very much."

"She's worried about how I'll cope when she's gone," sighed Alice.

"How will you cope?"

"I can't think that far ahead. The pressing problem is finding somewhere to live. We've got to move out in four weeks." Alice told Esther about Mum's letter.

"That's not a problem. You can both stay with me as long as you like. You know I've got plenty of room."

Alice hugged her friend.

"It's been hell this last year," continued Esther, "but you'll pull through, I know you will."

"Life was so good, and it was getting better. I thought I could achieve anything. Now my life's falling apart. I'm in quicksand, and the more I fight the worse it gets. I don't know if I want to keep doing this, Esther. I know I've got Mum, but... sometimes I feel so lonely." Tears trickled down Alice's cheeks.

"Hang on, girl." Esther dabbed Alice's tears with her napkin. "Remember the old Alice, full of energy and determination. She'll soon be back, don't you worry."

"Not soon enough to save her job," groaned Alice. "Maybe it's for the best.

What I need is a completely new life."

"Don't say that. You mustn't even think about giving up psychology. You may be a bit rough around the edges, and you may be a little too quick with your opinions at times, but you have something special, something that can't be taught. And you care deeply about your clients, more than anyone else I've worked with. You have the potential to become one of the best." The cake and coffee arrived. "And the world is always a better place with a slice of cinnamon cake in your hand!"

They grinned at each other and, in perfect unison, lifted the sizeable chunks of cake to their lips. Alice felt the warm glow of friendship and knew that Esther was feeling it too. They enjoyed a few moments of silence.

As Esther topped up their coffee cups, Alice said: "There's something I want you to do for me. I need a favour."

"Oh yes, what's that?"

"Last night I saw someone on the roof of the prison. I think he intended to jump, but they got him down."

"It was on the news this morning," said Esther. "That was Harry Hart, the illusionist. I expect you know he owns a house in Watertown."

"I've never met him, but I've seen him on television."

"Brilliant magician and funny too. Gay and proud. He had an absolutely stunning transvestite assistant called Greta."

"A guy?"

"His real name was Grant. Harry's not one of my clients at the prison but I know some of the story. He crashed his car last year. Grant died instantly. There was something wrong with the brakes. Harry pleaded guilty to manslaughter."

"That's terrible," said Alice. "How's he coping?"

"I haven't heard, but I'd imagine that someone like Harry would be extremely popular with certain fellow inmates."

Alice shuddered. "It might sound crazy, but I want to meet him. Can you arrange it for me?"

"Are you sure that's a good idea? You've just been telling me how much you've got on your plate."

"It's important, Esther. I wasn't there when Jamie needed me. I can't explain it, and I'm probably going mad, but this feels like a chance to put that right, at least partly. It's something I have to do."

"If you put it like that I'll see what I can arrange. I suppose I owe you one."

Alice pecked Esther on the cheek.

When she got home, Alice found Sofia watching the lunchtime news. She sat down next to her, taking her hand. "Anything interesting?"

"Same old news. Politicians stealing our money, Europeans taking over our country. We let too many come here. We are too soft." Sofia turned off the television and grabbed the paper. "Have you read your stars today? You will meet a rich man and be very happy. See, I told you!"

"Yes, Mum." Alice knew from experience not to take Sofia's bait.

Sofia picked up her crochet work.

"Mum, there's something I meant to show you. I was sorting through some of Dad's books the other day, and I found something tucked into The Day of the Jackal."

Alice left the room, returning after a few moments holding a photograph. "It's a photo of Dad holding me when I was a baby."

Alice handed the photo to her mum and waited for the anticipated smile. A startled look materialised instead. Sofia's face turned white.

"Mum, are you alright?"

Sofia stared at the photo.

"Do you feel ill?"

Sofia collected herself. "I am fine."

"You never told me you wanted a boy."

"What?"

"I'm dressed in blue."

"Yes, I see. I think we had all different colours."

"And what about that moustache!"

Sofia said nothing.

"I don't recognise the room," continued Alice. "Where was it taken?"

"I do not remember, darling. Is it important?"

"No, Mum, not at all. I thought it might bring back a happy memory, that's all. I'll put it back where I found it."

Alice was troubled by the realisation that Sofia's memory might be failing.

CHAPTER 7

Angus lifted the guitar strap over his head and plugged his Fender into the Vox amp. He turned to the poster on his basement wall, as he did at the start of every rehearsal, and searched into Jimi Hendrix's eyes for inspiration. Pulling a plectrum from his jeans pocket, he nodded to his companion who adjusted his headphones and cried, "One, two, three, four," before thumping out the opening beats of Angus's latest composition, Insanity Rules.

Halfway through the number Angus stopped playing without warning.

A few beats later the drummer followed suit. "Sorry, Mate," he said, "my timing's all over the place. From the top?"

"You've got to concentrate," snapped Angus. "It's only ten days to the biggest gig we've ever played."

"It's just a rehearsal, Mate."

"We've got to be spot on," insisted Angus. "We've got to be perfect."

"You know I'm not a perfectionist like you."

"All the great musicians are perfectionists!"

"What if I don't wanna be one of the great fucking musicians!" The drummer threw down his sticks, one of which bounced upward, flicking a cymbal as it arced sideways onto the floor.

Angus hesitated, trying to calm himself. "What's up with you?"

"Nothing, Mate. Everything's fine."

"Come on, Stix." He unplugged his guitar. "What is it?"

"Angus, I know how much all this means to you, how obsessed you are with making it to the top. It's your dream, I know that."

"Our dream."

"You've always been so focused. But for me, well, I started playing drums for fun. Things have got a bit out of hand."

"What are you talking about?"

"I've been meaning to tell you for a while, Mate, but..."

"Tell me what? Oh, bollocks! It's that crazy woman of yours, isn't it?"

"Yeah, Stella's been a big influence since she came into my life."

"You mean a big distraction," grumbled Angus. "She's on another planet. She's a Woodstock hippy time-warped into the future."

"Since I met Stella, I've been seeing things differently."

Angus threw his head back and groaned.

"I've wanted to tell you," continued Stix, "but you've been so stressed out that…"

"What the hell are you talking about?"

"I've got a job, starting Monday. It's all sorted."

A wave of nausea twisted Angus's stomach.

"Stella thinks I should have a break from the drums, at least until I get settled into the job."

"That's insane! We've got a monster gig coming up. We're on the verge of something big. All the work we've put in, the hundreds of hours, it's about to pay off."

"Don't worry, Mate, I'll play the gigs you've already booked, you know I will. I wouldn't let you down."

Angus dropped onto a stool in front of the bass drum, and stared at the words 'Spear Thistle' painted on the front skin. He picked at his fingernails.

"This isn't easy for me either, Mate. The cash we've been making from gigs has come in very handy, but it's never gonna be enough to…" Stix took a deep breath. "Look, Mate, I need to start saving some money. Stella's been on at me for a while to get a proper job. Recently she's stepped up the pressure."

"Classic. She won't be happy 'til she's cut you off from all your mates."

"What bleeding mates? You're the only bloke I ever spend time with."

Angus stood up. "Stix, you've got to listen to me. She'll have you burning incense and hugging trees before you realise what's happened."

"No, Mate, you're the one who needs to listen. Okay, she's different. But she knows what's important. You know she works as a carer, don't you?"

"What the fuck has that got to do with anything?" whined Angus.

"Some days she comes home from work in tears. Some of her clients have tough lives, really tough. It eats away at her, so I've tried to get her to give it up. Instead she persuaded me to spend a day with her at work. Christ, what an eye-opener that was. I went the next day, and the next. It didn't take long before I knew. I've got myself a job as a trainee carer."

"What?"

"She didn't have to twist my arm, Angus. I really want to do this. I'm fed up with living life as if my needs are so important. It's time to come out of my own world and start thinking about people who aren't as lucky as I am."

"And you think this is going to make you happy? You've just told me your girlfriend can barely cope with the stress of her job."

"She gets tons of support. She's got loads of friends."

"Unlike us you mean? Well, I bet you anything they're all as mad as she is."

"Is she mad? Really? Look at us, then tell me who's mad."

"What sort of life is that?" scoffed Angus. "Working yourself to death for peanuts."

"There are people out there whose lives are much worse than hers, and Stella's the kind of person who can't turn away and ignore that. To her every human being's important, and her life is worthwhile as long as she can help their suffering."

"Most people have easier lives than her, but I don't see any of them queueing up to make her life better."

"I told you," insisted Stix, "she's special. She has as much right to be happy as anyone, yet she's prepared to sacrifice that for the sake of other people."

"The best way to help other people is to get rich and famous. Look at Bono, and Bob Geldof. They can influence governments, really change the world. People like Stella hardly scratch the surface."

"If we all scratched the surface, every one of us, it would make a real difference. Anyway, I can't wait around for fame that may never come. I need to make a difference now, however small that might be."

Angus clasped his hands together. "I don't believe what I'm hearing."

"It's not just that, Mate. Truth is, I've found someone special, and the thought of losing her frightens me."

"If she loves you she'll stick with you through thick and thin, no matter where you go, no matter what you do."

"How can I be sure of that? Look what happened to you. You were engaged to Jess, a great girl, but you pushed her away, didn't you?"

"I didn't push her away," growled Angus.

"Of course you did, you idiot. You ignored her until she couldn't take it any more. You and your obsession with the band. I'm not making the same mistake. Can't you see we're suffocating in our own little world? We're human, Mate, and without other humans we're gonna waste away. That's what you've been doing since Jess left. You're wasting away."

Angus held out his hands. "We'll be fine as long as we stick together. I've told you before, you're like the brother I never had. We've come on so fast, it's like we've been playing together for years. We're so tight we can read each other's minds. All that effort, rehearsing day and night, it's paying off."

"You'll find another drummer. A better one."

"No chance. I'll give it all up."

"Don't be daft."

"Sod it then!" screamed Angus, grabbing the neck of his guitar and lifting it high into the air.

"No!" shouted Stix, jumping out from behind the drums to grab Angus's arm. He rescued the guitar and placed it carefully down.

"This world is so full of shit," moaned Angus. "How can anyone expect to be happy? But we've got something going for us, a chance to get a decent life. All we have to do is concentrate on the music. Everything'll be great once we've made it."

"No, Mate. The world will still be full of shit, even then. There's no bloody Shangri-La. Better to have a life now."

"Don't you wanna know if we can get there," pleaded Angus, "to see if we've got what it takes?"

"Part of me does, I admit that."

"What about that thrill we get when we're tight and everything's perfect. Surely you'll miss that."

"Of course I'll miss it. But it doesn't last, does it? It's gone before you can start to enjoy it. I don't wanna spend my time looking for the next thrill. There's got to be more to life than that."

"What about the buzz we get from a great crowd?" argued Angus. "Think about that, and imagine it multiplied a hundred times when we start playing bigger venues. What an experience that's gonna be."

"However great the buzz, it's soon gone. I want a life that gives me a buzz all the time. Maybe without the highs, but much more satisfying."

Angus sat down on the stool, rubbing his hands across his face. "I don't mean to be a pain, but you know how long I've dreamed of us being signed by a label. We can't let that go now."

"You don't have to, Mate."

"I admit I've been difficult lately. And you're right, I let a fantastic girl slip through my fingers. But honestly, despite all the heartache, I don't think we should give up. All I want is for us to achieve our potential, even if it's all over in a year or two. Fighting to get there is what's kept me going. Without that there's no point."

"Don't say that," pleaded Stix.

"Don't think I haven't thought this through. I lie awake every night thinking about it. I just know that we've got what it takes to be famous."

"That's another thing. Don't you worry about the person you'll become when you're famous? A lot of stars start out okay but end up total bastards. I don't wanna take that risk, ending up as some arrogant wanker, taking drugs, spending a fortune on cars, clothes and women."

"Surely that's up to us. Nobody forces these stars to behave the way they do."

"I don't know if I'd have the strength to resist."

"Okay, some of the greats had troubled lives. I don't suppose Elvis or Michael Jackson died happy. But they achieved immortality. People will be playing their music for decades, maybe centuries to come."

Stix shook his head. "Even if I was certain we'd be famous, even if I knew we'd be immortal, that wouldn't be enough. I want to make people's lives better. I want to make a real difference."

"Great music makes a real difference to people's lives! How many people survive depression with the help of music? How many people make lifelong friendships and find their soulmates through their love of music?"

"Look, Mate, I know how much the band means to you. You won't give up, even though you know it might not make you happy."

"I don't care about being happy!"

"What about my happiness? Do you care about that?"

"Of course...you know I do."

"You're going to carry on, whatever the consequences. You won't give up, however long it takes, even if you end up miserable. Even if it kills you. Well, I'm not giving up either. I've got my own struggle ahead, to become who I want to be." Stix put an arm around Angus's shoulders. "You know how much I care about you, don't you?"

Angus stared into space.

"You've got a dream, Mate, and there's nothing wrong with that. But it's your dream, not mine, and I can't help you achieve your ambition without giving up my own."

Angus turned his face away.

"It's important to me," pleaded Stix, "that you understand, and respect my decision."

"I understand all right. What I want counts for nothing! However successful the band might be, you'd feel a failure, you poor sod. Come on, you'd better go. You should be with that mad tart of yours, making plans to become a decent person. And deciding how many kids she wants!"

Angus followed Stix to his car.

Stix started the engine and wound his window down. "Have you seen It's a Wonderful Life, Mate?"

"What are you on about now?" groaned Angus.

Stix reached across to the glove compartment and took out a DVD box. "Stella bought it for my birthday. I've been meaning to lend it to you."

"You know I'm not into films."

"Please watch it. It'll help you understand."

Angus took the DVD box and watched Stix drive off down the road. As he walked towards his front door he spun the box against the wall of the building. It shattered on impact, the disc flying out onto the ground. Angus slammed the front door behind him and headed for the basement to smash his Fender.

CHAPTER 8

Saturday had always been Sammy Rice's favourite day of the week. When he was a lad Saturday meant going to Brunton Park to watch Carlisle play. If Carlisle were playing away, Saturday meant Grandstand on the telly. The last place Sammy wanted to be on this or any other Saturday was in his GP's consulting room.

"You do realise, Mr Rice, that Saturday surgery is meant for emergencies only!"

"Yes, Dr Cartwright, I know. It wasn't me who rang for the appointment."

"I see. Here under duress, are we?"

"You could say that."

Her chubby fingers tapped away at the keyboard. "Anyway, all of your test results seem to have come back. Hmm, interesting."

Sammy monitored her tone of voice and facial expression for signs of reassurance. He found none.

"Let's start with the good news, shall we?"

"Yes please," muttered Sammy.

"The endoscopy, the camera examination of your stomach, showed that you do have an ulcer as suspected. But it's a small one, and it doesn't look as if it's been bleeding."

"That is good news," gasped Sammy.

"So the blood you vomited didn't come from there."

"Oh," he groaned, "that doesn't sound so good."

"I'm afraid it isn't, Mr Rice. In addition to the ulcer, they found some varicose veins at the lower end of your oesophagus. That's the bottom of your gullet. The bleeding probably came from there."

"Varicose veins? Have they spread from my legs?"

"They haven't spread from anywhere. These veins are called oesophageal varices. They've become swollen."

"How did that happen?"

"The most common cause of oesophageal varices is liver disease, specifically cirrhosis of the liver."

"But I haven't got cirrhosis of the liver...have I?"

"In addition to the endoscopy they performed an ultrasound scan of your liver. The scan images are consistent with moderate to severe liver cirrhosis."

Sammy's jaw dropped.

"Have you followed my previous advice and given up alcohol?"

Sammy's mind was blank.

"I thought not." She took her hands from the keyboard and leaned towards him. "I cannot stress this enough, Mr Rice. You must stop drinking alcohol immediately, or you will surely die."

"Everyone has to die sometime, Doc."

"That's true. But do you want to die within the next eighteen months?"

His jaw dropped again.

She sat motionless, waiting.

"What if I cut down?" begged Sammy.

"You have to stop completely!"

"Please, Doc, one step at a time. I'll add more water."

She brought her hands together firmly on the desk. "You have a daughter, Mr Rice, don't you?"

"Yes."

"What is your daughter's name?"

"Emily."

"Does Emily have children?"

"Not yet."

"Is she likely to?"

"I hope so. She'll make a brilliant mother."

"Do you wish to live long enough to see your grandchildren?"

"My God! Is it as bad as that?"

"Yes, Mr Rice, it's as bad as that."

Sammy gulped. "The thing is, Doc, my job's stressful. I need the occasional drink to help me unwind."

"If that's the case, I suggest you start looking for a less taxing occupation."

"I can't give up my work. It's the only thing I know, and it gives me the chance to make a difference. As a GP you can understand that, can't you?"

"If stress is unavoidable there are various ways of coping with it. Some people manage without resorting to alcohol."

"How do you cope, Doc?"

"We're not here to talk about me, Mr Rice, are we?"

"No, Doctor, sorry."

"You must start taking responsibility for your own health."

"Yes, Doctor, you're right."

"That's better. Now what about your weight?" She glanced at his belly. "You seem to have put on quite a lot."

Pot, kettle, black, thought Sammy.

She took a tape measure from a drawer. "Stand up please."

As she passed the measure around his waist, Sammy resisted the impulse to take hold of it and measure hers instead.

"One hundred and twenty centimetres," she said, tutting.

"What's that in English?"

"Forty-seven inches."

"Blimey."

She weighed him, then checked her computer screen. "You've put on twelve kilos."

"Is that a lot?"

"That's nearly two stones. What on earth have you been eating?"

"I've put it all on since you got me to give up smoking, Doc," he pleaded.

"Are you suggesting it's my fault that you're obese?"

"Of course not, it's just that-"

"I'm glad to hear it!" She took a booklet from another drawer and dropped it on the desk. "There's some good dietary advice in here."

Sammy scanned the front page, focusing on a colourful picture of a variety of vegetables, many of which he didn't recognise. "You're not suggesting that I become a…" He couldn't bring himself to say the word.

"Vegetarian? No, but I must insist that you cut out red meat."

"I can do that, Doc, no problem. As long as I can have my bacon sandwiches for supper."

"What?"

"Bacon doesn't count as red meat, does it?"

She closed her eyes.

"Okay, okay, no bacon sandwiches," he whined.

"And I advise you to stick to skimmed milk. I assume you know which…it's the one with the red top."

"I tried it once," he grimaced. "It tasted like water."

She tapped at the keyboard. "What about exercise? Do you get any at all?"

"I walk up and down the stairs to my office, when the lift's out of order."

"May I suggest that you use the stairs even when the lift is working?"

Sammy took a moment to absorb this suggestion. "An excellent idea," he said without the slightest conviction.

"Have you heard of Parkrun?" she asked.

"I don't think so."

"It takes place at Chances Park once a week. People run five kilometres. Each person's time is recorded and published on the website. It's a good way to improve fitness, and it's free."

"I don't think I'll live as long as eighteen months, Doc, if I try to run."

"Many people walk round to start with, then see how they get on."

"Sounds great. I'll definitely give it a go."

She peered at him through half-closed eyes. "Alternatively, you could book a week or two at a health farm, to get some professional advice about exercise and diet."

"Is that available on the health service?"

"No, given the current financial state of the NHS-"

"I'll stick to the running then."

"I'll check the Parkrun website to see how you get on," she emphasised, one eye raised. "One more thing. Your blood results."

What now, thought Sammy?

"They show significant inflammation of your liver, though that's not a surprise."

"I suppose not."

"And your blood sugar is borderline."

"What does that mean?"

"It means that you're at high risk of developing diabetes if you don't lose a lot of weight. Assuming that you live long enough to get diabetes, that is."

"Okay, Doc, I've got the message."

"Diabetes will put you at risk of various complications. Kidney failure, heart disease, poor circulation, blindness, and of course impotence."

Sammy's face flushed. "Actually, Doctor, that is something I've been told to ask you about."

"I see. We've already missed the boat, have we?"

"You could say that."

"How long have you been having problems getting an erection."

She doesn't beat about the bush, thought Sammy. "About six months."

"Does it ever get hard, even partially?"

"Not really."

"What about first thing in the morning?"

"That's stopped as well," he sighed.

"Why didn't you come to see me earlier?"

"Well…"

"Never mind. It's probably caused by a combination of your alcohol intake and early diabetes. I'd better check you over though, just in case."

"I beg your pardon?"

"Remove your trousers and pants please," she ordered, gesturing towards the couch.

Sammy held onto his chair. "Do I have to?"

"No, Mr Rice, you don't have to! But I assume you do want to know if you have some kind of unpleasant disease down there?"

Sammy was not at all sure he did want to know. He got up, walked over to the couch, and started to undress.

"Lie down when you're ready," she said, pulling on a pair of latex gloves.

He hauled himself up, rolled onto his back, and held his thighs together as tightly as he could.

"Legs apart please." She started to examine his testicles.

It would be just my luck, thought Sammy, after it's been dormant all these months, if it decided to wake up now. He was sure that he could feel it growing. "Ooh!"

"Am I hurting you?"

"No, Doc, everything's fine."

She was now checking his penis.

Sammy closed his eyes and tried to think of anything that would take his mind off what she was doing. Into his brain popped an image of a meadow covered with a blanket of pastel-coloured flowers. A herd of deer nibbled at the lush grass. That's better, he thought. He noticed a group of mushrooms, and held his breath in horror as one of them increased in size, as if in a time-lapse film, until it stood tall and proud in the shape of an erect penis. "No!"

"Are you sure you're okay?"

"Yes," squeaked Sammy, eyes tight shut.

"Nearly finished."

A deer approached the mushroom and trampled it into the ground. "Thank God," he whispered. In the next moment a magnificent stag mounted the deer and began thrusting into her with gusto. "Go away!"

"For goodness sake relax," groaned Dr Cartwright. "I think you've had enough for now. We can do the rectal examination next time. Get dressed please."

Sammy rolled off the couch, exhausted. "Is everything okay?"

"There's no sign of anything abnormal."

He puffed his cheeks and blew out.

"Please make an appointment to see me again in four weeks."

Four years would suit me better, thought Sammy. "Will do."

"And remember everything I've said."

"Definitely." He made for the door.

"Aren't you forgetting something?" She held out the diet booklet.

"Thanks, Doc, you're a star."

CHAPTER 9

Angus stood paralysed in the centre of his basement, fists clenched, staring into Jimi Hendrix's eyes. His Fender was still in one piece.

Since Stix had left, almost an hour ago, Angus had replayed the argument over and over in his head. Finally, he screamed at Jimi, "Aaargh!"

Full of adrenaline, he found himself storming out of the house, jumping into his Chrysler Crossfire roadster, and screeching off in the direction of Stella's flat. He knew Stix would be there. If I can talk to them both, he thought, reason with them.

Stella answered the door. "Angus, hello." She glanced past him into the street. "Stix has just popped out to get a Chinese." She waited for Angus to say something. "D'you want to come in? I expect there'll be more than enough for three."

Angus felt something brush against his leg and looked down to find a black cat curving around his calf. Stella smiled nervously, picked up the cat, and retreated into the flat.

Angus followed for a few steps then hesitated. "It's okay, I'm not hungry. I'd better go."

"Sit down," said Stella, pointing at the sofa. She dropped onto a giant bean-bag and stroked the cat. "Stix was very upset when he got home. He didn't say a word for half an hour. What happened?"

"You know what happened."

"I guess he told you then?"

"After all the time and effort we've put in, it's over..." Angus clicked his fingers. "...just like that."

"I understand how-"

"You understand nothing! Can't you see we're on the verge of something big? If we don't take this chance there may never be another."

"What d'you mean by something big? Late nights, alcohol, drugs? Is that your ambition?"

"I'm not interested in any of that crap. The music means everything to me."

"What if Stix doesn't share your obsession? What if he believes there's more to life?"

"He's a bloody good drummer. He can be one of the best."

"Perhaps."

"Please, Stella, you must talk to him, make him understand."

"Stix has made up his own mind. You see only one purpose in your life, but he-"

"Stix shares that purpose! He's just confused. It's nerves, that's what it is. He's shitting himself because we've got a top record producer coming to a gig. He'll be fine when that's over."

"Are you sure, Angus?"

"He'll listen to you. If you don't talk to him, by the time he comes to his senses it'll be too late. It'll be your fault. He'll realise you denied him the chance of being somebody. He'll hate you."

"We'll see."

"Look, I know what you want. You want him to settle down, get a steady job, have kids."

Stella's face reddened.

"You've got plenty of time for that. We'll get a contract and make a couple of albums. It'll all be over in a year or two. If we do hit the big time Stix can leave and I'll find another drummer. The two of you can settle down, have kids, and spend the next fifty years together."

"It's not that simple, Angus. There are more important things in life than satisfying our own selfish needs. There's work to be done. Work that can't wait a year or two."

"You mean your missionary work? I see you've brainwashed Stix into joining you. Surely you can hang on. It won't be that long before you can have him all to yourself!"

Stella leapt to her feet. "You have no idea what you're talking about! There are people out there who can't wait for our help. A few days can make all the difference." She took a step towards him. "Have you heard of Dr Barnardo?"

"What?"

"It's a simple question."

"Of course I have," protested Angus. "What's he got to do with-"

"When his first home was full, he turned away an eleven-year-old boy who was found dead two days later. After that he put up a sign saying, 'No Destitute Child Ever Refused Admission'. If help is needed today it needs to be given today, otherwise it may be too late. We must make the most of the time we have, make every day count. Otherwise how can we sleep at night, knowing there are people suffering and not doing anything to help?"

"That's a load of shit. If everybody spent all their time looking after everyone else, nothing would ever get done. The world just doesn't work like that."

"No one's stopping you from doing what you want, Angus. I'm proud of what Stix is trying to achieve. If only you were proud of him too."

Angus jumped up. "You can twist things round all you want! You've trapped him and you're not gonna let him go, it's as simple as that."

"I'm not going to lie to you. We're in love, and yes, I do want children. There's nothing strange about that. What better purpose is there? Don't you want kids, one day?"

"Why would anyone want to bring a child into a crap world like this? But what do I know? I'm just an arsehole who doesn't give a toss about anyone but himself. Whereas you...you know everything! You get all the answers by freeing your mind, attuning yourself to the rhythms of the universe, all that bollocks. You think you have some kind of awareness that escapes other people. Well, it's time to wake up. You might think you're at one with the universe, but you're not living in the same universe as I am."

"You're right, Angus, it's a harsh world. Which is why we all need to be less wrapped up with our own problems and learn to care about each other. I do like to free my mind, attune myself to the rhythms of the universe, all that bollocks. But I'm not a fool. Meditation helps me stay calm, at peace, able to accept what goes on in the real world. It doesn't do any harm, so why should you mock it?"

"What about the paranormal? Spirits, hauntings, all that claptrap. I bet you've got fairies at the bottom of your garden."

"There is more to this world than we can possibly understand. I like to think that nature is able to transcend ordinary existence."

"As I said, claptrap."

"You've clearly made up your mind about me," she sighed. "I had hoped we could be friends."

Angus dropped down onto his chair, eyes shut, the strength draining from his body. "If the world blew up tomorrow, it wouldn't matter at all. Nothing really matters."

Stella kneeled at his feet. "Don't you ever feel at peace?"

"Only when I play guitar," he murmured, picking at his fingernails.

"Playing helps you escape?"

He nodded.

"What are you trying to escape from, Angus?"

No reply.

"Do you miss Jess?"

Angus's eyes snapped open. "How do you know about...?"

"Stix told me about her. It's been tough since she left."

"It's been tough all my bloody life! I was screwed up before I met Jess. We never had a chance."

"Have you seen her recently?"

"She's found someone else."

"I'm sorry."

"Don't be. She's better off without me."

"Because you're screwed up?"

"Right."

"Do you have any brothers or sisters?"

He shook his head.

"What about your parents?"

"My mother lives in Inverness."

"And your father?"

Angus turned his face away.

"It might help to talk about it, Angus."

"There's nothing to talk about. I never knew my real dad, my step-dad left when I was eight. That's it, no big deal."

"Are you sure about that?"

"What is this, some kind of therapy session?" He moved to get up.

Stella touched his arm. "Tell me about your step-dad."

Angus sank back into the chair.

"Was he strict?" she asked.

"No way! Callum was great. We played football in the garden every day. Even if it rained, which it usually did."

"Why did he leave?"

"You'll have to ask my mother that."

Stella raised her eyebrows.

"It's complicated," muttered Angus.

"Do you keep in touch with Callum?"

"I haven't seen him since he left. He emigrated to New Zealand after the divorce. He obviously wanted to get as far away from her as possible."

"What about your real dad? You say you never knew him."

Angus bit his lip.

"Have you tried to find him?"

"I know roughly where he lives."

"But you've never met him. Why not?"

"Mother always told me that he didn't want anything to do with me. She made me promise never to contact him. She made me swear on the Bible."

"Is your mother very religious?"

"Religious? She's a Catholic fundamentalist! Why d'you think Callum left? He couldn't stick it any longer."

"I'm sorry."

"Like I said, it's no big deal."

"Are you religious, Angus?"

"I know the Bible inside out and back to front."

"Do you believe there's a greater power, someone looking after us?"

"I don't know what I believe any more. And I'd rather not talk about it."

They heard the front door open.

"Hi, Stella, I'm back." Stix entered the room.

Angus stood up, Stella at his feet.

"Holy shit!" blurted Stix, dropping the plastic bag of Chinese food.

"It's okay," replied Stella, rising. "Angus came round to apologise, that's all."

"Some apology, by the looks of it."

"Don't be daft," she replied.

"Right, Boss." He picked up the bag. "Are you staying for dinner, Mate?"

"No thanks, I'm not hungry."

"Just as well." Stix smiled at Stella. "Someone's eating for two!"

CHAPTER 10

At 2.45pm the school fete was in full swing. It was a scorching afternoon, with the occasional respite granted by a fluffy white cloud drifting across the sun's path. The bouncy castle was actually a bouncy dinosaur, which was even better judging by the excited cries from within. Assorted objects were being hurled at various targets. Children with painted faces roamed from stall to stall nibbling candy floss. The aroma of barbecued sausages filled the air.

For half an hour Alice criss-crossed the field searching for Leo. Her mood slipped from excitement to disappointment. He's not here, she thought. I might as well head off home.

A resonant voice from the cakes stall attracted her attention. "You can't have another one, Tom, or you won't eat your dinner."

Alice's heart fluttered. She took a step towards the voice, hesitated, then turned to walk away.

"There you are!" called Leo, stopping Alice dead in her tracks. "Tom, come and say hello to Miss Alexander."

Alice smiled at Tom and held out her hand. She flinched as he gave her a surprisingly manly handshake.

"I need to speak with Miss Alexander for a few minutes," said Leo, offering his son a coin. "Just one more cake, then you can go and find your friends."

Tom grinned, paid for his treat and trotted off.

They found a small bench in a secluded part of the field, in the shade of a sycamore.

Alice's gaze flicked between Leo's eyes and the cross-shaped scar on his cheek. Both fascinated her. The scar is very unusual, she thought. "It's very unusual," she murmured. Her hand covered her mouth. "I didn't mean...actually, it's quite attractive...oh!" Alice clenched her teeth.

"I'm glad you like it. Two lads took a dislike to me after school one day. They had one cut each."

Alice grimaced. "Mr Mason, would you-"

"Please, call me Leo."

I'd like that very much, thought Alice. "Leo, would you tell me about Bonny's anxiety problem, from your own perspective?"

"She explained what happened?"

"Yes."

"I was allocated her case a few days after the attack. When I first met her, she was a nervous wreck. There was no eye contact, she hardly said a word. It took me a while to win her trust, but in time she told me everything."

"You must have been very patient."

"I soon realised she was falling in love with me. I should've had myself removed from the case, but I felt sorry for her and wanted to help. She was so vulnerable... and beautiful."

Alice blushed.

"I tried to persuade her to resume her circus career," Leo continued, "but she was far too anxious. I wish I'd had the chance to see her perform, even once, but it wasn't to be."

"That's such a shame."

"Since we married she's never been out of the house without me. She's too frightened. I've encouraged her to go out with other people, but..."

"It must be hard for you."

"It is, sometimes."

"Do you have any idea why Bonny's anxiety has been worse recently?"

"No idea at all. I'm sure she would've told me if there was anything wrong."

"Yes, I'm sure you're right," responded Alice with an uneasy smile.

Tom came closer to them, shouting: "Can we go home, Daddy?"

"In a few minutes."

"He's a lovely boy," smiled Alice. "He has your eyes."

Leo looked down for a moment, then back at Alice. "Bonny hasn't told you?"

"Told me what?"

"She became pregnant...after she was..."

Alice's hand shot to her mouth. "Oh, Leo, what have I said! I'm so sorry."

"Don't be. You're not the first person to think Tom and I are alike."

"Does Tom know?"

"Of course," he nodded. "Everyone knows."

"You've brought him up as your own?"

"Absolutely."

"Did you consider having more children?"

"I wanted to, very much. I'd love a daughter. But Bonny doesn't eat properly, and she's always so anxious. I suppose that's why...I'm sure there's nothing wrong on my side."

Alice wanted to change the subject, but all she could think about was giving Leo a daughter. She shook her head to make the thought go away.

"Before Tom comes back," said Leo, "there's something else I want to talk to you about."

"What's that?"

"I've heard on the grapevine that you're going to see Paul Ireland."

Alice startled at the name. "Sorry, Leo, I'm not allowed to discuss-"

"No, of course. But you need to know what you're up against. We were partners, so I know how his mind works better than anyone. Ireland is a devious, dangerous man. Don't trust a single word he says. And never turn your back on him. That's all I need to say."

"Thanks, Leo. I suspected as much, but it's good to hear it from such a reliable source."

They stood up. Both hesitated.

"Thank you so much for helping Bonny," said Leo. He bent down and kissed Alice softly on the cheek. She kept perfectly still.

Leo jerked backwards. Tom was running towards them.

As she left the fete, Alice tried to analyse her feelings for Leo. Why are things we can't have so much more attractive? What would Bonny think if she realised? All Alice knew for sure was that she came alive in Leo's presence. How could that be a bad thing?

Alice spent the rest of the afternoon doing housework and preparing dinner. Shepherd's pie followed by lemon meringue, Mum's favourites.

She watched Sofia pushing the food around her plate. "Try to eat a little bit, Mum. You've got to keep your strength up."

"I know, Aliki. I will eat more tomorrow."

After dinner they played rummy until Sofia nodded off in the chair.

Alice grabbed her laptop, opened YouTube, and typed in Harry Hart. She found a video of a show which featured Harry and Greta performing an illusion using a large wooden chest. Harry was about thirty-five, medium height, with short dark hair. He was wearing a white tank top, white waistcoat and trousers, and white shoes. Around his neck was a black and red tartan choker. An interesting look, thought Alice. Greta was younger. She was tall, dark, and stunningly beautiful. She wore a St Trinian's-style schoolgirl outfit, with a tartan tie and matching pleated mini-skirt. Her long legs looked fabulous in black hold up stockings. Alice said out loud, "There is no way she's a guy, no way!"

Sofia murmured, "Who, darling?" but did not wake up.

Alice settled back to watch Harry locking Greta inside the chest before springing effortlessly up onto it. With both hands he lifted a black silk curtain between the audience and himself. A moment later the curtain dropped, revealing Greta standing in his place, wearing a tartan catsuit. The audience reaction was ecstatic. Wow, thought Alice, they were good. Greta unlocked the chest, out of which leapt Harry, arms aloft, with a beam from ear to ear. Alice couldn't help smiling with him.

That evening, with Sofia safely tucked in bed, Alice sat down with the photo she'd found in The Day of the Jackal. It fascinated her. Dad looked so proud cradling her in his arms. And it was the only picture of him she'd ever seen sporting a moustache. It was impressively thick, and even redder than his ample locks. She decided to keep the photo on her bedside table.

"Hi, Jamie," she said later in the direction of her open bedroom window. "It's been another interesting day. Esther took me for a drive, then I went to the fete to meet Leo Mason. I think I might have a bit of a crush going there. I expect I'll get over it soon enough." She played with her engagement ring. "I'm worried about Mum. She's not eating properly and her memory's dodgy." Alice yawned. "I'm really tired, so I'll say night night."

As she closed the window Alice gazed in the direction of the prison. She wondered how Harry was coping? Will they allow me to see him, she thought? What if he refuses? What could I possibly say or do that would help him anyway?

Alice was soon asleep. Within minutes a nightmare began. She was in Watertown prison, in an enormous room with no furniture and bare grey walls. A solitary light bulb was swinging like a pendulum from the ceiling. The room was full of men, all staring silently at her. They were a mixture of guards and prisoners together, their shadows swaying to and fro across the walls and across each other's faces and bodies. Alice pleaded with the men to watch out for Harry, to protect him. The men looked at each other, then back at Alice, and started sniggering. They laughed louder and louder until they were roaring hysterically. The sound was deafening.

Alice woke, her bedroom silent. She stared at the print of Van Gogh's Landscape at Twilight on her bedroom wall until she nodded off. She didn't wake again until the church bells started ringing.

CHAPTER 11

The hoot of an owl entered through the open bedroom window. It didn't disturb Angus. He'd already given up trying to sleep. Having tossed and turned for hours, he lay on his back, eyes closed, breathing slowly, attempting to keep his mind blank.

It was no good. Every time his mind cleared, the same image jumped into it. Stella's face.

Angus wanted to hate Stella. That would make it so much easier for him to persuade Stix to reconsider. He wanted to dislike her, even a little. But it was hopeless. He'd already relived their entire conversation, and realised that he agreed with her. Agreed with every word she'd said.

All his life Angus had been asking himself the same questions. Why are we here? What's the point of existence? Is my life serving some greater purpose? Whenever he'd asked his mother these questions, she'd told him to have faith in God, that all would be revealed. Whenever he'd asked Father Barrington, long conversations followed, after which he'd be more confused than before. When he'd asked God, there was no answer.

So he stopped asking, and focused on playing guitar. Playing every moment he could, day and night. Until one day he dreamed he would be a star. He'd been dreaming that dream ever since. Until today.

"Damn you, Stella!" he cried. "There goes my reason for living. What am I supposed to do now?"

It was already getting light when he finally dozed off, exhausted.

In the morning Angus hid under the duvet, trying not to ask himself the same question. He rolled himself up in a ball, desperate to get back to sleep. It was no good. What am I supposed to do now?

He yearned to see Jess's face, but knew that meeting her again would only make him worse. He decided to do the next best thing. He would go to Oxley Park.

Angus and Jess used to visit the park once a week. They'd sit on the bench under the old oak tree by the pond, feeding the ducks, talking about anything and nothing.

As Angus entered the park he saw that the bench was occupied by a couple having a cuddle and a kiss. He waited on the grass nearby, watching them from the corner of his eye.

"Where's your young lady?" asked a trembly voice.

Angus turned to find a white-haired old lady standing by his side.

"I've seen the two of you here many times," she recalled, "sitting on that bench. But not recently. Is she alright?"

"She's fine," replied Angus.

"But you're not?"

"Not really."

"You're waiting to sit there, I suppose."

"That's right."

"Do you think sitting on that bench will help you feel better?"

"I don't know. I doubt it."

She tilted her head, lifting one corner of her mouth. "I don't think you're going to find what you're searching for here, young man."

"What am I searching for?"

"Love, of course! What else?"

"I already found love. I lost it. It's gone, forever."

"Don't you think it's possible to find love again, to give your heart to more than one person in your lifetime?"

Angus stared at the ground. "Not if it's broken."

"Don't be so sure, young man. Many people recover from a broken heart and learn to love again. You can take my word for that."

"Maybe, but…"

"I suppose your case is different?"

"That's right. Jess is one in a million."

"One in a million? Yes, I expect she is. But there are countless millions of young ladies in this world. So there are countless one in a million young ladies to choose from. The sooner you start looking, the better."

"It's not as simple as that."

"Are you sure? I think it's very simple indeed. You just have to decide to start."

"What's the point? I could search forever and never find another Jess."

"What will happen if you don't try?"

Angus didn't answer.

"Give yourself time. Everything will be fine, you'll see."

The old lady squeezed Angus's hand and waddled away.

Angus stood bemused, considering the old lady's words. Bemusement turned to frustration, and frustration to anger. Who does she think she is, he thought? Just because she's old, doesn't mean she's got all the answers. He decided to follow her. He'd give her some advice of his own.

The old lady had a head start and was more sprightly than she appeared. She was through the gate and across the road in no time, disappearing behind a bus.

Angus ran across the road without checking. He jumped onto the bus as the door was closing.

"How far are you going?" asked the driver.

"Back here," replied Angus, knowing that the bus had a circular route.

"Are you sure? It'll take an hour if you're lucky."

"That's fine. I've got nowhere to go."

Angus paid the fare and looked around for the old lady. She was nowhere to be seen.

He sat by a window and watched the world go by. He saw a girl in a crimson dress getting into her banana-coloured VW Beetle. She caught up with the bus, matching its speed for a while before turning off at a roundabout filled with marigolds and dahlias.

Angus surveyed the flowers. The world is full of colour, he thought, full of life. My world is grey, and it's turning black.

Angus knew that he was dying.

CHAPTER 12

Alice parked as near to the gates as she could. Sofia struggled to walk steadily despite the help of her stick, so Alice took hold of her arm.

"I can manage on my own," moaned Sofia.

Alice held on.

The sun had been up for a few hours, but the Sunday morning mist hung around the tombstones, clinging on for dear life. A solitary rabbit nibbled at the grass between two graves. The liquid warbling of a skylark descended from above a neighbouring field. Alice remembered reading somewhere that a skylark's song is like sunshine translated into sound. The thought comforted her.

When they reached their destination, Alice opened the collapsible chair she'd brought with her. Sofia sat without complaint. The gravestone was still shiny, as if the burial had taken place a week ago rather than a year.

Sofia scolded her husband. "You could have waited until our thirtieth anniversary, Richard! I was looking forward to a beautiful pearl necklace. But I would have settled for diamonds."

Sunday had always been Alice's favourite day. She thought back to the happy Sundays of her childhood. Playing Scrabble with Dad while Mum prepared roast lamb with her homemade mint sauce. Going for a late afternoon walk followed by cheese sandwiches and ice cream for supper. Heaven. A year ago, she'd learnt to hate Sundays. I should have been there, she thought. Dad made me stay at home because I had a temperature. A stupid temperature! If I'd been in the water with them, I would've got Dad to safety with Jamie's help. The two best men in the world, gone. Because of me.

"What are you thinking about?" asked Sofia.

"Dad and Jamie," replied Alice.

"They are happy in Heaven."

"You think so?" Alice covered her mouth.

"What do you mean, darling? Of course they are happy there."

"Yes, Mum, you're right...of course."

The skylark began a new verse.

Alice stroked the mole in the centre of her forehead.

"Stop it, Aliki!" groaned Sofia. "You will make it bigger if you keep touching it."

"Don't be daft, Mum." Alice sighed, recalling how Dad used to kiss the mole gently when it was time to say goodnight. "You know it relaxes me...and it's the same size it's always been."

Sofia jerked her head upwards, tutting as loudly as she could.

A thought jumped out of Alice's mind and was instantly at her lips. "Mum, do you think there are themed areas in Heaven, for people from different backgrounds?"

"What on God's earth are you talking about, Aliki?"

"You know, like an area for the Scots, with mountains, lochs and bagpipes."

"And haggis, with neeps and tatties," added Sofia. "Perhaps."

"What about the Greek area? What d'you think they'd have there?"

Sofia pondered. "I know something I would like to see when I get to Heaven. The house and garden where I grew up in Piraeus."

"What a great idea. To re-experience times from your past."

"Happy times."

"You've told me about your childhood, Mum. You said it was tough!"

"Yes, darling, it was. We had nothing, but life was simple then. I loved the animals." She closed her eyes and breathed in through her nose. "I can still smell them all. We had rabbits, chickens, and a goat."

"Sounds dangerous," mused Alice.

"Kiki was very gentle with me. She was rough with the others, but never with me. I would stroke her fur for hours."

"Didn't your family have to eat her in the end?"

"No, Aliki. We ate her children, but not Kiki. I would have protected her with my life."

"I know you're not going anywhere, Mum, but when the time comes, what will you do if Dad's already settled in Scottish Heaven?"

"We will live there, and go to Greek Heaven for our holidays."

They chatted on while Alice tended Richard's grave.

"Mum?"

"Yes, darling?"

"Did Dad ever take you up to Inverness before I was born, to visit his family there?"

"Yes, two or three times. We stayed with Grannie and Granda."

"Did he have the moustache in those days?"

"No, darling, I hated it. I told him I would not marry him until he shaved it off, and that I would leave him if he ever grew it again." Sofia's shoulders jerked as if she'd been poked in the back. "I did let him grow it again! I changed my mind, when I was pregnant with you. But he looked better without it. No more questions, Aliki. I am too tired to remember these things. Do you want your mother to have another stroke?"

"No, Mum, of course not. Come on, let's get you home."

"What about Jamie?"

"You're too tired. I'll come back another day."

They made their way back to the car.

"You are not going to Moston today, are you?" begged Sofia. "Please, stay at home with me."

"Mum, how many times? You know I have to be there, every Sunday."

"Yes, I understand. But do you have to go in the water? It frightens me, Aliki."

"I wasn't there when they needed me! I'm not going to make that mistake again."

CHAPTER 13

Angus sat in his Crossfire struggling to block out the world.

Barbecue smoke trespassed via the air vents, coaxing in the aroma of sizzling bacon. A carefree little boy, hand in hand with his dad, skipped by clutching a kite. A passing ice-cream van chimed O Sole Mio. The world carried on as if nothing was wrong.

Angus had been parked around the corner from his mother's house for half an hour. He couldn't face going in. He couldn't face not going in and having to talk to her on the phone. He couldn't face the thought of her existence.

His mobile rang. It was her.

With gritted teeth Angus thumped the phone against the steering wheel. It kept ringing. He jabbed at the receive button.

"Angus, where are you? You're late!"

He drove around the corner. She was at the window.

"I was worried," she fretted as he entered the house, "so I prayed, and here you are, safe and sound."

"Yes, Mother, I'm here."

"Dinner's ready. It's your favourite."

Angus didn't finish his beef and potatoes.

"What's wrong?" she asked. "Don't you like it?"

"It's fine. I'm not hungry."

"Finish it up, there's a good boy. You know there are people starving in-"

"I said I'm not hungry!"

"I see," she replied, eyebrows raised. "Never mind, I've baked a Dundee cake."

"Which part of I'm not hungry don't you understand?"

"There's no need for rudeness, Angus. You know better than that."

"Do I?"

"What in God's name is that supposed to mean?"

"Just forget it! I'm sorry I wasn't hungry."

"There is something wrong, isn't there?"

"I told you, it's nothing."

"Don't lie to your mother."

Angus slumped back in his chair. "If you must know, my drummer has quit."

A fleeting smile crossed her face, followed by a dramatic frown. "Oh dear, what a shame. I suppose you'll have to give it up now." She took both his hands. "Maybe it's for the best."

Angus jerked his hands away. "You never wanted me to play the guitar. At last, your prayers have been answered."

"What do you mean? I pray every day for you to be happy. If God thinks you'll be happier not playing that...music, who are we to disagree?"

"Do I look as if I'm happy?"

"You must be patient. God will take care of you. Have faith."

"I've had faith since I was born. Where has it got me?"

"Don't talk like that, Angus!" She made the sign of the cross on her chest. "On the Sabbath of all days. What would Father Barrington think if he could hear you?"

"Why should I care what he thinks?"

"How can you say that, after everything he's done for you? Iain has been like a father to you, you know that!"

"My life's a mess."

"You should never have left home. I knew it was a mistake to let you go. Why not come back? It'll be just like old times. Remember how content we used to be, reading the Bible together, discussing the stories? We didn't need anyone else."

"If you say so," he growled, disgust covering his face.

"Dear God!" she cried. "You've changed, Angus. What's happened to my little boy?"

"He's been doing a lot of reading. And a hell of a lot of thinking."

She sat forward, elbows on the table, placing her palms together.

"Don't bother," muttered Angus. "I stopped praying months ago, when I realised no one was listening."

"It's alright," she gasped. "God understands that we are weak. We all have doubts occasionally. You remember the story of doubting Thomas, don't you?"

"Of course I do. It's one of your favourites."

"Thomas refused to believe that Jesus had risen from the dead, until he saw Jesus for himself. When he did, Jesus asked Thomas to place his hands in his wounds. Thomas was so ashamed. Jesus said, 'Blessed are those who have not seen and yet have believed'. You remember?"

"The whole point of that story," scoffed Angus, "is to contrast faith with common sense. Thomas was wrong to ask for evidence, so he failed the test of faith. It takes faith to trust children to strangers."

"Lord, forgive us," she murmured.

"Then there's the story of Abraham, another one of your favourites. God told him to sacrifice his own son! He was about to go through with it until an angel stopped him at the last minute. Abraham had faith, and it meant he could kill his own son without taking responsibility."

She whispered a prayer under her breath.

"Even today faith means people can do things that are morally wrong and accept no blame whatsoever. The result is a world of terror."

"God made a beautiful world," she said with pride.

"If God made the world he's made a bloody mess! Awful things are happening in God's world."

"It's people who've made the world a mess, Angus."

"Who made my world a mess, Mother?"

"I don't know. But you must have faith that one day you'll be happy."

"When will that be?"

"Trust in God and you will live a contented life. If not in this world, then certainly in Heaven."

"Another fairytale!"

"You're not well, Angus. Have you been taking drugs?"

"What?"

"How can you doubt the existence of Heaven? Without Heaven, how would all the poor souls who suffer so much carry on? Yes, there is despair in the world, but however hopeless people's lives are, they'll find redemption at God's side, as long as they believe."

"Belief may offer comfort for the hopeless, but it gives everyone else an excuse to look the other way. All they have to do is have faith that God will take care of the hopeless. It should be our responsibility to make sure that everyone has a chance of a decent life."

"You know that most people look to God to provide them with a decent life. Do you suppose they're all fools?"

"Not fools," replied Angus, "just human. Religion takes full advantage of our human needs. Today's religions survive because they've adapted so well to trap so many people."

"There is only one faith," she declared, "one true God."

"In this house maybe. But there are countless religions across the world, and they contradict each other so much that they can't all be correct. It's more likely they're all wrong."

"I can't believe what I'm hearing!" she cried, tears welling up in her eyes. "What have I done to deserve this?"

"What have you done? Do you really want to know? You brainwashed me. You programmed me to believe in a fairy story, then trained me never to question it. You filled my childhood with prayers, Bible lessons and church services. You did nothing at all to prepare me for the real world. And worst of all, you pushed Callum away, so you could have me all to yourself. You're a selfish bitch!"

"How dare you speak to your mother like that! After everything I've done for you. I don't know where these crazy ideas have come from. Perhaps God is testing us. Yes, that's it." She shivered. "Or it's the Devil's work."

"I've had enough of this!" screamed Angus. He got up and stepped towards the door.

She jumped at him, grabbing him round the chest. "No, Angus," she howled, tears streaming down her cheeks. "Please don't go. You must listen!"

He shoved her body away from his with a growl. She threw herself onto the floor and held out both hands to her son.

Time stood still. Angus stared at his mother. She was out of focus. He could feel the anger draining from his being until he reached a state of perfect numbness. For a few moments he was weightless, drifting upward, gazing down on the scene.

"Angus!" echoed his mother's voice.

He blinked, focused on her face, and stretched out a hand to help her up. He was now totally calm.

She dropped back onto her chair, signing the cross on her chest. "Please, Angus," she begged, "you must try to remember everything I taught you. Your future depends on it. Do you want me to explain it all again?"

"You're joking," mocked Angus.

"You have to listen to me!"

"You're serious, aren't you? You really mean it." He sat down, took off his watch and placed it on the table. "Okay, you've got five minutes. Then you'll never see me again."

"You remember?" she yelped. "God created Heaven and Earth for us in six days."

"Astronomers have proved that the earth is a microscopic fragment of the universe. We're here by complete accident due to the process of evolution."

"Our ancestors were animals?"

"Fossil records prove it. The evidence is overwhelming."

"The universe appeared all by itself, out of nothing?"

"The origin of the universe is a great unanswered question, but not knowing the answer doesn't mean we have to make something up. If your God doesn't need a creator, why must everything else?"

"God made all of us, Angus. You know he did."

"Just remind me, why exactly did he do that?"

"To serve him, and to fulfil his purpose."

"That's it, is it? And what precisely is his purpose?"

"We must trust in God. All will be revealed."

"When?"

"When we reach Heaven."

"Does that include the Muslims, the Hindus, the Buddhists? Are they all going to Heaven?"

She stared at her hands, gripped together on the table.

"The truth is, there is no Heaven. It's all a lie." He tapped his watch. "Four minutes."

She sat up, startled. "We know there is life after death. Auntie Mary went to a seance and spoke to Uncle Jack. She told us all about it."

"She was tricked. How much did she have to pay them?"

"What about near-death experiences, people going through a tunnel towards a brilliant light, hearing the voices of the departed begging them to stay back. How do you explain that?"

"Who knows what people dream about when they're at risk of death, when their brains are not working properly?"

"Non-believers change their minds on their deathbeds though, don't they?"

"When they're at their most frightened, in pain, or delirious. That says it all. The idea that fear drives people to believe in God only shows that religion is based on fear rather than sense."

"What about scripture?" she pleaded. "You know everything in the Bible is true. You've spent so much of your life reading it."

"Just because something is written in a book doesn't mean it's true. You know perfectly well the Bible is full of contradictions. The truth is that the Bible was written over a long period by many authors, based on stories passed from mouth to mouth until they'd changed beyond memory. The Bible is a work of mythology. Three minutes."

"What about miracles?" she implored. "Miracles happen every day. They prove the existence of God."

"That depends what you mean by miracles. If I suddenly grew wings and could fly, that would be a miracle."

"Mrs Green was told by her doctor that she had three months to live. Everyone prayed for her, and now she's fit and healthy five years later. You know that's true, we prayed for her together."

"The doctor made a mistake. Surprising things happen all the time, and people remember them. However unlikely something is, there's always a natural explanation."

"People see visions and hear God's voice!"

"Yes, and many of them are mentally ill or deluded. Others are lying, or just mistaken. Have you ever had such an experience?"

"No."

"But you're happy to trust the word of people who say they have? People you've never met, people you know nothing about? Two minutes."

"Please, Angus, stop this."

"Fine, I'll leave now." He put his hands on the table.

"No!"

"Two minutes."

"I taught you to pray before you could walk. You know from your own experience that God is listening."

"When something good happens, you attribute it to God. When a disaster occurs, you say that God's will is mysterious and cannot be understood by mortals. If God's will cannot be understood, how can you know that God has good intentions at all?"

"God loves and protects us, Angus. I'm at peace when I pray. I feel his presence inside me, and I know you do too."

"Not any more. Those feelings are real, but they're not based on anything outside of your own mind. People feel what they want to feel. Believing something doesn't make it true."

"But the smartest people in history have believed in God."

"Don't confuse intelligence with knowledge. If someone is indoctrinated, and never questions their belief, they will continue to believe, intelligent or not."

"Thousands of martyrs have given their lives for God. You're not going to tell me they all died for nothing!"

"People have always been willing to sacrifice themselves for something they believe in, especially if they think their earthly death is only the beginning of an eternal afterlife. Dying's not such a big deal if you're not really dying. One minute."

She grasped her hair with both hands. "Without God there'd be no purpose to life, no point."

"No point? What about helping each other, caring for each other, loving each other?"

She held out her hands. "I beg you, Angus, at least admit that you cannot prove that God doesn't exist."

"I can't prove that you're not an assassin hired by the Pope to kill me, but I'm not going to spend any time considering the possibility, because there's no evidence whatsoever to support it. The same is true for the existence of God, although you being an assassin is more likely."

"So that's it, is it? I have to accept that my only child, the son I brought up to love and respect God, has become…" She twisted her face. "…an atheist."

"Hallelujah!"

"Well, I hope you're proud of yourself. You're in good company. Remember Joseph Stalin and Chairman Mao? How many innocent people did they have killed?"

"Millions. Dictators are only right because they say so. Their regimes are built on fear and discourage freedom of speech. They're no different from religious leaders. Time's up."

"God help me, my son has been brainwashed. Can't you see, Angus? You're just repeating what other people have told you, and what you've read in books."

"It's me who's been brainwashed, is it?"

"Enough!" she cried. "You have an answer for everything. But you have no respect for your mother."

Angus's mind snapped, releasing an explosion of rage. "I don't have a mother," he roared, "and thanks to you I don't have a father! I should have two dads and I haven't got one. I've never even met my real dad."

"I've told you a thousand times, forget about him. He didn't want you."

"Yes," screamed Angus, "you've told me that a thousand times!" He stood up and gazed around the room. "I had faith in you. I believed everything you told me."

"It was for the best, Angus."

"Go to Hell!"

She covered her eyes and shrieked.

"That's not going to work, not this time."

She held out her arms in desperation. "I've always done my best for you," she wailed. "All I ever wanted was to make you happy. Now I know that I've failed."

"Don't worry," he growled, "you may have failed me, but you haven't failed God. You'll go to Heaven."

CHAPTER 14

The sun was on its return journey to the horizon. An eager tide advanced through barricades of pebbles towards the welcoming sand. Ochre boulders, crossed with cheerful orange streaks, cast lengthening shadows along the shore.

Alice stood on the beach, listening to the crashes of breaking waves, enjoying the coolness of the water splashing her ankles. The unmistakable scent of the sea rode the onshore wind as it massaged her face and body. Gusts attempted to push her back from the ocean's edge. Alice resisted. During the past year she'd swum in this water in worse conditions. It was something she had to do.

Alice steered forward across the stones and rocks until the waves were soaking the lower half of her costume. She plunged into the water, gliding along the bottom until she was startled by seaweed slithering across her face. On surfacing she took a deep breath, focused on Tern Rock, and swam directly towards it. Her purpose as usual was to swim around the island until she got tired. Very tired. It was a duty. And a punishment.

As Alice reached the island the wind was picking up. Crags afforded her protection on the near side, but the waves around the far side were powerful and tried to force her towards the rocks. She swam on undeterred.

On the sixth circuit Alice was tiring. Come on, she thought, my record is nine times around. I've got to keep going for at least one more.

As she reached the far side she took a shortcut closer to the rocks. A giant wave threw her violently sideways. She screamed as intense pain tore through the left side of her body. The next wave forced her head against the rocks with a mind-numbing thud. Alice could no longer scream as sea water entered her mouth. Her limbs stopped working. She lost consciousness.

Alice dreamt that she was deep underwater, rocking to and fro in the silence, gazing up at the sun playing on the surface. It was showing off its endless repertoire of shapes, throwing out golden spikes in all directions.

A further blow brought Alice back to reality. Stretching her neck to push her face out of the water, she coughed as hard as she could and struggled to get precious air into her lungs. My only hope is to get clear of the island, she told herself. Despite everything that was wrong in her world, Alice now realised how much she wanted to live. She swam.

Her eyes filling with seawater, Alice quickly lost all sense of direction. A powerful wave heaved her forwards. That's it, she thought, go with the waves! She paddled on, but her waning reserves of energy were rapidly used up. All she could do now was hold up her head as best she could and hope that the waves would see her back to land. The opportunities to snatch a breath came further apart as her face spent more and more time in the water. This is it, she thought.

From nowhere a powerful creature encircled her body. The beast dragged her along the surface before hauling her completely out of the water. Alice was too weak to fight. She squinted at the sun until it became eclipsed by the creature's body. She realised she was being carried through the shallows by two powerful arms, and twisted her neck to catch a glimpse of the creature's face. It was Leo's face. She rested her head against his chest and passed out.

Alice came round as Leo was drying her eyes and mouth with the towel she'd left on a boulder with her clothes. She sat up and spluttered. Leo placed the towel around her shoulders and across her chest.

"Are you okay?" he asked. "Have you inhaled any water?"

"I don't think so," wheezed Alice. She barked to clear her throat and sucked in a deep breath. "I'm fine."

"You're a lucky girl."

"Lucky you were here. Where did you come from?"

"There's been a break-in at the seaside cafe. I was just leaving when I saw someone in trouble. I never thought in a million years it'd be you."

Alice struggled to stand up. "I must get home."

"I'll drive you."

"No," she protested, "I'm fine, thank you."

"I'll walk you to your car."

Alice got dressed as quickly as her fumbling fingers would allow, then staggered ahead of Leo towards the road. Her ankle turned on a stone, throwing her backwards into Leo's arms. With no further objections from Alice, they continued side by side.

At the car they stood face to face. Leo placed his hands on Alice's shoulders. "I'll follow you home, just in case." Before she could reply he bent forwards and kissed her lips. Their faces remained inches apart.

Alice threw her arms around Leo's neck and pressed her lips against his. She jerked back. "I must go!" She scrambled into her car and drove away.

The blood drained from Alice's hands as she gripped the steering wheel, tears running down her cheeks. She pulled into a layby and wound her window down, inviting the wind to dry her eyes. She didn't want Mum to know she'd been crying.

What's happening to me, she thought? One minute I'm trying to get my world under some sort of control, the next I'm behaving like a person I don't recognise.

As she drove home Alice did see one thing clearly. She wasn't ready to die. But had she found a reason to live?

"Where have you been?" asked Sofia with a trembling voice. "Something has happened, I know it!"

"Everything's okay, Mum, relax. You know you're not supposed to get wound up." Alice kissed Sofia's cheek.

"I may be stupid, Aliki, but I know when my daughter has been crying."

"I'm fine, really."

Sofia tutted as loudly as she could.

Alice picked up the newspaper and found the TV page. "There's a Columbo on in a minute. Remember how Dad used to hate missing an episode? Why don't we watch it?"

Columbo was Alice's favourite programme. Dad loved Columbo, and they'd often enjoyed it together.

"It's Agenda for Murder, Mum, one of the four episodes with Patrick McGoohan as the murderer."

"That's nice."

Alice recalled how her interest in psychology began when Dad first introduced her to the programme. Columbo always knew who the murderer was, and the murderer always knew that he knew. The murderer's mistake was to underestimate

Columbo. Each episode involved a game of cat and mouse, played out until Columbo got the upper hand, often by hounding his opponent into making a mistake. Psychology heaven.

Alice hadn't watched an episode since Dad died. There'd been no point. But today was different. Something had changed. She switched on the TV and made herself comfortable next to Sofia. Columbo did not disappoint.

Later, in her bedroom, Alice slid off her engagement ring. "I know you won't mind, Jamie. It's been a whole year after all." She kissed the ring and placed it carefully in its box.

That night, Alice didn't have nightmares. She had dreams.

CHAPTER 15

It was a full moon, but a thin layer of cloud dampened its glow. Sammy Rice stood in the darkness under Nelson Bridge, leaning against the brickwork, waiting. He felt the vibration of a lorry crossing above.

The moonlight found a gap in the cloud and ignited the wavelets on the River Caldew as it streamed towards the bridge. A broken beer bottle on the opposite bank reflected a beam of green light into Sammy's eye. He stepped sideways out of the beam.

A hooded figure approached along the riverbank path. As it moved into the shadow of the bridge the figure stopped and twisted round.

"No one's following you, Jake," muttered Sammy.

"Can't be too careful."

Jake walked up to Sammy with his hand held out. Sammy placed a folded twenty-pound note in the palm.

"You takin' the piss, Sammy?"

"There'll be more when I get information."

Jake took another look behind him. "When you told me what you were after, I figured you must be on somethin'. A boy with a paw print tattoo on 'is face? A mobile phone covered in diamonds? The whisky's caught up with Sammy, I reckoned, he's really lost the plot."

"Never mind that. Have you got anything for me?"

"Course I 'ave, Sammy. When did I ever let you down?"

Sammy shook his head.

"Yeah, well…" Jake coughed up a mouthful of phlegm and spat it into the river. "I can't 'elp with the tattoo. I've asked around and no one's seen anythin' like that."

"What about the phone?"

"That's a different story." Jake slipped the twenty-pound note into his pocket and held out his hand.

Sammy produced another note and handed it over. "This better be good, Jake, or I'll have both twenties back."

"'Ave you 'eard of Micky Sullivan?"

"No," replied Sammy.

"You will. 'E's new in town. Flash git, by all accounts. 'E's bought the King's Arms."

"What, that dump? It should be called the King's Arse."

"Yeah, I know," chuckled Jake. "But 'e's done it up. They reckon it's like a five star 'otel now. 'E's usually in there drinkin' champagne and doin' 'is business. Nasty piece of work they reckon. 'E's been seen with some of Carlisle's 'ardest. I wouldn't go in there if you paid me!"

"What about the phone, Jake?"

"Oh yeah. Sullivan's been flashin' round this really posh mobile. 'E reckons it's made of solid gold, and it's covered in diamonds. Must be worth a bloody fortune."

"Probably a fake."

"You can tell 'im that if you like. The story goes 'e was given it by some countess 'e met in Monte Carlo. If you ask me, it's more likely 'e nicked it and killed the owner."

"I'll let you know."

"You're not thinkin' of goin' there, are you?"

"Is that it?"

Jake nodded.

Sammy held out a final twenty-pound note.

"Thanks, Sammy, you're a gentleman." Jake grasped the money and checked around before setting off back along the path.

Sammy left in the opposite direction. He got in his car and headed for the pub.

The King's Arms had been a dying pub for years. The last time Sammy had gone in he'd interrupted a deal in progress between the landlord and a shifty-looking character in a hoodie. The man's face had been well covered, but his sagging jeans granted an excellent view of a pair of tattooed upper buttocks. Sammy had walked straight back out of the pub, vowing never to return.

Sammy parked his black 1966 Citroen DS a short distance from the pub, on the opposite side of the road. He switched the engine off, and the car's cassette player on. Muddy Waters' voice sang out, 'I'm ready, ready's anybody can be. I'm ready for you, I hope you're ready for me'. Muddy was always good value for settling Sammy's nerves, and boosting his confidence.

Sammy spied across the road at the pub entrance. In front of it stood two stocky men in dark suits. Bouncers at the King's Arms, thought Sammy, times have changed. He sank back into the fifty-year-old leather seat and waited for something to happen.

The final track of the Muddy Waters album ended. Sammy listened to the hiss from the car's speakers as the cassette tape wound to its end. His eyes started to close.

A series of sharp taps on the driver's window made Sammy's heart leap. He peered through the film of moisture coating the glass's inner surface. On the outside was a hand, covered in rings, waving. Behind the hand was a pretty face. Even through a misty window Sammy knew a pretty face when he saw one.

The hand made a rapid circular motion through the air. Sammy grabbed the handle and wound his window down a few inches.

"Are you waitin' for summat, darlin'?" asked the girl.

Hello, thought Sammy, it's Geoff Boycott's granddaughter! "I'm waiting for a friend," he answered.

"You've bin waitin' ages, darlin'," she chuckled. "Ah don't think your friend's comin'. Maybe ahl do instead!" She gave him a flirty wink.

"I don't think so," said Sammy, his hand regrasping the window handle.

A car sped past, narrowly missing the girl. "Crikey, tha' wur close!" she cried, squeezing up against the car door.

"You shouldn't be standing there in the middle of the road," advised Sammy.

"It's nice o' you ta offer!" chirped the girl. She skipped around the bonnet, opened the passenger door, and bounced in.

Sammy's eyebrows jumped up. "I'm sorry, young lady, I don't think-"

"Me name's Kylie," she announced, shutting the door before adjusting her skimpy dress. "What's yours?" She held out her hand, smiling from ear to ear.

He wanted to be annoyed but found his hand reaching for hers. "Sammy."

"Nice ta meet you, Sammy. Shall wi go sumwhere wi can get better acquainted?"

"You don't understand, Kylie. I didn't come here looking for company."

"Oh," she giggled, "my mistake!"

"I'm happily married," he lied. "I'm here on business. So, if you don't mind..." He gestured at the door.

"You want me ta leave?"

"That's right."

She placed her hand on his knee. "You sure you won't change your mind?"

Sammy nodded. "I'm sure."

"Tell you what. When your business is finished, cum 'n find me. You can buy me a drink."

"I'll look forward to it, Kylie. Now, if you don't mind." Another gesture towards the door.

She leaned across to give him a peck on the cheek. "Ah like you, Sammy. You're nice."

"Thank you," said Sammy, wiping away the lipstick.

She jumped out of the car, slamming the door loudly enough to make Sammy flinch. She walked around to the bonnet, stopped to blow him a dramatic kiss, and skipped across the road.

Sammy followed her with his eyes through the partly open window. She was wearing a tight red mini-dress and the highest pair of heels he'd ever seen. Her walk reminded him of Marilyn Monroe's, though her bottom was much smaller than Marilyn's.

"Stop it," he rebuked himself, "she's younger than your daughter!"

Kylie walked down to the King's Arms and started chatting with the two bouncers. Sammy wound his window further down but could only just make out the conversation.

Out of the pub came a cigar-smoking man dressed in a Crombie coat with a velvet collar. He stopped behind the bouncers and pulled the cigar from his mouth. "What the fuck's goin' on!" he shouted. "I'm not runnin' a fuckin' brothel here. Get rid of her, you useless pair of morons!"

Sammy willed Kylie to make a run for it. Instead she started talking to the man. Sammy leaned his ear out of the window.

"Hiya, Mr Sullivan!" she bleated.

"Who the fuck are you?"

"It's me...Kylie. You remember me, don't you?"

Sullivan pushed forward between the bouncers. "Piss off, you stupid cow!" He drew back his hand.

Sammy had no difficulty hearing the slap as Sullivan's hand sent Kylie into the gutter.

"If I ever see you round here again, I'll kill you." Sullivan turned to the bouncers. "Get rid of her!" he screamed, disappearing back into the pub.

The bouncers stepped towards Kylie who was getting up onto all fours.

She held up a hand to stop them. "It's okay, fellas, ahl be off as soon as ah can get me shoes back on." She turned around to sit on the kerb. "Oh shit, me left 'eel's knackered!"

One of the bouncers lifted her up and sent her stumbling across the road, a shoe in each hand. She trundled away.

Sammy waited for the bouncers to stop watching her, then started his engine. "This is all I need," he muttered as he wound up his window. He drove past the pub and pulled over to the kerb in front of Kylie.

She opened the passenger door and leaned in. "'Ave you changed your mind then?"

"Just get in the car!"

"Anythin' you say."

The moment she shut the door Sammy drove off. "I'm taking you home. Where do you live?"

"Ah can't go 'ome tonight, Sammy. It's Sandra's night."

"What?"

"We tek turns. There's only one bed. It's 'er night tonight. She'll 'ave a customer."

"Is there somewhere else you can go?"

"Don't worry 'bout me, Sammy. Just drop me anywhere 'ere. Ahl be okay."

Sammy sighed. There's nothing else for it, he thought. "You'll have to stay the night at my flat."

"So you 'ave changed your mind! What 'bout your missus?"

"I'm not really married."

"What, you arl alone?"

"I've been living at my girlfriend's house," explained Sammy, "so the flat's empty. I expect I'll be back in there soon, though, the way things are going. It's a mess, I'm afraid."

"What, your relationship or your flat?"

"Both."

Sammy stopped at a petrol station to get some crisps for his guest.

"Keep the noise down," he whispered as they entered the flat.

"Got nosey neighbours, 'ave you?" joked Kylie. She walked straight into the bedroom. "This'll do nicely, Sammy!" she shouted.

"Shhh!"

"Sorry," she giggled, returning. "'Ave you got a bottle o' wine?"

"I'm not a wine drinker." Sammy pointed at an empty whisky bottle by the bin.

"A girl could die o' thirst." She opened her tiny red handbag and took out a hip flask. After taking a swig, she handed the flask over.

Sammy sniffed at the fumes and grimaced.

"Not a vodka fan?" she asked.

"Can't stand the stuff." He took a gulp and passed it back.

She grabbed his hand and led him to the threadbare settee. "Cum on, Sammy, let's get comfortable. Why don't you tell me arl 'bout yourself?"

"There's not much to tell."

"Don't be daft. What's your job?"

Sammy didn't make a habit of telling strangers about himself. But this girl didn't seem like a stranger at all. "I'm a private investigator."

Her face lit up. "Wow, a private dick?"

"I started out as a policeman, but I was never any good at following rules."

Kylie ran her hand across the frayed arm of the settee. "Not much brass in private dickin' by the looks o' it."

"I'm not great at sending out invoices."

"Why d'you do it then?"

"I enjoy my work, Kylie. What about you?"

"Ah 'aven't bin on the street that long, but ah can tell you there's sum serious money ta be made, if a girl plays 'er cards right."

"Have you managed to save up a bit?"

"Not really, but I've nearly got enough fur me train ticket ta Scotland."

"Heading up north?"

"Yeah. I used ta live in Bradford, but I got mixed up wi' sum bad people, so I 'ad ta leave. And 'ere ah am, Sammy, drinkin' vodka wi' you!" She took a sip and beamed at him.

"Have you got any family?" he asked.

"Ah grew up in a kids' 'ome. Ah did 'ave a family when I wur right little, but it wur better int' 'ome, ta tell you the truth. Me dad used ta beat me mam, you see. He wur a right bastard. Not like you, Sammy." She kissed him on the cheek. "'Ave you got kids?"

"One daughter."

"What's 'er name?"

"Emily."

"That's a luvly name."

"She's a lovely girl."

"D'you see 'er much?"

"Not as much as I'd like. It was difficult, after her mum left me. We lost touch for a while, but we're getting to know each other better now."

"That's nice. Did you get married again?"

"A few times."

"You've lost count 'ave you?" she chuckled. She drank some more vodka and shook the flask next to her ear. She handed it to Sammy. "You can finish it."

He allowed the few remaining drops to land on his tongue, one by one.

"'Ang on a minute! That's why you wur sittin' there int' car. You wur snoopin', undercover like."

Sammy smiled at her, shaking his head. He knew he was going to tell her anything she wanted to know.

"Ah bet you wur watchin' that Micky Sullivan bloke, wurn't yer?"

"That's right."

"'E's a nasty piece o' work, 'e is. Ah'd be careful if I wur you."

"I always am, Kylie. You seem to know Sullivan quite well."

"'E's a customer. Likes t' 'ave lots o' girls. 'E's loaded, so 'e can 'ave whatever 'e wants."

Sammy realised that his fists were clenching.

"What are you watchin' 'im for?" she asked.

Without pausing to think, Sammy told Kylie all about Zoe, her brother's disappearance, and the diamond-studded mobile.

"Ah've seen that phone!" cried Kylie. "'E makes sure arl the girls get a good look at it, the flash git. Reckons 'e got it from sum millionaire film star who 'ad 'im on 'er luxury yacht. You think 'e's lyin', do you?"

"It's highly likely."

"D'you reckon it's that lad Robbie's phone then?"

"I'm sure of it."

"What you goin' ta do?"

What the hell am I going to do, thought Sammy. Micky Sullivan is my only link to Robbie. I need to find out how Sullivan got hold of the phone.

"You need ta find out 'ow Sullivan got 'old o' the phone, Sammy."

"Yes, Kylie. But even if I could manage to talk to him, he's not going to tell me that, is he?"

"'E might tell me though!"

"I beg your pardon."

"'E might tell me. A fella will tell a girl anythin' when she's treatin' 'im nice. You know, really nice."

"No, Kylie. You must stay away from Sullivan at all costs. He threatened to kill you."

"Tha' wur just for show. 'E didn't want 'is men knowin' 'e'd bin wi' me. Anyway, ah'm off ta Scotland soon. 'E'll never find me there."

"No, it would be too dangerous."

"It'd be fun though."

"Fun?"

"An adventure. Anyway, ah'd like ta 'elp you, Sammy. You've bin good ta me." An air of wonder appeared on her face. "Wait a minute! 'Ave you got one o' them bugs, Sammy? You know, the sort you can 'ide in your clothes?"

"What?"

"If I wur talkin' ta Sullivan, could you wire me up so you could 'ear what the two of us wur sayin'?"

"Yes, of course, but-"

"That's it, Sammy. Problem sorted!"

CHAPTER 16

Alice woke in the same frame of mind. She couldn't remember the last time she'd felt this good on a Monday morning. Why should I be nervous about meeting Paul Ireland, she thought? He'd better think twice before messing with Alice Alexander!

She arrived at the clinic early to brush up on the theory of compulsive lying. She found some useful notes in one of her old university folders.

> Compulsive lying:-
> Is under-researched and poorly understood.
> Is associated with personality and mental disorders,
>> substance and alcohol abuse,
>> abuse in childhood,
>> low self-esteem.
>
> Compulsive liars:-
> Experience no guilt when lying.
> May learn to lie very convincingly.
> Cannot control the impulse to lie.
> Show few, if any, physical or vocal signs of lying.
> Often believe in the lies themselves.
> Lie to cover up failures.
> May feel pleasure when lying.
> Insist they are telling the truth, despite evidence to the contrary.
> Cannot maintain relationships.
> Often lose their jobs due to their lying.
>
> Treatment:-
> Is ineffective if the client does not recognise that they suffer from the condition (getting compulsive liars to admit they are lying can be almost impossible).
> Options include medication, and psychological therapies such as CBT.

Reading this took the wind out of Alice's sails. Just my luck, she thought. I'm under pressure to deliver, and I'm given a client who'll be tricky to handle, to say the least.

At 8.55am she had a surreptitious peek into the waiting room. Seated there was a man in his thirties wearing a suit and a Donald Duck tie, reading Gardeners' World magazine. He doesn't look that frightening to me, she thought.

She wandered into the office to see if the coffee was on.

"Alice," said one of the staff, "your nine o'clock appointment just rang to say he'll be late."

"But he's already...oh, I see. Thanks."

Fifteen minutes later Alice was sitting at her desk trying desperately to ignore the bouquet of ashtrays permeating the room. The taste made her irritable.

Facing her was a man in his thirties with facial stubble and a clean-shaven head. He wore a black T-shirt, blue jeans, and Doc Martens boots. Across the chest of the T-shirt, in block capitals, was the word 'TRUTH'. Under that, in smaller letters, were the words 'has no agenda'.

Reading this encouraged Alice. A compulsive liar with no insight, she thought, would have no reason to wear a shirt with such a message. Surely he must have some understanding of his condition. This may not be quite as tough as I thought.

"Good morning, Mr Ireland."

There was no reply. His face was devoid of expression.

"I'm Alice Alexander. I trust you had no difficulty finding your way to the clinic this morning."

"Let's get straight to the point, shall we? I'm sure Esther Williamson filled you in, but in case she left anything out, I'm a bent cop with a personality disorder and a drug problem. My partner turned me in, so I tried to ruin his reputation. I'm a hardcore compulsive liar. I either believe in my fantasies, or I'm devious enough to convince people that I do. I'm big trouble."

It was clearly her turn to say something, but Alice was speechless.

"The big question is," he added, "are you interested in hearing the truth?"

"Which truth are you referring to?"

"What if I tell you my version? Then you can decide if you believe it or not."

Alice found his purposeful tone and emotionless features unnerving. "Whatever your version of the truth may be," she replied, "I'm not sure that I'm the right person to help you."

"You're the right person alright. It's not just me who needs your help."

"What d'you mean?"

"You've been seeing Bonny Mason."

Alice's heart jumped. "How would you know that?"

"I'm a policeman."

"An ex-policeman. Anyway, I couldn't possibly comment. That information is confidential."

"Let's just say we both know you're seeing Bonny. There are certain things you need to know before you can even begin to help her."

"Mrs Mason will tell me everything I need to know."

"I doubt that. You clearly have no idea of her situation."

Stay cool, thought Alice.

"She's terrified of Leo," insisted Ireland, "always has been. She'll never tell you the truth about him, not in a million years. He's a tyrant."

"Leo Mason is a fine man!" snapped Alice. "He would do anything to make Bonny happy." She shook a finger at Ireland's face. "I know exactly what you're up to. You think you can trick me into helping you get closer to Bonny Mason. Who the hell do you think you are?"

"It's not what I think that counts."

"Do you realise how busy I am? I've got enough on my plate without having to sit through this garbage!"

Ireland stood up. "We're not going to achieve anything like this, are we? I want to speak to your manager."

Alice jumped up as if an electric shock had shot through her chair. "There's no need for that." She looked at her watch. "Alright. You've got twenty minutes."

They both sat down.

"Leo and I worked together for a couple of years. He was my senior partner, taught me the ropes. We became mates, in and out of each other's houses. Our wives got on well. It turned out that Bonny had a way with dogs, adored them, so she started taking my two for walks. She never took them out on her own though, Leo was always with her. One day, when he was in the next room taking a call, I asked Bonny if she'd like to take the dogs out with me sometime. She panicked, whispered that he'd never allow it, begged me not to say any more. I'm telling you, she was terrified. That's when I knew."

Alice bit her lip.

"He pretends that Bonny can't go anywhere without him, because of her anxiety, but it's not that at all. He dominates her, controls her. He won't let her out with anyone else, and she doesn't answer the door if he's not there. He owns her."

Alice couldn't let that go. "That's plainly wrong. Bonny sees me here without Leo."

"But I guarantee that he brings her here, and waits outside until you're finished."

What's the point, thought Alice? Just let him have his say.

"I wasn't sure what to do," he continued. "I made the mistake of asking Leo some questions about Bonny, about her past, how they met, that sort of thing. He must have worked out what I was up to, because his attitude to me changed straight away. The following week I was busted for drugs. You work it out."

"You can't expect me to believe that Leo would do a thing like that! If he thought you were interested in his wife, he'd have it out with you, man to man."

"You don't know Leo Mason."

Alice shook her head and said nothing.

"The irony is, I was chuffed when I got teamed-up with him. Everyone told me he was a star. His arrest rate was the best in the county. I looked up to him, respected him. Then he screwed me. I lost my wife, my home, everything. While I was inside I had plenty of time to think, and it all fell into place. When we were first getting to know each other, Leo and I went out one night for a few beers, then onto the Jack Daniels. Anyway, we got pissed. We were laughing about something, then out of the blue he got stroppy, said he shouldn't have drunk so much. Turned out he hardly ever touched the booze. He got emotional, started crying, feeling sorry for himself. He began telling me about his childhood, how his dad left home, his mum was an alcoholic, used to beat him and his brother. He said he'd hated her, hated his life. Then one day it all changed. He watched this film called Scarface on TV. About this psycho gangster with a scar on his face." Ireland touched his left cheek.

"Al Pacino," said Alice. "I've seen it."

"He told me he cut his own face, with a knife. Twice, to make a cross. He wanted a scar that was identical to the one in the movie. He said doing that completely changed his life. After that he stood up to his mother, gave as good as he got. He ended up leaving home and never looked back. You're the psychologist. You see it, don't you?"

"Yes, I see it. You want me to believe, despite evidence to the contrary, that Leo Mason was so messed up by his childhood that he cut his own face, framed his partner, and terrorises his wife!"

"He's not normal."

"First of all, I've never heard of anyone crazy enough to cut their own face like that. It's ridiculous. Leo already told me how he got the scar, and I believe him. Second, who would risk his own police career by framing a colleague for no good reason? It doesn't make sense, he'd have to be bonkers. And third, I've got to know Bonny Mason well over the last few weeks, and I don't recognise the Bonny you describe."

"There's more. When I was fitted up, I wasn't sure at first who was responsible. A few days later Leo came to see me. I was desperate, in a state. I asked him to help me find out what was going on. He didn't answer, just stared at me. But not at me, if you know what I mean. He looked right through me, as if I wasn't there. Then he just smiled." Ireland gave an almost imperceptible shudder. "I'll never forget that smile. Like something out of a horror movie."

"You're reading too much into-"

"I was there. I'm telling you, he's evil."

Alice was near the end of her tether. "Mr Ireland!"

"Yes."

"Why don't we cut the crap and get to the heart of the matter. You're in love with Bonny Mason, aren't you?"

He hesitated. "I care about her, yes, very much."

"You've been following her, haven't you?"

"She needs my help."

"The best way for you to help Bonny is to leave her alone. You know there's a law against stalking, don't you? Yes, of course you do. Bonny may be frightened of you, but I'm not! I'm warning you. If it doesn't stop I'm going to the police. With your criminal record they'll throw the book at you."

"I wouldn't do that if I were you. You should consider the consequences."

"Are you threatening me?"

"Something bad is going to happen."

"Yes, you're going to end up back in jail."

"And where will Bonny be then? I'm her only chance to get away from that scumbag. If you can persuade Bonny to back my story, together we can nail him. With your help, we can-"

"That's enough!" snapped Alice. "I've listened patiently. Now it's my turn. You trick your way into seeing me, pretending you want psychological help, then proceed to give me this cock and bull story. You don't deny you're in love with Bonny Mason, and you expect me to help you win her. Nothing's changed, has it? You continue to live in your own little world, with no concept of the damage you're doing to other people. You've wasted enough of my time!"

Alice stood up and ushered Ireland towards the door.

"Everything I've told you is true," he insisted. "We're her only chance."

Alice turned her face away as he left the room. She shut the door behind him and sat down. That's it, she thought, that madman has cost me my job. Thanks, Esther.

She took a few minutes to compose herself, then went into the office for some sanity. "I hope I never set eyes on that man again," she groaned to the receptionist.

"Really?" came the reply. "That's strange. He said you wanted him back on Thursday. I gave him an appointment at ten."

Later that morning Alice had changed into her running gear and was saying goodbye to the girls.

"Before you go, Alice," said one, "there's a letter for you. Dropped in by that pretty blonde girl."

Alice's heart missed a beat. "Bonny Mason?"

"That's right."

"Was anyone with her?"

"Not that I could tell."

"Did she say anything?"

"Not a word. She was in and out like a shot."

Alice took the envelope to her room and tore it open using the chopstick she kept on her desk for that purpose. Inside was a sheet of A4 paper. As she unfolded it her jaw dropped. She was looking at a circus flyer.

Emblazoned across the top in gold and red lettering were the words 'CIARAVOLO BROS. CIRCUS'. The lower third was filled with coloured stars containing entries extolling the wonders of fire breathers, jugglers, contortionists, tightrope walkers, acrobats, and a human cannonball. One of the stars contained the words 'Marvel at the Astonishing Knife Throwing Skills of the Incredible FIRE and her Hyper Intelligent Hounds SPARK & FLASH!'

Wow, thought Alice, knife-throwing dogs. I'd pay to watch that.

The rest of the page was taken up by four photographs. One showed a group of clowns of various shapes and sizes, another a tightrope-walker wearing wellington boots, and a third a human tower of impressive proportions. Alice's attention focused on the fourth picture. In it was a beautiful girl holding an impressive knife above her head. The girl had long blonde hair and was covered from her neck to her ankles in skin-tight white lycra. At her feet, gazing up at her face, was a black and white border collie which appeared to be grinning. Behind them was a section of the audience, most of whom were caught in various excited poses.

It can't be Bonny, thought Alice. This girl is so confident, so alive. She has luxurious hair, and a figure to die for.

Alice turned the flyer over. On the back was written, in Bonny's unmistakable hand: 'Dear Alice, you asked if I had a photo of me at the circus. I said no, but then I remembered this. It was taken during one of my last performances. It brings back memories, especially the crowds. Look how every single one of them is smiling. Thank you for helping me. Bonny.'

Alice turned the flyer back over and re-examined Bonny's picture. Members of the audience were laughing, screaming, and waving their hands in the air. Her act must have been something to behold.

Alice was setting off on her run when the strain of Fossils by Saint Saens emanated from her pocket. She stopped, took out her mobile, and read a text from Esther. 'Prison visit on for tomorrow. Pick you up at clinic 11am. Esther x'.

As Alice circled the lake she had mixed emotions about visiting Harry. She wanted so much to speak to him, but was uncertain what she hoped to achieve. Is this for Harry's benefit, she thought, or mine?

She turned off the lakeside path and entered the woods. Clear your mind, she thought, concentrate. There's no need for a repeat performance in the nettles. She felt stronger than she'd done for weeks, and pushed on between the trees and over their roots.

Alice had just started the downhill stretch when she was knocked out of her stride by the sudden clamour of startled birds taking off from amongst the branches. She stopped running. The sound of the birds died down, leaving silence.

Alice jumped at the echoing crack of a snapping branch. She turned towards the sound and stood motionless, holding her breath, listening. Nothing. Her heart pounded as she turned two full circles on the spot, searching through the trees for any movement. Nothing.

If there is someone there, she thought, I'm a sitting duck if I stay here. So I'd better get running!

Alice continued through the woods, reassuring herself that she had nothing to worry about. She looked over her shoulder from time to time, just in case. Better not mention this to Mum, she thought.

CHAPTER 17

Angus parked two streets away from his mother's house. She was always out on Monday evenings at a church meeting, but there was a danger of being spotted by one of her neighbours. The last thing Angus needed was another brush with the law.

He crept up to the door and let himself in with his spare key.

I may not have a mother worthy of the name, he thought, but I do have a dad, even if I haven't seen Callum for twenty years. New Zealand may be on the other side of the world, but it's a small world.

Angus knew where his mother hid her address book. He flicked through the pages until he found the entry for Callum MacMicking. There, sure enough, was Callum's address in Christchurch. It had a line through it. Angus turned the page, allowing a triangular piece of card to escape onto the carpet. It had been cut from the corner of a greetings card.

Angus picked up the piece of card and turned it over. He recognised Callum's handwriting. 49, Springfield Road, Elgin. He blinked hard. What the hell's going on, he thought? Callum has never lived in Elgin.

Within seconds the penny dropped and he was heading back to the car. Elgin was less than an hour's drive away.

Fifty minutes later Angus was gazing through his driver's window at the front of number 49, Springfield Road. There were lights on in the house. He imagined Callum sitting inside with his family, watching television or playing cards.

Callum loved playing cards. He taught Angus the rules of whist, rummy and poker. Angus remembered how much they'd also enjoyed board games together, especially Angus's favourite, El Tesoro, the pirate game. Callum would pull one of his heels up against his bum and put on a ridiculous pirate accent which always had Angus in stitches. After a game Callum would play tunes on his ukelele. He taught Angus to play that too.

"How do I know he'll want to see me?" muttered Angus to himself. "What am I even doing here? Sod it!" he cried, thumping the steering wheel.

He was about to turn the ignition key when the door of the house opened. A middle-aged lady leaned out to place an empty milk bottle on the step. Angus turned his face away. By the time he turned it back she'd gone inside.

Without a thought Angus jumped out of the car and approached the house with his heart thumping. He knocked. A teenage girl opened the door.

"Who is it, darling?" asked an antipodean voice as its owner appeared behind the girl. "Hello," she said to Angus. The teenager disappeared inside.

"I'm sorry," muttered Angus, "I've come to the wrong house." He turned to go.

"Who are you looking for?"

Angus hesitated. "Callum," he murmured. "Callum MacMicking."

"I'm Kate, Callum's partner. He's away on a fishing trip. Can I help you?"

"No," replied Angus, taking a step back. "I'm sorry to have bothered you."

Kate lifted her hand. "Wait." She half-closed her eyes. "It's Angus, isn't it?"

The strength drained from Angus's legs as she offered him her hand and led him inside.

"I'm glad you've come," she said as they sat down. "I'm very pleased to meet you, Angus."

Angus forced a smile.

"Callum told me all about you. He showed me some photos of you and your mother. You were only a kid, but you haven't changed that much."

"How long have you been in Elgin?"

"Almost six months. Callum always missed bonnie Scotland, and I fell in love with the place while listening to his stories. So here we are."

"I see."

"But you knew that surely. Callum sent a card with our new address just after we arrived. He wasn't sure if you'd want to meet with him, so he sent it and waited to see what would happen. He'll be so disappointed to have missed you."

"The stupid cow!"

Kate raised her eyebrows.

"Sorry," said Angus. "It's just that my wonderful mother forgot to mention it to me."

"I take it she hasn't improved with age? Callum told me all about her. And about you, Angus. He's very fond of you. You know that, don't you?"

"Is he?"

"I'm sorry the two of you haven't kept in touch all these years. I'm partly to blame for that, I'm embarrassed to say."

"What d'you mean?"

"Callum took it badly when your mother asked him to leave. He knew the relationship was coming to an end, but he still loved her, despite her increasingly strange behaviour. As time went on he wanted to see you again but couldn't face contacting her, so he kept putting it off. We met just after he moved to New Zealand, and he told me all about you. After we fell in love he thought it was better not to look back. I'm ashamed to say I didn't try to persuade him otherwise. It suited me to have a man without baggage. I'm sorry, Angus."

"Don't be. You're not to blame for anything. I wanted to keep in touch, but Mother went mad whenever I mentioned it. She controlled my life. She still does."

"I'm going, Mum!" called the teenager from the hall.

"Don't be late," replied Kate.

The front door slammed.

"What's your daughter's name?" asked Angus.

"Beth. Her brother Rory is fishing with Callum."

"You have a nice house," he said, surveying the room.

"Thank you."

He noticed several photos of smiling faces. "You're a lovely family."

"We're very happy, Angus."

The last thing you need is me in your lives, he thought.

"I hope you don't mind me prying," said Kate, "but are you in touch with your... biological father? Callum said his name is Iain, if I remember right."

"I've never met him. His name's Richard."

Kate flushed. "Oh yes, that's right," she stammered. "How stupid of me...

Richard." She got up. "I'll put the kettle on. Tea or coffee?"

"Tea please."

Kate left Angus alone. He looked once more around the room. By the window was a card table, on which lay an old-fashioned bagatelle. Angus walked over and ran his fingers across its prongs. There was a magnificent globe in one corner, straw-coloured with an ornately carved stand. He spun it around to find New Zealand.

Callum's found himself a good life, thought Angus, and I've come here to mess it up.

He closed the front door quietly as he left.

CHAPTER 18

As soon as dinner was over, with Sofia sitting comfortably watching Gentlemen Prefer Blondes, Alice took out the circus flyer to have another look. She examined the picture of Bonny, and shuddered to think how much she'd changed, how pale, underweight, and lifeless she was now. The world's a frightening place, thought Alice, if you stop to think about it. She decided not to. Instead she closed her eyes and listened to Marilyn Monroe singing Diamonds Are a Girl's Best Friend.

By the end of the song Alice was relaxed, her mind clear, when into it jumped an idea. It's a long shot, she thought, but worth a try. She picked up her laptop, opened YouTube, and typed 'Ciaravolo Brothers Circus'. There was only one hit, but it was a gem. The notes explained that the video was filmed to record the tenth birthday treat of a girl named Sally.

Alice clicked play. After footage of Sally, her friends, and the audience in general, the ringmaster appeared. He removed his top hat, took a deep bow, and welcomed the people of Watertown. Alice was open-mouthed. Oh my goodness, she thought, it was filmed here!

The arena filled with clowns, tumblers, jugglers, a unicyclist, and a Victorian lady riding a penny farthing. Alice settled down to enjoy the fun. She shrieked with the audience as the human cannonball flew through the air, landing in a lifeless heap on the ground. She laughed with them when she realised it was a dummy. She marvelled at the grace and timing of the trapeze artists, the twists and turns of the acrobats.

Then came the moment she'd been waiting for. The ringmaster proudly announced that the next act contained a feat never before attempted, anywhere in the world. "Ladies and Gentlemen, please welcome...Spark!" A border collie ran on from one side, wearing a collar studded with red flashing lights. "And Flash!" A second collie appeared from the opposite side, her collar flashing blue. "And, of course...the one...the only...Fire!" The audience screamed as Bonny strode into the arena, arms aloft. Each hand was holding, by the blades, five impressive knives fanned out.

During the first part of the act the dogs sat under a row of balloons attached to a wall. Bonny threw her knives, bursting each one in turn, releasing titbits of food which dropped into the mouths of the dogs. Spark and Flash then retrieved the knives one by one, jumping up and biting onto the handles, and hanging on until each knife came loose. The audience cheered as the collies proudly returned the knives to Bonny.

More balloons were attached to the wall, this time in two diagonal rows meeting in the middle, in the shape of an inverted V. Spark and Flash sat, one at each side, staring along the rows towards the top. Bonny threw her first two knives, bursting the lowest balloon on each side. She then burst the next two balloons, and so on until they were all gone. At Bonny's command the dogs bounced along the knife handles until they stood at the top, noses almost touching, tails wagging furiously. At another command from Bonny the two crossed over and skipped down the opposite sides, returning to their mistress to share in the wild acclamation of the audience. Bonny took a bow and left the arena, the dogs running circles around her feet as she strode off.

Alice couldn't wait to tell Bonny how impressed she was. Her heart was filled with a mixture of elation and sadness. Sadness at the knowledge that Bonny's future had been stolen from her by one man. A man who'd paid nothing at all for his crime.

That night, as Alice sat on her bed, the same thought went round and round her mind. Whatever it takes, she thought, I must help this girl. But Bonny begged me not to tell anyone about Ireland. I can't go to the police and risk losing her trust completely. Maybe I should ignore her wishes and tell Leo, ask his advice.

She gazed through the open window. "What should I do, Jamie? How can I decide when both choices are bad?"

Desperate to think about something different, Alice grabbed her laptop and typed 'Al Pacino Scarface' into Google Images. She examined several pictures of Tony Montana's face. The scar was on his left cheek, just like Leo's. But there the similarity ended. Montana's scar was a line, not a cross. Nothing at all like Leo's.

During the night Alice dreamt she'd told Leo what Ireland was up to. She looked on as Leo felled him with a single punch. Standing over him, he screamed at Ireland to leave his girl alone. With his foe cowering at his feet, Leo turned to Alice with a smile.

The following morning Alice got into Esther's passenger seat. "That's good," she breathed, sipping the coffee that appeared in her hand.

"Yours is a large mocha," grinned Esther, "with an espresso added for good measure."

Alice took a larger sip. "What's the plan?"

"I emailed the governor to say that I've asked you to interview Harry Hart, as part of some research I'm doing."

"How long will I have?"

"I said you'd need a couple of hours. You've got an hour today and another on Friday."

"What? That's hardly enough time to break the ice, let alone establish a clinical relationship."

"Hold your horses! Who said anything about a clinical relationship? You're not Harry's psychologist. Remember, this whole thing is extremely irregular. It's a case of take it or leave it."

Alice knew it was pointless arguing with Esther. "Fair enough. Is there anything more you can tell me about Harry, to give me a head start?"

"I spoke to a contact at the prison yesterday. It's as I suspected. He's having a rough time, physically and mentally. He comes across as a nice guy, but that won't help him in there."

"How long's his sentence?"

"Three years, but from what I've heard he won't last another three months. You'll have to be realistic about what you can hope to achieve." Esther finished her coffee and started the engine. "We'd better set off. You can tell me en route how you got on with Paul Ireland."

At the mention of the name Alice's temperature shot up. "What a complete waste of time that was! He's a weirdo if ever I saw one. He may have told you he's ready to move forward, but all I heard was a string of bizarre fantasies. Mind you, I'm not convinced he believes all that stuff. I reckon he knows full well what he's up to. He enjoys stringing people like us along. It makes him feel powerful."

"You may well be right. That's what makes him so interesting. Does he have insight or doesn't he?"

"He gives me the creeps," shuddered Alice. "He's got this monotonous voice, and there's no emotion, so it's hard to tell what he's thinking. The worst thing is, after I sent him packing he went and made another appointment to see me on Thursday."

"That's simple enough. Get one of the staff to ring him and cancel it."

"That would go down really well with Diana Foster, don't you think?"

"If you explain the situation to her, I'm sure-"

"That woman is waiting for an excuse to get rid of me. I'd be handing her one on a plate! There's no way out. I'll have to hope he doesn't turn up."

"I suppose you're right," nodded Esther. "What if he does?"

"I'll just have to keep my cool. I've always had a problem with liars...especially the male variety."

"That sounds interesting! Tell me more."

"Nothing to tell," blushed Alice. She'd never told anyone about the schoolgirl crush she'd had on her maths teacher. She'd never forgiven his lies. "Ireland didn't deny stalking Bonny Mason. I threatened to tell the police, but he replied that something bad would happen if I did. Can you believe that?" She turned to Esther. "Do I have to get Bonny's permission to go to the police on her behalf?"

"If you think she's in genuine danger, you should try to persuade her. If she refuses, you have a duty to act. Her safety comes before client confidentiality."

"Or maybe I should say something to Leo."

"No," replied Esther. "If he finds out, it should be from Bonny herself."

"I'm seeing Bonny this afternoon. Hopefully I can persuade her to see sense."

"First things first," said Esther as they approached the prison gates.

As a child Alice had often imagined what the inside of the building was like. Now part of her didn't want to find out.

"Your first visit to a prison?" asked the officer as Alice signed the visitors' register.

"Yes," she replied, "how did you know?"

"Experience," he said with a wink. His tone altered as he recognised her name. "Hold on, you're not...yes, you're Richard's girl!" He held out his hand.

Alice smiled as she accepted it.

"Spitting image. Except you're much prettier."

"Yes. I mean, thank you," blushed Alice.

"We all miss him, you know. Richard put his heart into his work. They don't make 'em like him anymore."

Alice was proud to hear those words.

With the formalities over she was taken by a guard through a metal detector, then via a series of doors to an interview room in the heart of the building. It had bare walls, no windows, and was empty apart from a functional table and two chairs.

"I'll get Hart," said the guard. "He's harmless. There's no need for me to stay, unless you want me to."

"I'm sure I'll be fine, thank you."

The door clicked shut as the guard left the room. Alice shivered. What am I doing here? Stay cool, she advised herself.

The door reopened. The guard ushered in a weary figure in a cotton prison uniform. Alice tried to hide her shock. Harry was thinner than he'd appeared in the video. He looked several years older. And he looked ill.

Alice pulled back a chair. "Please sit down, Mr Hart. My name is Alice. May I call you Harry?"

He sat down, staring at the table.

Alice took her seat, leaning forward to examine the rows of stitches on his face and hands. She wasn't sure how to break the ice. "You're not as tall as I thought you'd be," she offered. Her hand covered her mouth.

Harry's lifeless eyes remained fixed on the table.

"Do you know why I'm here?" she asked.

He showed no interest. "Something about research."

"Do you know who I am?"

Harry tilted his head and glanced in her direction. "Should I?"

"We have met, in a way."

Harry's eyes focused on Alice's face, then widened as if he'd seen a ghost. He sat up, hands trembling. "It's you, isn't it? The girl...in the window!"

"Yes." Alice waited for Harry to absorb this.

"I don't understand," he said. "Why have you come here? It's because of you I lost my only chance to escape."

Alice was taken aback. "I'm so sorry, I didn't mean to...I thought you didn't want to die."

"I don't know why I said that. Anyway, I'm already dead."

Alice tried not to betray pity in her voice. "Harry, I'd like to help you."

"Help me? No one can help me. Do you have any idea what it's like in here? It's hell, and I'm living it!" His fists clenched. "Every hour is like a day. Every day lasts a year. I can't eat, I can't sleep. Oh, what's the point. It'll soon be over, one way or another."

Alice didn't know what to say. "Would you like me to leave?"

No reply.

She remembered that she was a psychologist. "Would you like to talk about what happened? There was an accident."

"It was all my fault," moaned Harry. "The brakes failed. My brakes, my car, my fault!" He started to weep. "I miss Grant. I miss him so much. I can't stand it any longer."

Alice reached across to touch his hand. He withdrew it.

"I don't want your sympathy." Tears trickled down his cheeks. "I deserve this."

"It could've happened to anybody."

"The tax and MOT were a month overdue."

Alice gasped.

"We were on tour so I didn't get the reminder," he sobbed. "I didn't even think about it. Now I think about it all the time." He screwed up his eyes.

Alice felt a knot in her stomach. "Is there anything I can do to help? Anything at all."

Harry shook his head. Moments later his eyes opened. "There is one thing. A gold locket. Grant gave it to me for Christmas. If I could have my locket..." He peered at Alice with a child's eyes.

"Where is it?" asked Alice.

"At home in my jewellery box. I've asked if I can have it here, but they said no." He thumped the table. "It's not as if I'd wear it when anyone could see it!"

"I'm not sure what I can do about-"

"You're coming back on Friday, aren't you? You could bring it with you. I'll give you my address. There's a back-door key in the shed, and a shed key hidden in the garden." Harry's eyes begged Alice to agree.

"I'm sorry, Harry, it's impossible."

"Please."

He asks me for just one thing, thought Alice, and I can't help him. She heard her voice asking: "Exactly where are the keys hidden?"

CHAPTER 19

Alice gave Harry's back door a thump of frustration. She'd found the keys without trouble, but the back-door key wouldn't turn in the lock. She had another go while pulling and pushing at the handle. If the key breaks in the lock, she thought, I've had it. If I go back to Harry without the locket he'll be devastated. I must get in, even if it means breaking down the door.

The key started to bend in the lock. "I bet this is the wrong bloody key!" she blurted. Covering her mouth, she turned to check if anyone was near.

Alice noticed a crack in a glass panel near the door frame. This gave her an idea. She examined another panel next to the lock. No crack in that one. What the hell, she thought, as she picked up a chunk of flint and smashed the glass. The sound echoed from the wall of a neighbouring house. Alice squatted down to make herself small.

She waited. No sign of anyone nearby. She removed a few pieces of the broken glass and cautiously put her arm through. She gripped the inside handle and pulled it down in the vain hope that the door would open. It didn't.

"Ow!" A spike of glass pierced the back of Alice's upper arm. "Shit!" Her available hand covered her mouth. She looked around. Nobody there. Adrenaline masked the pain, but not the shock of seeing blood trickling down her arm. A few drops landed on Harry's carpet. Good thing I'm not on the police DNA database, she thought.

Alice gingerly withdrew her arm and yanked out the offending shard. She put her arm back through, this time with key in hand, and managed to steer it into the inner lock. As she turned the key the bend in its shaft increased. With a rush of blood Alice went for broke, forcing the key with all her might. It flipped around in the lock, snapping into two at the same instant.

Alice pulled down the handle. "Gotcha!" she whispered. Within seconds she was inside.

Following Harry's directions Alice ran up the stairs and into the master bedroom. Her feet sank into the luxurious white carpet. She slipped off her shoes and twisted to check the cut on her arm. It had stopped bleeding. Crimson satin sheets covered the king size bed. On one wall was a giant black-framed mirror. "No time to admire the decor," she told her reflection.

At the back of the wardrobe, just as Harry had said, was an Indian jewellery box of ornately carved wood with a brass inlay in the form of an elephant. The instant Alice opened the box the smell of camphor escaped. She held the box to her face and breathed in the pungent scent. The locket held pride of place and was instantly in Alice's hand. It was heart-shaped, engraved with a floral design. She couldn't resist opening it. Inside was a tiny photo of Grant's face, smiling, handsome. Alice had never met Grant, but she liked him very much.

A siren in the distance! Alice's heart thumped as she stood statue-like, listening for the blare to get louder. It faded instead. Her mind now focused, she replaced the box, picked up her shoes, and ran down the stairs.

She was about to leave when she was startled by movement at the other end of the hall. A wave of nausea hit her as she turned to discover her reflection in the hall mirror. "Don't do that!" she squealed. She walked to the mirror to check her arm. No bleeding.

Alice was now standing at an open doorway into a spacious room. She dropped her shoes and walked in. In the centre were two white leather sofas, each with a set of red and black tartan cushions. There's a bit of a theme going on here, she thought. Even for a Scot, Harry's into tartan in a big way.

She cast her eyes around the room. On one wall was a cherry-red rectangular glass clock. It had stopped. Beneath the clock was a bookcase upon which rested two picture frames. One was facing her and she instantly recognised the figures of Harry and Greta in costume. As she approached to get a closer look the picture in the second frame came into view. Alice couldn't believe her eyes. It was a circus flyer, a smaller version of the one Bonny had given her. Alice started to wonder if she was losing touch with reality.

She picked up the frame and imagined the police dusting it for prints. What the hell, she thought, they've already got my blood. In tiny writing, in the bottom right-hand corner, were the words, 'To Harry, with love, Bonny.'

Something on the bookshelf caught her eye. A pile of letters. Alice blinked hard as she recognised the same handwriting. Without stopping to think, she grasped the pile and sank into the nearest sofa. She opened and read the top letter.

Dear Harry,

I know you're away so you won't get this for a while. I hope the tour is going well. Sounds like you're all over the country. Reminds me of my circus days.

Thanks for the lovely letter. The photos are amazing, especially the one with Greta hovering in mid-air. I wish I knew how you did that. Are you serious about learning to throw knives? You asked if we could meet, but that would be difficult. Hope you understand. Do you like the flyer? That's me with Flash. It was a great crowd. Thanks for writing to me, it means a lot.

Love, Bonny

Alice put the letters back. It was time to get out. She was creeping towards the back door when she realised she wasn't wearing any shoes. Within a minute she'd retrieved them, escaped via the now unlockable door, and was driving back to the clinic. She had an appointment with Bonny in half an hour.

"Relax, Alice," said a voice as she rushed into the office. "Mrs Mason rang to say she'll be ten minutes late."

"Thanks," replied Alice, slowing her breathing down. "I'll be in my room."

This was not the first time Bonny had been late for an appointment. Alice wasn't pleased, but she understood.

"Sorry I'm late again," whispered Bonny as she sat down.

"Usual reason?" asked Alice, indicating the white cotton gloves covering Bonny's hands. Blood had soaked through in places.

"They're worse. The more I wash them the dirtier they get. I think I'll try soaking them in disinfectant."

"No, Bonny. Washing your hands isn't the answer. The real problem is deeper, and harder to face. If we can't deal with something that's too painful, or seems impossible to control, we focus on an alternative, something that feels more manageable."

"It doesn't help, I know. But how do I stop?"

Alice touched Bonny's arm. "You have to be brave."

"I'll try. Did you get the envelope I left for you?"

"Yes," beamed Alice. "Thank you so much, it's wonderful!" Her smile faded as she imagined the Bonny in the poster and compared her with the Bonny before her. "You've lost weight since then."

"Did you read what I wrote on the back?" asked Bonny, searching into Alice's eyes.

"Yes. You don't have to thank me, Bonny. It's my pleasure to help in any way I can."

Bonny's head dropped.

"Is something wrong?"

"No." Bonny stared at her lap.

"Before we start," said Alice, "there's something I need to tell you. Don't be alarmed, but I saw Paul Ireland yesterday."

Bonny stiffened. "Where?"

"He had an appointment with me here."

"You said everything I tell you is confidential!"

"You don't understand. I didn't ask him to come. He's a client here. He has his own problems."

"I know that," moaned Bonny, "but what if he sees me?"

"Don't worry, I'll make sure that-"

"Or he could meet Leo in the car park! No, it's no good." Bonny stood up, trembling. "I can't come here anymore."

Alice held out her hands. "Please, Bonny, trust me."

Bonny hesitated. "I don't know…" She sat down on the edge of her chair.

"Are you sure you won't go to the police?" asked Alice. "I'll come with you."

"No! I've told you, I can't." Bonny began to weep.

"I won't mention it again, I promise." Alice was cross with herself. I'm losing her, she thought. She decided to change the subject. "I met someone interesting this morning. A friend of yours, I think."

"Who's that?"

"Harry Hart."

Bonny's shoulders jerked upwards. "Harry!" She sank back. "But that's impossible. Harry's in prison."

"I visited him there today."

"Why did you talk to Harry about me? You're not allowed to do that."

Oh no, thought Alice, this is going from bad to worse. She decided to tell a white lie. "I wasn't aware that he knew you, until he told me today. We were talking about his career, and he said he wanted to learn how to throw knives. He mentioned your name, said he hoped you might teach him one day."

Bonny breathed out, visibly relieved. "We're pen friends. Or at least we were, before his accident. He's a lovely man. How is he?"

"He's doing...quite well. How do you two come to know each other?"

"Harry lives locally, but I've never met him face to face. We saw him and Greta... Grant...on TV last year. They were brilliant, so I asked Leo if we could go to a show. He said no at first, but Tom was desperate to go. Tom usually gets his way in the end."

"He's a lovely boy."

"The show was great. Tom wanted Harry's autograph, but there was no chance on the night, so I wrote a letter. I thought his secretary would send a signed photo, but Harry wrote back himself. He's so sweet." Bonny paused, smiling. "We've been writing ever since. I've got a boxful of letters." Her body jolted. "You won't say anything to Leo?"

"Of course not."

"Only, he doesn't know about the letters. He can get a bit...jealous sometimes."

"I understand."

"It was terrible, what happened," said Bonny. "Do you think they'd let me write to Harry in prison?"

"Yes of course, though I think one of the officers might have to read it first."

"Maybe it's not such a good idea."

"Wait a minute! Would you like me to arrange for you to visit him?" During these last few words Alice began shaking her head instinctively as she remembered how ill Harry had looked.

"I couldn't," replied Bonny, "I'd be too frightened."

Alice sighed internally with relief.

CHAPTER 20

Angus gazed up at the blue and white sign for the first time since he'd been eight years old. He remembered vividly the day he'd first stared in awe at the iconic words INVERNESS CALEDONIAN THISTLE FC. The sign was so much bigger then. He licked his lips and summoned up the singular flavour of Caley steak pie.

He circled the stadium with butterflies in his heart. Callum had first taken him to see Caley Thistle play on his eighth birthday. The match went ahead despite the snow. It was a good thing Callum had brought a blanket and a flask of hot chocolate. A nil-nil draw. Callum said he was sorry there were no goals. Angus wanted to know when they could go again. Within six months Callum was gone.

Angus had a clear view of the impressive Kessock Bridge which spanned the nearby Moray Firth. He recalled the nickname it had when he was a kid. Check Out Bridge. He decided to have a closer look.

As he reached the bridge the wind stiffened, sending his red hair into a highland dance. He found himself counting the paces as he strode out towards the centre. At five hundred he stopped. Turning to his left, he was stunned by the awesome view across the firth. The wind had dropped, but Angus began to shiver.

He replayed the argument with his mother. "It should be our responsibility to make sure that everyone has a chance of a decent life," he'd told her. Stella would have been proud of his words. He cringed as he imagined what Stella would think of the disgraceful way he'd treated his mother.

Angus leaned forward against the barrier. He remembered how the kids at school used to argue about how long it would take a jumper to die after hitting the water.

A shag flew under the bridge. Angus followed its flight to the mouth of the Ness, losing sight of it as it veered left along the river. It must be a Catholic shag, he thought, St Mary's is only a mile downriver. Angus knew where he needed to go next.

He felt numb as he entered the church. The pews were all empty. He recognised

Father Barrington's voice resonating from somewhere at the back. The priest was rehearsing a sermon.

Angus sat down in his old pew and stared at the altar. He didn't pray. Footsteps echoed behind him. Footsteps he recognised.

"Testing, testing!" cried Angus. "Can you hear me, God?" He paused. "I know you're here, 'cause you're everywhere aren't you?" Another pause. "Looks like our chat today's gonna be a bit one-sided. No change there then. I thought you'd be interested to know that I've been doing some research. It seems opinions vary about the deal you're offering. I know you'll agree that it's good to get both sides of a story."

A gentle cough reached Angus's ear.

"For nearly two thousand years," he continued, "people were told that without you life had no meaning, and without you there'd be no morality, just a world full of sin. Then a rumour started that you'd died, that the human race would have to look out for itself, and be responsible for its own behaviour. What a frightening concept, being abandoned in a cold, purposeless universe. No heaven to compensate for the misery of life, death the only relief."

Another cough.

"That was over a hundred years ago, but most people still believe in Christianity, Hinduism, whatever. Which reminds me. You gods really should get your heads together and your stories straight. One god or multiple gods? Reincarnation or no reincarnation?" Angus paused, tilting one ear to the ceiling. "Anyway, here's the thing. Life does have meaning without you. It has meaning to people, for its own sake. We don't need you to live happy lives that are constructive and good. And as for morals, I've got news for you. Immorality is alive and kicking on your watch."

Footsteps followed by silence.

"I'm sure we mortals can get things sorted with a few simple rules. Let's see...each one of us has an equal claim to the good things in life...and it's wrong to make any person's life worse than it needs to be. That's about it really. Not rocket science, is it? There'll be mistakes of course. We're not perfect like you. But we'll sort ourselves out in time. Then we'll start making the best of the only life we have."

Angus peered behind him from the corner of his eye. Father Barrington was sitting in the back row.

"We'll keep the Bible though. Some great stories in there, plus excellent lifestyle advice, such as how to keep your slaves in check without killing them, and helpful guidance on when to put people to death, fight wars, that sort of thing. Mind you, they don't seem to be executing people any more for lying about their virginity, or cursing their parents. Don't you just miss the good old days? I'm surprised you haven't brought out new editions to keep up with the changes. But that would be a sign of weakness, wouldn't it?"

Angus heard movement behind him. Father Barrington was getting up.

"Do you mind if I ask a question about your rules on morality? You know, such as when is it okay to use violence, and when is violence a sin? I'm dying to know, where did the rules actually come from? Did you get them from your own god, or did you make them up yourself?" Angus cupped an ear for a moment, then shook his head. "One last thing. Would you do me a favour and have a word with my mother? She thinks you've still got the energy to answer all her prayers, even at your age. I've pointed out that people die young, become disabled, or live horrible lives despite praying to you. It's obvious you can't cope with the demand. I've advised her to cut down and give you a break. Trouble is, I think she's addicted."

Footsteps.

"It's been good to talk, God. Sorry if I've been blunt. It's just that...I've not been myself lately."

Father Barrington sat down next to him. "Is there anything I can do to help, Angus?"

"I don't think so, Father."

"I've always been here for you, you do know that?"

"You've always been here," murmured Angus.

"I've done my best to steer you in the right direction, since Callum left."

A tear ran down Angus's cheek.

"Now you seem lost."

"Not lost...disappointed."

"I understand, Angus."

"I doubt it."

"You feel that God isn't listening, that he's let you down."

Angus's body stiffened. "How can I be let down by someone who doesn't exist!"

"Do you think someone else has let you down?"

"My mother I can understand. She believes it all. Universe in six days, virgin birth, the lot. But you?"

"You think I've deceived you, Angus?"

"Haven't you?"

"Not intentionally."

"So you really believe that your God is all-powerful and all-loving? Despite the terrible things that happen every day. Children dying of cancer, natural disasters wiping out communities, millions living intolerable lives. Your God is righteous and compassionate, is he? You're certain he's not in fact powerless, or cruel...or non-existent?"

Father Barrington was nodding repeatedly.

"You're convinced that prayer is the answer to all life's problems? You're happy that some parents pray for their sick children rather than seek medical assistance? That so many people pray for victims of disaster rather than volunteer to help them?" Angus began to shake. "You really believe that your God, who can perform miracles at the drop of a hat, finds it acceptable that people hate and murder each other, as long as they love him?"

"That's not-"

"You really believe it's acceptable to promise people, against all sense and without any evidence, that they'll meet their loved-ones and live happily ever after in Heaven? To indoctrinate children so thoroughly that questioning their faith is impossible without psychological trauma?" Angus clenched his fists. "A lot of people have paid a high price for believing those lies. I should know...I'm one of them!"

Father Barrington placed his hand on Angus's shoulder. "I'm sorry you feel this way, Angus. I've always tried to...I genuinely do believe..."

"You brainwashed me," sobbed Angus, "you and my so-called mother. When the doubts surfaced the guilt was terrible. Slowly but surely, I learned to hate myself. If it wasn't for my music I would've ended it all. Believe me, now I wish I had!" He collapsed in tears.

Father Barrington put his arm around Angus's shoulder. Angus pulled away, escaped from the pews, and from the church.

CHAPTER 21

"'Ere wi are," chirped Kylie. "The car park's be'ind the 'otel."

Into Sammy's view appeared a sign displaying five gold stars above the words 'Ambassador Hotel and Spa' in calligraphic writing. He drove to a secluded corner of the car park.

"Ah'm ready when you are, Sammy. Are you sure you'll be able to pick up what me and 'im are sayin'?"

"No problem. It's a state of the art micro transmitter. I got it second hand, but it works like a dream."

"Wi'd better switch it on now," she suggested, tapping her side. "Ah won't manage it once ah'm in there wi' 'im. It's inside me corset."

Sammy was having second thoughts. "What am I doing, letting you risk yourself? This is never gonna work. He's bound to find it when you take your clothes off."

"Ah won't 'ave to take anythin' off at all. It's 'im who'll be strippin' off!"

"What?"

"Wi' 'im it's always the same routine. Ah take 'is kit off, tie 'im ta t' bed, then pretend ta torture 'im. 'E goes for all that weird stuff. You should see the gear ah've got on under me coat."

"I can't believe a man like Sullivan would let anyone tie him naked to a bed. Sooner or later he'll get robbed, or worse."

"'E won't let me tie 'im too tight. 'E can get loose if 'e wants to. It's just pretend."

"No!" snapped Sammy, reaching for his seat belt. "This is madness. We're leaving."

She stopped him from connecting the belt. "Ah want ta do this, it's excitin'. Ah've always wondered what it'd be like bein' a spy."

"You're crazy, d'you know that?"

"O' course," she chuckled. "All the best people are crazy."

Sammy struggled to reach the transmitter switch without touching Kylie's body.

"Cum on, Sammy, ah've got nowt catchin' you know. Testin', testin'."

"It's working fine."

"'Ere goes!" She got out, winked at Sammy, and walked off towards the hotel entrance.

Sammy heard her voice in his earpiece. "Ah'm comin' up ta t' door...goin' in now...walkin' o'er ta t' lift."

He forgot that she couldn't hear him. "Cut the running commentary, Kylie, for God's sake."

A robotic female voice called: "Doors closing, going up." After that, silence.

"Shit," grumbled Sammy, "I've lost her."

Thirty seconds later Sammy heard a crackly voice. "Ah'm nearly there. Room thirteen as usual. Good thing ah'm not superstitious eh, Sammy?"

"Shut up, Kylie," groaned Sammy. He heard knocking and held his breath.

"'Ello, Mr Sullivan. 'Ow are you?"

"Come in, Kylie."

Sammy's hands tightened.

"Ah don't know why you don't 'ave a diff'rent room, Mr Sullivan. Sum people say thirteen's bad luck."

"There's no such thing as bad luck," he replied, "only bad decisions."

"Damn right!" shouted Sammy at his reflection in the rear-view mirror.

"Hope I didn't hurt you too much," grinned Sullivan, "outside my place."

"That's okay, Mr Sullivan. Ah think a man shud always treat a girl firm, when she steps out o' line. 'Specially a powerful, good-lookin' man like you."

Sammy jumped as he heard the sound of a gunshot.

"Ah luv champagne," purred Kylie. "You're class, Mr Sullivan, real class."

"Bottoms up," said Sullivan.

"Son of a bitch!" cried Sammy, fists clenching.

"Ooh, the bubbles are ticklin' me nose."

"There's plenty more, Kylie. Come on, drink up."

"It's so sparkly, Mr Sullivan. Reminds me o' that flash phone you've got."

"You like my phone?"

"O' course ah do. It's covered in diamonds. It's amazin'!"

"You can have it if you like. As long as you do everythin' you're told."

"No, Mr Sullivan, ah didn't mean...ah just wondered where you got it from, that's all."

Sammy groaned. "Too sudden, too sudden."

"Are you interested in me, Kylie, or my phone?"

"Stuff the bloody phone, Mr Sullivan. Can ah 'ave sum more champagne?"

Sammy shut his eyes.

"If you must know," said Sullivan, "I got it from a young punk."

"'Ow much did you 'ave ta pay for it?"

Sullivan laughed. "I didn't pay a penny. It was a gift."

"Blimey, that's one 'ell o' a gift."

"Let's just say he did somethin' to annoy me. The phone was his way of sayin' sorry."

"Ah'd like ta meet this punk. What's 'is name?"

"Mind your own business."

"D'you know where ah can find 'im?"

"I said mind your own fuckin' business!"

"Sorry, Mr Sullivan, it's just that 'e might 'ave sum other good stuff, that's all. Ah didn't mean..."

Sammy recognised the sound of a Sullivan slap.

"Ah'm sorry, Mr Sullivan, ah'm really sorry!"

"Don't worry," he growled, "you're gonna make it up to me."

"Please, Mr Sullivan, you're 'urtin me."

"Shit!" shouted Sammy as he heard the unmistakable sound of fabric tearing.

"You said I should treat you with a firm hand, didn't you? Well, I'm happy to oblige." Another slap.

"Stop it, Mr Sullivan!" shrieked Kylie.

"What the fuckin' hell's this?"

The transmission went dead.

"He's found it," bawled Sammy at his reflection. "Shit, shit, shit!" He opened the glove box, grabbed a brown paper bag, and jumped out of the car as fast as his hefty frame would carry him.

The receptionist was too busy to notice Sammy puffing past and into the lift. On leaving it he struggled to squeeze past the chambermaid's trolley. She appeared from one of the rooms to find him jammed between the trolley and the wall.

"I'm sorry, Sir," she said, pulling the trolley away.

"No problem," replied Sammy, clenching his teeth as the trolley scraped across his waist.

The moment he reached the door of room thirteen Sammy looked back along the corridor to check the coast was clear. He took a three-hole balaclava from the bag and pulled it over his head. His hand went back into the bag and came out holding a replica Colt 45.

"Police, open up!" cried Sammy, thumping repeatedly against the door with the grip of the revolver. Moments later the door flew open and Kylie dived past him into the corridor. Sammy entered the room holding the gun in front of his face with both hands.

Sullivan was in the middle of the room, clutching his face. "You've scratched my eye, you stupid bitch!"

Sammy turned to Kylie. "Come in and shut the door."

Sullivan peered at Sammy through his good eye. "Who the fuck are you?"

"Get down on the floor," screamed Sammy, pointing the gun at Sullivan's head. "Now!"

Sullivan dropped down.

"Tie his hands together."

Kylie's torn corset was almost falling off her. "'Ang on." She put on her coat, took off its belt, and used it to tie Sullivan's wrists behind his back.

"You're not police," growled Sullivan.

"No," replied Sammy. "Worse."

"What do you want?"

"Where's the phone?"

"What?"

"Don't mess with me. The phone, where is it?"

Kylie took the phone from Sullivan's pocket and handed it to Sammy.

Sullivan laughed. "If that's what you came for, you're wastin' your time. It's a fake."

"Not according to my boss it isn't," advised Sammy.

"Then your boss is a liar, or a fool."

"You'll get the chance to tell him that yourself," threatened Sammy, "if you don't answer my questions. Someone stole my boss's phone, and he's not a happy bunny. Whoever's responsible is gonna have to pay, big time."

"That's nothin' to do with me. A teenage punk gave it to me. It was a present."

"What's this punk's name? Where can I find him?"

"I don't know his name. I don't know anythin' about him. You've got the fuckin' phone, haven't you? Take it and piss off!"

"You haven't been paying attention, have you? My boss isn't the forgiving type. If the thief doesn't pay, someone else will have to. And that someone else, my friend, is gonna be you." Sammy held the gun against Sullivan's head.

"Alright! But I'm tellin' you, I don't know anythin' about the boy. Except that he had a tattoo on his face. Like a bear print or somethin'."

Sammy jabbed the gun hard into Sullivan's temple.

"Alright, alright! I met him at the Hacienda club. He seemed friendly with the barman there. He should know somethin' about the little shit."

"And this barman's name?" asked Sammy.

"No idea. But you can't miss him. He's about seven feet tall, and black as the ace of spades."

"Is that it?"

"That's all I know. If you're not satisfied, you'll have to fuckin' shoot me!"

Sammy took a step back. "We'll see about that. Now, before I go, a bit of advice. If you make any attempt to get this phone back-"

"Sod the fuckin' phone. I never want to see it again, as long as I live."

"And if you try to discover the identity of my boss, or me, you can kiss your arse goodbye. Do I make myself clear?"

"Perfectly."

Sammy moved to the door. "Come on, Kylie, time to leave Mr Sullivan in peace."

"Hang on," whined Sullivan, "don't forget to untie me."

"Sorry, Micky," grinned Sammy, "we're in a bit of a hurry. We'll send room service up if you like."

"Arsehole!"

Sammy gave Kylie a peck on the cheek as they got into the car.

"What's wi' the gun, Sammy?" she asked as he put the paper bag and its contents back in the glove box. "You're breakin' the law usin' that."

"Don't worry, it's a fake," he chuckled. "Like the phone."

"It's still illegal though, int' it?"

"Yes, it is. But the people I point it at are hardly likely to complain to the police."

"Ah suppose not."

Sammy took Kylie back to his flat.

"Can ah cum wi' you, Sammy, ta see this seven-foot giant?"

"No, Kylie. You've got to leave Carlisle as soon as possible. I'll take you to the station first thing in the morning. You won't be safe here."

"Ah can't go yet. Ah 'aven't got enough fur me train fare."

"I'll give you whatever you need. You must go."

"Ah suppose you're right. Anyway, ah'm lookin' forward ta gettin' ta Scotland, ta start me new life."

"Why Scotland? What's the attraction?"

"The accent. It's so sexy, Sammy. Ever since ah saw Sean Connery in Goldfinger ah knew ah 'ad to find me a fella wi' a Scottish accent!"

Sammy sighed and gave Kylie a kiss on the forehead.

CHAPTER 22

Alice stood at her bedroom window watching the roof of the prison. She thought about Harry. How much longer can he survive in there, she wondered. She thought about Bonny. How will she cope if anything happens to poor Harry? Most of all she thought about Leo. Thoughts that went round and round until they made her head dizzy. For the first time in a year she forgot to say goodnight to Jamie.

Next morning Alice sat doodling at her desk. She had admin time on Wednesday mornings but was struggling to focus on the paperwork.

A knock. "Come in," she sighed.

The consulting room door opened and half an arm appeared. It was holding a large brown mug with steam rising from it. A moment later a grin emerged above the arm. "Thought you might need this," said the grin. "It's disgusting, as always, but it'll get your day started."

As the door closed Alice took her first sip and grimaced. The phone rang.

"Sorry to disturb you, Alice. There's a gentleman in the waiting room who'd like a word with you. He says he's the husband of your client Bonny Mason. Shall I tell him you're busy?"

Alice's hand shook, splashing coffee across her desk. "Shit!"

"Okay, I'll get rid of him."

"No! Ask him to wait, I'll be out in a minute."

Alice trembled with a mixture of excitement and panic. She quickly wiped up the coffee, checked her face in the mirror, and dashed out to the waiting area.

Leo was standing at the window. Alice got her first decent view of his rear perspective. She liked what she saw.

Leo turned around. "Good morning." He waited for Alice to join him by the window. "It's a beautiful day. Would you like to go for a walk? There are one or two things to discuss."

"I'm afraid I've got tons of paperwork..." Alice remembered that her boss had taken the day off. "...but I suppose I'll find time to catch up."

Minutes later they were strolling by the lake. Sunlight frolicked on the surface. Birdsong filled the air.

Alice waited for Leo to speak.

"Sorry to pounce on you like this, but I'm concerned to know how you got on with Ireland."

"Don't mention his name."

Leo grinned. "I see you're a fan."

"He's crazy. Actually, I don't think he's crazy at all. That's what worries me."

"Did he mention me at all?"

"You're not going to believe this," replied Alice with a glance at Leo's scar. "He told me you cut your own face, on purpose."

"He told you what?"

"He's on another planet. He said you did it because your mum was an alcoholic."

"Ah, yes," murmured Leo, "that part is true."

Alice stopped, putting both hands over her mouth. "Leo, I'm so sorry."

"Don't worry. It's not a problem for me, talking about it I mean. It was a long time ago. My dad left when we were little. I don't remember him. Mum struggled to bring us up on her own. All I can say is, she did her best."

"How sad," replied Alice. How forgiving, she thought.

"What else did Ireland say?"

"That you copied your scar from the film. You know, Scarface. The daft thing is, Al Pacino's scar looks nothing like yours. I checked online."

"You did what?"

"Sorry, that came out wrong. I don't mean I believed him. I was just interested, that's all."

"Glad to hear it. When are you seeing him again?"

"Tomorrow." Alice stopped and turned to Leo. "He makes me nervous. Ever since I met him I've felt as if I should be looking over my shoulder."

"Don't you worry about Ireland. Everything's gonna be fine, you can take my word for that." Leo lifted his hand slowly and stroked Alice's hair. She blushed and walked on.

They reached a bench and sat down. A pair of swans cruised past.

"A friend of mine noticed you at the prison yesterday," said Leo.

Alice was taken aback. "You've got eyes and ears everywhere."

"My friend thought you were there to see that magician, Harry whatshisname."

"Harry Hart."

"Any particular reason?"

"Just routine," lied Alice. "I'm helping a colleague with some research."

"How did you get on?"

"Do you know Harry?"

"No. It's not important." Leo pointed at a group of oaks nearby. "There'll be squirrels in there. Shall we take a look?"

They walked towards the trees. Alice listened to the birdsong. She was starting to remember what romance used to feel like.

"There's one!" she cried. They laughed together.

The squirrel scampered away along the ground, leading them into the trees. They soon lost sight of it but walked on. They reached a fallen tree lying across their path. Leo turned to Alice. He took both her hands.

"There's something I need to tell you, Alice. I know we've only just met, but...do you believe in love at first sight?"

His eyes burned into hers. Alice's legs weakened.

"I can't stop thinking about you," he moaned.

Alice pulled back. Leo gripped her hands tightly.

"What about Bonny?" she asked.

"I'll divorce her, I promise."

"Don't say that! You shouldn't promise anything unless you're certain you can deliver."

"I am certain," he pleaded.

"How can you be? Never ever break a promise. That's something Dad taught me."

"But Alice-"

"No, Leo, this isn't right." She tore her hands from his grasp.

He clasped her shoulders. "I can't live without you." He pulled her up onto her toes and kissed her lips.

Alice jerked herself away and slapped Leo across the cheek. He froze, his face on fire. Alice turned, tears trickling down her face, and ran.

The admin was left untouched. Alice spent the rest of the morning pacing around her room, arguing with herself. It's impossible, she thought. I can't have him, but I can't stop thinking about him. He loves me. I wouldn't be the first girl in the world to break up a marriage. Is that really such a terrible thing? He wants children. I'll give him as many as he likes! But it's impossible.

Eventually she realised she was going around in circles. Only one thing would help to get her head straight. It was time for her run.

Alice got changed into her running gear and set off. As she circled the lake she glanced at the oaks where the squirrel had been. She told herself to focus on the ground ahead. Concentrate.

She took a detour onto the grass to avoid a lady walking three greyhounds. They were straining at their leashes and paid no attention to Alice.

Soon enough she left the path and was running between the trees. Okay, she thought, no distractions today please. Personal best here I come.

She glimpsed at a red deer far ahead. A buzzard soared above the trees. Concentrate!

As she started to run downhill Alice jumped sideways to avoid a branch and tripped over her own feet. She managed to avoid tumbling but her ankle twisted over. "Ow!" she screamed, hopping in a circle. She put the injured foot gingerly to the ground and dropped down on the opposite knee to examine it. The ankle was tender. She got up and made circles in the air with the foot. It seemed okay. Time to set off again.

A movement in the distance! Alice stood bolt upright and stared. There, now perfectly still, was a figure spying on her from behind a tree. Only a head and one arm were visible, but Alice knew what she was looking at. This was no squirrel or deer.

The figure disappeared from view. Alice heard the rustling of disturbed branches. He's running away, she thought.

"What are you frightened of, Ireland?" she screamed, hobbling forwards. "Afraid of a girl, are you? Coward!"

Despite her adrenaline Alice could feel her ankle throbbing. She took a few more paces forward, then realised how vulnerable she was and began to retrace her steps. Little by little her bravado was matched by fear. She looked over her shoulder every few paces as she limped towards safety.

By the time she got back to the clinic Alice's blood was back at boiling point. She grabbed her keys. "I know where you live, you bastard," she muttered. She struggled to her Mini and screeched around to Ireland's house.

Alice jumped out of the car, leaving the door wide open. She hobbled as fast as she could to the front door and rang the bell. He must be back by now, she thought. She pounded against the door with her clenched fist. "Come on," she cried, "I know you're in there!"

An explosion of barking forced Alice backwards. She imagined the door bursting open and a pack of bloodthirsty hounds tearing at her flesh. She limped onto the small lawn in front of the house and peered through the window. The sunlight bounced off the glass into her eyes. She inched forward until her nose rested against the pane.

Two sets of fierce teeth leapt up at her. "Aaagh!" screamed Alice as the dogs thudded into the window and barked at her hysterically, their paws pounding repeatedly against the glass. She threw herself away and fell backwards onto the grass.

"Having fun?" said a voice behind her. "Don't worry, they can't get out. If they could they'd probably lick you to death."

Alice tried to get up but collapsed in a heap after putting weight on her injured ankle.

Ireland offered his hand.

"Leave me alone," she growled, her face distorted by pain.

"Suit yourself," he replied, walking to his front door.

"What d'you think you're up to?"

He stopped. "I was about to ask you the same thing."

"I know where you've been."

"I've been for a walk. It's important to get plenty of exercise, don't you think?"

Alice scrambled to her feet. "You think you're so smart, don't you?"

Ireland stared at her, shaking his head.

"The truth is, you're a waste of space!" She limped back to her car, slammed the door, and drove away.

When Alice got home she was surprised to find Sofia sitting on the carpet in front of her chair, watching television.

"You hate Australian soaps, Mum. How long have you been sitting there?"

"Only two hours," shrugged Sofia. "I got up to go to the toilet but I did not get very far. I am a little wet."

"I'll get the frame from the spare room."

"No, Aliki. Do you think I am an old woman?"

Alice lifted her mother and helped her to the bathroom. She stood outside the door as Sofia washed herself.

After dinner they were browsing through an old family album. Alice turned the pages.

"Orkney," smiled Sofia as they came across a photo of a standing stone as tall as a house. In front of it stood Richard with toddler Alice sitting on his shoulders, clutching her father's ears for balance. "The Stenness stones."

Sofia pointed to a picture of the magnificent Orkney cliffs towering above a choppy North Atlantic Ocean. Alice was sitting on the grass, holding out her hand to the camera. Between her thumb and forefinger was a small dark pellet.

"You spent most of your time there trying to eat sheep poo," laughed Sofia. "I had to watch you like a hawk."

"Here's one of a Macclesfield Town match we went to," said Alice. Behind the blue and white stand climbed the rolling foothills of the Peak District. "Do you remember we used to drink Bovril, and eat sausage rolls?"

"All I can remember is the freezing cold wind," replied Sofia.

Alice's eyes moistened as she discovered a photo of Richard sitting on the edge of her bed, reading her a story. She squinted to make out the title of the book in his hand. "It's Adventures of The Little Wooden Horse, my favourite!"

"Your father read you bedtime stories while I did the washing up. I could not read very well in those days."

"He made me laugh so much with his weird and wonderful accents. But the best thing of all was the way he'd start to make up the story himself, while pretending to keep reading from the book." Alice grinned. "Once, the Little Wooden Horse was sailing the seven seas with a band of jolly pirates when for no obvious reason they made him walk the plank. Another time he was on a tightrope at the circus when he nearly fell and was hanging on to the rope by his teeth. If I got worried Dad would laugh and go back to the real story. He was so good that I nearly always fell for it. Then once in a while I'd be sure he was making the story up when he wasn't! It was the best fun. I tried my hardest not to fall asleep."

Sofia sighed. "I'm tired now, Aliki. No more photographs."

Alice put the album down. "I really did have the best dad in the world. Whenever I wanted to play, however tired he was, he'd stop what he was doing. Hide and seek, murder in the dark, horsey rides."

"Yes, darling," murmured Sofia.

"He'd be on all fours, carrying me to bed on his back, neighing for all he was worth."

Sofia's eyes closed.

That night Alice gazed out of her bedroom window. Jamie was back in favour.

"I'm a fool, Jamie. He'll never be mine, I know that. Remember how we used to say, if anything ever happened to one of us? Well, you can forget all about that. I never want to see another man as long as I live."

Leo found his way into Alice's dreams. She was trying to persuade him to leave Bonny. She begged him repeatedly but he wouldn't reply. Tom ran into the room shouting: "Daddy! Daddy!" Leo turned to his son, crouched down, and hugged him. Tom, arms around his father's neck, stared at Alice with bitter eyes.

CHAPTER 23

"How's the ankle?" enquired Paul Ireland, scraping his chair across the floor as he sat down.

Alice grimaced. "Why are you here?" she growled.

"You're very direct this morning."

"Answer the question!"

"I'm here to be honest with you."

"A little honesty would be nice."

"You asked if I'm in love with Bonny. The answer is yes, I am, very much."

Alice struggled to keep calm. My priority is to protect Bonny, she reminded herself. "If you really loved her you'd know that she'd be happier if you left her alone."

"She'll never be happy with him."

"You think she'll be better off with you?"

"I'd do anything for her."

"You're messing around with people's lives," pleaded Alice. "Haven't you got a conscience?"

"You don't understand."

"If you carry on like this there's only one possible outcome, you do know that?"

"I'm prepared to risk anything."

"Even prison?"

"Anything."

"Have you stopped for one second to consider there's a child involved? How will Tom cope when Bonny has a mental breakdown?"

Ireland said nothing.

Alice jolted with the shock of realisation. "It's not just Bonny, is it?"

His eyes narrowed a fraction.

"You want them both, don't you? Bonny and…" She jumped up. "Are you Tom's father?"

"Would you believe me if I said I wasn't?"

For a moment Alice imagined Paul Ireland and Bonny Mason together. That would leave Leo free. She forced out the thought.

"The only reason I haven't gone to the police already," she insisted, "is that Bonny asked me not to. But if anything happens to Bonny…or me…the police will work out what happened, you can be certain of that. And they'll use DNA evidence to prove you're Tom's father. They'll lock you up and throw away the key. This is your last chance. Leave Bonny alone!"

Ireland rose, his hands closing.

Alice was too angry to feel fear.

He thumped the desk and stormed out of the room, slamming the door behind him.

Alice sat with head in hands. What am I doing, she thought? I'm pushing him to the edge. If he reacts it'll be my fault. Maybe I should phone Esther, but I know what she'll say. Go to the police. I've got myself into a corner and there's no way out.

The door flew open and thudded against the empty chair, knocking it sideways.

"Alice, come quick. There's going to be a fight!"

Alice ran after the receptionist into the waiting area. Through the window she could see Paul Ireland and Leo Mason out in the street. Leo was squaring up to Ireland, shouting something at him. Ireland stood still, facing Leo, hands by his side.

Alice ran out of the building to confront the pair. "Stop it, you two! What the hell do you think you're doing?"

Ireland concentrated on his foe. Leo's eyes turned towards Alice.

"Leave him alone, Leo," she insisted. "He's not worth it."

Leo growled and moved forward. He gave Ireland a violent push, sending him flying onto his back in the road.

Alice jumped forward and grabbed Leo round the waist. "No, Leo, that's enough!"

Leo made no further movement. He watched Ireland hawk-like as he climbed to his feet.

"There," said Ireland, jabbing a finger at the face of his adversary, "is the real Leo Mason."

Leo jerked forward. Alice tightened her hold. Ireland turned his back on them both and walked away.

"What the hell are you doing here?" cried Alice, steering Leo towards the building.

"I don't trust him. I decided to hang around, in case he tried something."

"Why on earth did you let him spot you?"

"I'm not afraid of him."

"That's not the point!" Alice threw her hands up. "You're a policeman. You can't go around beating people up."

"I'd better go."

"Promise me you'll leave Ireland alone."

Leo nodded once and headed for his car.

Alice went inside. She sat for a few minutes drinking coffee with the girls.

"Men!" said one. "It's either sport, sex or fighting with them."

"You've forgotten alcohol and food," said another.

"And cars," chipped in a third.

"You see," said Alice, "they're more multifaceted than we think." She gulped down her coffee. "I'm popping home to check on Mum. I haven't forgotten my appointment with Mrs Mason. I'll be back by then."

Sofia wasn't expecting her, so Alice called out as she opened the front door. There was no reply. Alice called again, louder. Still no sound. The living-room was empty, as was the kitchen, and Sofia's bedroom. After searching every room in the house Alice checked around the outside. She looked down the garden and noticed that the shed door was open. What on earth is Mum up to, she thought?

The strains of a Greek melody reached Alice's ears. As she entered the shed the smell of oil and petrol fumes made her choke. Sofia was sitting on an old dining-room chair in the corner, singing.

"Mum, what are you doing out of the house?"

"Hello, Aliki. Are you spying on your poor mother?"

"I came home to see if you needed anything." Alice scanned the shed. "Where's your stick?"

"In the house where it belongs." Sofia gazed around the shed at the assorted tools, the petrol lawnmower, the shelves covered with cans of oil and various other liquids. "Your father and I used to spend hours in here," she sighed. "I love these smells. They bring back so many memories."

Alice sat down on Dad's workbench.

Sofia smiled. "We used to sit here and talk." She winked at Alice. "That is not all we did in this shed."

"Mum!" spluttered Alice. "You don't mean...what I think you mean?"

"Only before you were born. After that I would not let you out of my sight. Your poor father could not get near me for months." They laughed.

"Mum, can I ask you something?"

"Yes, darling."

"I've always wondered why you didn't have any more kids. I'm not complaining, it's just that...it would've been fun to have a brother or sister."

Sofia shrugged. "We tried, Aliki, we tried. God gave you to us, so we were lucky." She held her arms outstretched. Mother and daughter embraced.

Alice got back to the clinic with ten minutes to spare. She was surprised to find that Bonny had arrived early for her appointment.

"Leo said I mustn't be late again," explained Bonny. "He has to come home from work to bring me, so he gets cross if I'm not ready."

"Perhaps one day, when you're better, you might feel able to come on your own."

"I don't know."

"How are your hands?"

"A little better...I think."

"And the housework? Have you made any progress?"

"I'm trying to spend less time cleaning and tidying like you said, but Tom makes such a mess. It doesn't matter how much time I spend, the house is always in a state. I'm a terrible mother."

"Of course you're not. You have a wonderful son, and I'm sure you have a wonderful home. Perhaps you might like to invite me round for coffee sometime."

"No!" Bonny held up her hand. "Sorry, I don't mean...it's not that…"

"I understand. It would be too stressful for you."

"Yes, that's it," nodded Bonny, "too stressful. I'd like you to come but it's impossible. You do understand, don't you?"

"Never mind. Maybe one day."

Bonny began to tremble. "Have you seen Paul Ireland again?"

"I shouldn't tell you, Bonny, it's confidential. But yes, I saw him earlier today."

"You will help him, won't you?"

"I'll try. I've already told you what I think."

"Yes, I know," frowned Bonny, "but if you can help him, stop him from...then everything will get back to normal, won't it?"

"And if I can't?"

Bonny stared into her lap.

Alice moved to the edge of her seat. "Bonny?"

"Yes."

"There's something I need to ask you. You said that, when you were attacked, he used a hood...to cover your head."

"Yes, that's right," quivered Bonny.

"Then, later on, he removed the hood?"

"Yes."

"So he let you see his face?"

Bonny screwed up her eyes and nodded.

"He wasn't trying to hide his identity."

"No."

"Did you tell that to the police?"

Bonny shook her head.

"Why not?"

Bonny's eyes opened wide. "You don't understand? They would never have trusted my word against his."

I knew it, thought Alice. "Bonny, was your attacker...was your attacker a policeman?"

Bonny gasped. "You know, don't you?"

"Yes, Bonny, I know."

"You mustn't tell anyone. You can't!"

"You're right, but I have a duty to persuade you to reveal the truth, for your own sake."

"It wouldn't do any good. No one would believe me."

"I believe you, Bonny. And there is a way of proving he was responsible." Alice took a deep breath. "If you'd give permission, a blood sample from Tom could be used to...these days paternity can be proven beyond doubt?"

"That's impossible. He'd never agree."

"He'd have no choice. The court would insist. If he refused it would be like admitting his guilt."

Bonny jumped up. "I've got to go home. I'm sorry, I have a lot to do."

"Bonny, please."

"Thank you for everything you've done. I'll never forget you. Goodbye."

Bonny hurried out of the room. By the time Alice had collected herself and gone after her, she'd disappeared.

CHAPTER 24

Angus dropped onto his sofa, a bag of chips in one hand, a can of Coke in the other. He took a sip of Coke and placed the can between his knees. He was on his third chip when a wave of exhaustion overcame him. His eyes closed.

There was a knock. Angus woke and put another chip in his mouth. He grimaced and spat the cold potato back into the paper. The can was on its side between his feet, his socks wet through.

Another knock. Angus threw the chips onto the table, dragged himself to the door and opened it. Father Barrington stood there, silent, motionless.

Angus said nothing. He walked away from the door and heard it close behind him. Grabbing the chip bag, he turned and held it out to the priest.

"No thank you, Angus, I'm not hungry."

Angus tossed the bag onto the table and sat down on the sofa. "Has God sent you?"

"No, I've come on personal business."

Angus gestured towards an armchair. Father Barrington sat down and waited.

"What can I do for you, Father?"

"We've known each other for many years," said the priest.

"Most of my life."

"I've always been very fond of you, and I hope our relationship has meant something to you too."

"You've been a major influence."

"I have no children of my own, Angus. After Callum left, I did my best to fill at least part of that gap for you."

"Did you, Father?"

"One of the things in life I value most highly is your good opinion of me. It troubles me greatly that I may have lost it."

"I'm sorry for your loss."

The priest closed his eyes. When they reopened he was staring down at his hands. "Is there anything I can do, Angus, to win it back?"

"It's too late for that."

"Please, I-"

"No, wait!" cried Angus. "There is something you can do to stop me hating you for the rest of my life."

"Anything."

"You can be honest with me, Father, just this once. You can tell me the truth."

"I'm sure I've never lied to you."

"What gave you the right," scowled Angus, "to tell me what to think?"

"I was only doing my job."

"Was it your job to give me one side of the story, instead of offering both and letting me decide what to believe?"

"That's how it works, Angus. That's how it's worked for two thousand years."

"That's not good enough."

"I understand how you feel, but-"

"You gave me every tiny detail about how God created Heaven and Earth, but you forgot to mention the theory of evolution. Do you believe in the theory of evolution, Father?"

"It has its merits."

"Do you believe that God created the universe in six days?"

"Many of the Bible's stories are best taken metaphorically."

"What about Heaven and Hell?" demanded Angus. "Are they metaphors?"

"To be truthful, I'm not certain."

"You're not certain! You taught me to trust in God and live my life according to his rules. And the reward for my obedience? An eternal afterlife in a place that you're not certain exists."

"I hope Heaven exists."

"Do you believe, Father, that in God's world all human beings are created equal?"

"I do, Angus."

"Even the Muslims, the Hindus? We're all the same, wherever we're born, whatever our beliefs?"

"Yes."

"Yet you taught me that only those who have accepted Jesus into their hearts can enter God's kingdom."

"I did," agreed the priest.

"So you lied to me!"

"No, Angus, I didn't mean-"

"Do you remember me asking you about the Pope?"

"I do. You were nine years old."

"Do you remember your answer? You told me that the Pope has a personal relationship with God. That he's infallible."

"Yes," replied the priest, "that's right."

"Despite the great diversity of faiths, the Pope is the only person in the whole world who has access to the absolute truth. And is incapable of making mistakes."

"That is what I told you."

"And now?" asked Angus. "Do you still believe I must accept his teachings without question? Or should I use my intelligence to assess the evidence and decide whether or not his teachings stand up?"

"That is something you must determine for yourself."

"I see. So now, all of a sudden, I get a choice. You didn't mention that when I was nine years old!"

The priest looked down.

"Do you remember telling me that God loves me and will look after me? That he is directly responsible for all the good things in my life?"

The priest nodded.

"I'm still waiting, Father. My life consists of one disaster after another. Is God only responsible for the good things, or is he to blame for all the crap as well? Perhaps he's forgotten about me. Or maybe he's just having a laugh!"

"God wants us all to live happy and fulfilling lives."

"Apart from the victims of murder, wars, discrimination and hate?"

"It's not that simple, Angus."

"It's perfectly simple! God created us to worship him, to serve him, to make him feel important. God is an egotistical tyrant, and like all tyrants he's not too bothered about the quality of life of his subjects."

"You're missing the point!" snapped Father Barrington. "The benefits of religion, particularly the Christian religion, vastly outweigh the negatives that you are so keen to highlight."

"Enlighten me," scoffed Angus.

"Okay, let me play devil's advocate. Suppose there is no God. Most of the world's population would find itself completely lost. People need to believe that their lives have meaning, but they can't imagine how that's possible without God."

Angus shook his head.

"Suppose there is no God. People are desperate for advice and direction. Without God, who would be there to look after them? Without the Bible, where would they look for guidance? Alright, I agree that some of the messages are unsuitable for today's world, but most people are good at ignoring those parts and using the rest to help them find rewarding lives."

"So they're following a simple rule," replied Angus. "Do what the Bible says if it supports a better life for all, and ignore it if it doesn't."

"Yes, I suppose so."

"But there's an even simpler rule. Do whatever supports a better life for all. We don't need God-given instructions to do that!"

"It's vital that the guidance comes from God," pleaded the priest. "Otherwise no one listens."

"The very problem is that the guidance comes from God," insisted Angus. "Every religion tells its followers that they are the chosen ones. There's no chance whatsoever that the people of the world can ever come together."

"The main purpose of religion is to bring people together! Churches host social events and encourage friendships. They provide emotional support and counselling for the vulnerable. Many charities have religious roots."

"What that proves is that people are capable of doing great things to help each other. Religion isn't necessary for that to happen."

"Religion leads people in the right direction. Without it they get lost."

"Not everyone in church has such a positive experience." Angus thumped himself on the chest. "Seeking my own way in life would've been far better than trusting it to your God!"

"People are able to make that choice for themselves, Angus. And the majority choose to follow God."

"There you go again. Choice. Does God really give people choice? Or does he hypnotise them with the promise of everlasting life, and blackmail them with threats of damnation?" Angus slapped the arm of the sofa. "I wasn't given a choice, damn you!"

"Choice isn't all it's cracked up to be. We don't allow children the choice to cross a busy road without looking. If people are given choice, then as likely as not they choose badly."

"Now the real truth comes out."

"I understand what you're saying," insisted the priest. "If this is the only life we have, and everybody realised it, then perhaps we could all work together to make the world a better place."

"Hallelujah! You'll make an atheist yet."

"It will never happen. Not in a million years."

"You're wrong, Father. You have to be wrong."

"You asked me to tell you the truth, Angus."

"No! There has to be a future in which we don't rely on religious doctrines and sacred texts. In which the rules of life are based on reason, and make sense to ordinary people."

"No, Angus-"

"A future in which we're not told that we're inherently bad and sinful, and that the only way to become good is by handing over our lives to faith."

The priest shook his head.

"In which we accept control over our own destinies, however frightening that might be, and face reality head-on without the comfort of a deception."

"Imagine there's no Heaven," muttered Father Barrington, "it's easy if you try."

"Yes!" screamed Angus.

"No, it's not easy at all. It's the hardest thing in the world." The priest stood up. "I'm sorry, Angus, I should never have come. Yet another mistake."

Angus escorted him as far as the gate. "I don't hate you, Father. I'm too busy hating myself."

"Bless you," replied the priest. He walked away.

Angus turned to go back indoors. A glint of light caught his eye. He stepped onto the grass and picked up the It's a Wonderful Life DVD. Rubbing it against his shirt, he went inside.

CHAPTER 25

The Hacienda didn't have a lift. It took Sammy ten minutes to crawl up to the bar on the third floor. He was the only customer there.

"Are you okay?" asked the diminutive female bar person.

"Not really," wheezed Sammy, hauling himself onto a stool.

"What can I get you?"

"Which whiskies do you have?"

She turned to her side and indicated a shelf of whisky bottles with a sweep of her hand.

Sammy grinned and scanned the labels. "I'll have an Ardbeg."

"On the rocks?"

He raised his eyebrows in horror. "Just a splash of water."

"I haven't seen you in here before."

"Not my kind of place." Sammy held up a hand. "No offence."

"None taken."

"I'm here to have a word with your colleague. The tall feller."

"Oscar?"

"Yes. Is he around?"

"He's busy. He'll be back in half an hour."

"I'll wait." Sammy downed his whisky. "Same again please." He spotted a surveillance camera in the top corner of the room. It was pointing directly at him.

The bar person replenished his glass before taking some clean ones down from a shelf and washing them.

Sammy was sipping his fifth whisky when he heard the sound of a door shutting.

"That'll be Oscar," she said. "I'll tell him you're here. What's your name?"

"He doesn't know me. Say I'm the friend of a friend."

She disappeared.

Sammy's jaw dropped as the giant came into view. He gulped down his shot.

"You wanted to speak to me?" asked Oscar.

"That's right."

"What can I do for you, Mr...?"

"Lane," replied Sammy, "Bob Lane."

"What can I do for you, Bob?"

"I'm looking for my nephew. He comes in here occasionally. I wondered if he'd been in recently."

"What's your nephew's name?"

"Robbie Johnson." Sammy monitored Oscar's face for any reaction. Nothing.

"I never forget a name, Bob. Haven't come across that one."

"You'd remember Robbie. He's got a paw print tattoo on his face." Sammy tapped his cheek.

There was an unmistakable flicker of anxiety on Oscar's face. "No, I don't remember seeing a tattoo like that."

"It's important. Are you sure you haven't seen him?"

"I told you, I've never met him," declared Oscar.

"I must speak to him."

"That's not my problem." Oscar turned away.

"I'll come clean with you. Robbie borrowed some money and I need it back. If you can help, I'll be more than happy to cut you in."

Oscar froze for a moment, then turned back around.

Sammy took out his wallet and counted five twenty-pound notes onto the bar. Oscar glanced from one corner of the room to the other before sliding the notes across the bar and into his pocket. The camera's obviously not switched on, thought Sammy.

"Okay, I served him once or twice. He didn't tell me his name."

"Has he been in recently?"

"Can't remember. A few days ago, I think."

"Do you know where I can find him?"

"He's a customer, not my best mate."

"Fair enough. What about friends? Has anyone been in with him?"

Oscar's face twitched. "No, he's always on his own."

Sammy counted another five twenties onto the bar.

"Okay, okay," growled Oscar, his voice now husky. "I might have seen him with a man, maybe once or twice."

"Does this man have a name?"

Oscar began to quiver. "Look, I've told you as much as I can. I don't want trouble."

"Why should there be trouble? All I'm asking for is-"

"Keep your money!" Oscar pulled the notes from his pocket, tossed them at Sammy, and left the bar.

That got me precisely nowhere, thought Sammy as he reached the stairs for the journey down. Oscar knows something but he's never gonna tell me. Has Robbie got himself mixed up with crooks? I suppose there's only one thing for it. I'll have to stake out the Hacienda until Robbie turns up, with or without Al Capone.

Sammy got into his car.

"You really should keep it locked, Sammy," said a voice from the passenger seat.

Sammy didn't have to look round. "Hello, Leo, long time no see. To what do I owe this pleasure?"

"I noticed your motor and thought it'd be nice to have a chat. How's the wife?"

"Which one?"

Leo chuckled. "You were with Jo last time we met."

"Let's not go there," shuddered Sammy. "How's Bonny? And Tom, he must be…"

"Ten years old."

"You're joking."

"Time flies, Sammy, when you're having fun. They're both well."

"That's good."

"So," asked Leo, "what brings you to this neck of the woods?"

Sammy's first instinct was to lie, but he reasoned that Leo might know something useful. "I'm looking for a missing person."

"What's his name?"

I didn't say it was a he, thought Sammy. "Robbie Johnson."

"Jimmy Johnson's boy?"

"That's right. He's got a half-sister called Zoe. She's asked me to find him."

"What makes you think you'll find him at the Hacienda?"

"A tip from an informant."

"What's your informant's name?"

"Sorry, Leo, that's-"

"Confidential? Fair enough. Well, Sammy, I can give you some info about Robbie, but you're not gonna like it."

"Try me."

"We've been keeping tabs on Robbie Johnson for a while."

"Why?" asked Sammy. "He's not a villain, is he?"

"No, he doesn't have the brains. But he's been keeping bad company, and we're hoping he'll lead us to bigger fish."

Damn, thought Sammy.

"I'm afraid I'll have to ask you to stay out of the picture. I know you wouldn't want to interfere with a police operation."

"No, Leo, that's the last thing I'd want to do."

"I knew you'd understand."

"How long is all this likely to take?"

"Impossible to say. You know how it is."

"Okay," sighed Sammy, "I'll sit tight for the moment. Let me know as soon as you're finished with the boy. You can put me in touch with him then."

"I'd be delighted. But don't expect a happy ending."

"What d'you mean by that?"

"If he doesn't get himself killed, odds are his sister will be visiting him in jail. Well, it's been fun catching up."

"Likewise."

"By the way, I've left you a present." Leo pointed at the glove box. "Cheers." He got out and walked away.

"Shit," muttered Sammy as he opened the glove box. To his relief the Colt 45 was still there in the paper bag. Behind it was a bottle of Tullamore Dew whisky. "Leo, you remembered."

Sammy eased back into the leather, opened the bottle and took a swig. There's nothing more I can do, he thought. I can't tell Zoe the truth in case she tries to find Robbie at the Hacienda. She'll just have to be patient.

CHAPTER 26

That night Alice knew she was the worst psychologist in the world.

"This is it, Jamie," she sighed, "the end of the road. I'll be out of a job by noon tomorrow, and we'll be out of our home within weeks."

Alice grabbed her pillow and hugged it tightly. She sat on the edge of her bed, rocking to and fro until tiredness overcame her.

She dreamt about the childhood picnics she'd loved so much. She was in a field with Mum and Dad. They were sitting around a multicoloured rug covered with sandwiches, apples and fairy cakes. The sun was shining, the sky clear blue. Alice sang Polly Put the Kettle On as she skipped away to find daisies for a chain. Black clouds appeared. Rain began to pour. Alice ran back to her parents. They were gone.

Next morning Alice was parked outside the prison building waiting for a dose of courage to materialise. The locket was hanging from a chain around her neck. She stroked its intricate pattern with her fingertips. As the time of her appointment passed she pictured Harry nervously anticipating her arrival, wondering if she would turn up. She positioned the locket under her blouse and got out of the car.

Her heart pounded as she approached the metal detector. If they don't find it today, she thought, they'll discover it soon enough and realise who smuggled it in. I'll have no job and a criminal record. You couldn't write this stuff.

The alarm screeched into action.

"Oh no," cried Alice, "I'm so sorry!"

"Please wait here," said the officer, "while I fetch a female member of staff."

The examination didn't take long. "I think your locket must've triggered it. It's beautiful. Where did you get it?"

"It's not mine," blurted Alice, "I'm smuggling it in for a friend." She put a hand over her mouth.

The examiner laughed.

"Did you bring it?" asked Harry as soon as they were alone.

Alice reached behind her neck to undo the clasp, slid off the locket, and refastened the chain. She held out her hand with the locket in her palm.

"Thank you," gasped Harry, lifting it with his fingertips. "Thank you so much." He opened the locket and gazed at the photograph. "This was taken when we first met in Barcelona, at the Park Guell. I was admiring the mosaic dragon when Grant appeared and asked if I'd modelled for it. Cheeky bugger. He said later it was his best ever chat-up line."

"A romantic place to meet," smiled Alice.

"Perfect. No one thought it would last. Holiday romances never do. I met the love of my life that day." He closed the locket and bent down to slide it into his sock. "I take it you found the house alright?"

"No problem." Alice screwed up her face a little, tilting her head to one side. "Had a bit of trouble getting in though. I had to break a small window by the door." She decided not to mention leaving the door unlocked with the key broken in the barrel.

"Never mind. As long as no one spotted you."

"I was really jumpy the whole time. Afterwards it felt good, in a crazy sort of way. Exciting."

"I hope you're not planning to enter a life of crime."

"I don't think so," she chuckled. "You've got a thing about tartan I noticed."

"It's the Rob Roy MacGregor tartan, in honour of Grandad. He was born in Argyll. The family moved to Cumberland when he was a lad, but he was always proud of his roots. Grandad taught me my first magic trick. How to make a coin go through a table."

"You've come a long way since then," declared Alice. She remembered where they were and covered her mouth. "I mean, before…"

"How the mighty have fallen, eh?"

"Sorry, I didn't mean…were you born in Cumberland?"

"Yes. It was Cumbria by then. We lived in Keswick."

"Keswick is my favourite place!" cried Alice. "We had family holidays in the Lake

District. I'll never forget, when I was nine, standing at the summit of Blencathra for the first time. I was on top of the world."

"If only we could stand there together one day," sighed Harry.

"Why not? Let's make a date. As soon as you're released."

"We'll see," he murmured.

"Harry, I hope you don't mind, but while I was at your house I went into the living room. I came across something interesting on top of the bookcase."

"The picture of Grant and me?"

"No, the other one."

Harry paused to think. "You mean the circus flyer? It was sent by a fan. Well, she started out as a fan, then became more of a friend."

"Her name is Bonny Mason."

"How on earth do you know that?"

"Bonny is...was a client of mine."

"It's a small world. We used to write to each other, until…" Harry gestured at the walls.

"She hasn't written recently?"

"I can't say I'm surprised. It's not just Bonny. I might as well have disappeared from the face of the earth."

"Did the two of you ever meet?"

"I suggested it, but Bonny preferred us to remain pen friends." Harry's face brightened. "Did you know she was a brilliant performer? She could hit a postage stamp with a knife from any distance you like."

"Have you ever been to one of her shows?"

"No, but I watched a video of her on-"

"YouTube," nodded Alice. "Yes, I've seen it."

"So you know exactly what I mean. Have another look at that video, and check out the crowd. Every single one of them is ecstatic."

Alice had a feeling of deja vu. It passed.

"Harry," she said, "this is our last appointment."

"I know."

"Would you mind very much if I came again, as a friend?"

"It's alright," he murmured, "you don't have to feel sorry for me."

"No, you don't understand, I want to come."

A tear appeared in Harry's eye. He wiped it away. "In that case, would you mind popping back to my house and bringing my forty-inch telly next time you come?"

They laughed together, now both with tears in their eyes.

Alice was due for her run. She went home first to check on her mother.

"I am fine," said Sofia. "You do not have to spy on me all the time, Aliki."

Alice poured her mum a glass of water and stood over her while she drank it.

"I am a child again," groaned Sofia. "One day, when you are old, you will remember how you treated your poor mother."

As she was about to leave, Alice felt a shiver run down her spine as the sensation of deja vu returned. The image of Bonny's flyer flashed through her mind. She ran upstairs, picked it up from her bedside table, and sat down on the bed.

Alice read the flyer and examined the pictures. She flipped it over and read Bonny's message. 'Dear Alice, You asked if I had a photo of me at the circus. I said no, but then I remembered this. It was taken during one of my last performances. It brings back memories, especially the crowds. Look how every single one of them is smiling. Thank you for helping me. Bonny'.

Alice remembered Harry's words. "Have another look at that video," he'd said, "and check out the crowd. Every single one of them is ecstatic."

She turned the flyer back over and peered intently at Bonny's photo. There in the crowd, amongst a mass of excited faces and waving arms, was someone she recognised. There, staring straight at Bonny, arms by his sides, with no emotion on his face, was Leo Mason!

Alice grabbed her laptop and started the YouTube video of the circus. Her hand trembled as she clicked again and again until she found the part where Bonny appeared. She wanted it to be the same performance. She wanted to find this man in the crowd, to prove to herself that he was merely a doppelganger for Leo. Time slowed. Alice held her breath.

"There he is," she gasped. There, motionless, as if in a trance, was the unmistakable face of Leo Mason. Leo Mason, who had never seen Bonny perform. Leo Mason, who had never even set eyes on Bonny before her attack.

Why would they both lie to me, thought Alice? What are they trying to hide? She searched her mind for an explanation, but could find none.

"See you later, Mum," she called to Sofia as she rushed out of the house. She jumped into her car and headed for the Masons' house.

I have to speak to Bonny alone, thought Alice. I'm more likely to get the truth from her. Leo's bound to be at work.

Alice knocked several times without response. She was on the verge of giving up when she heard movement.

"Who is it?" murmured Bonny from behind the closed door.

"Hello, Bonny. It's me, Alice Alexander. Can I come in please?"

The door opened a fraction. Less than half of Bonny's drawn face was visible.

"There's something I need to ask you, Bonny," said Alice, touching the door. "It would be better if we spoke inside."

Bonny retreated from the doorway. Alice followed, swinging the door behind her.

Bonny sat down at the dining table, picked up one of five circus knives that lay there, and began to polish it with a black cloth. There were two display cabinets on the wall. One contained a further five identical knives, the other was empty. Bonny's hand moved the cloth rhythmically back and forth along the blade.

Try to keep calm, Alice advised herself. "Bonny, I remember you telling me that you hadn't met Leo before he took charge of your investigation. You said he never saw you perform, that it was his biggest regret."

Bonny said nothing. She focused on the knife, her hand sliding back and forth.

"When I spoke to Leo he said exactly the same thing...exactly the same."

Alice waited for a response, but none came.

"I've looked again at the picture you gave me. He was there, in the crowd. Leo was there!"

Bonny's hand stopped for a moment, then resumed its rhythmic motion.

"Why, Bonny? Why lie? You knew he was there in the photo, didn't you?"

Alice heard the front door click shut.

"Bonny, I'm home," called Leo.

Bonny's hand stopped.

Alice froze. Did I shut the door on my way in, she thought? How long has Leo been here?

"I managed to get away early so that...Alice! What a pleasant surprise. What brings you here? Nothing wrong, I hope."

Alice shook her head repeatedly. "I was passing and thought I'd check on Bonny. You were a bit upset last time we spoke, weren't you Bonny?"

"How incredibly thoughtful of you," said Leo. "As you can tell, Bonny is absolutely fine."

"Yes, that's good." Alice took a step towards the door. "I'd better go. I'm late for my run."

"Are you sure you won't stay for a drink?" asked Leo.

"That's very kind of you, but Mum is on her own and-"

"I've got a Nespresso machine in my den. I can make two coffees in less than a minute."

Leo walked towards Alice. She took a step back as he moved past her towards a door she hadn't previously noticed. He opened the door and disappeared behind it.

From where she stood Alice could see one wall of the den. Hanging there was a mirror bearing the words 'Jack Daniel's Old No.7 Brand Tennessee Whiskey'. Most of the glass was frosted but there was a strip of mirror around the edge in which she could make out the back of Leo's head. The coffee machine gurgled.

Alice took a step towards the mirror and spotted a movement in the corner of her eye. She turned towards the movement and realised she could now see Leo through the gap between the door and its frame. She leaned forward and put her eye to the gap. On the wall opposite the mirror, partly obscured by Leo's head, was a framed black and white poster of a man carrying a machine-gun. He was dressed in a pinstripe suit and wore a fedora hat. On his left cheek was an ugly scar in the shape of a crucifix. Alice kept perfectly still. She focused on the scar.

Leo spun around, holding an espresso cup in each hand. As he moved towards the door of the den he no longer obscured the lower third of the poster. Alice's legs moved backwards but her eye stayed where it was. Across the bottom of the poster were the words, 'Paul Muni is SCARFACE'.

Alice blurted, "Scarface!" and threw herself backwards. She instinctively twisted with arms outstretched but was unable to avoid falling onto her side. She scrambled to her feet to find Leo standing motionless in the doorway, his eyes fixed on her.

"Did you say something?" he asked.

Alice put a hand over her mouth.

Leo handed her a coffee as he walked calmly past into the centre of the room. Alice turned to face him. Bonny was behind, polishing.

"I couldn't help noticing the poster..." stuttered Alice, "...on your den wall."

Leo drank his coffee in one shot. "An impressive image, don't you think?" An eerie smile came over his face. "My favourite film of all time, directed by Howard Hawks. Paul Muni played Tony Camonte, a man who really knew what he wanted, and was prepared to do anything to get it."

Alice was unnerved by Leo's trancelike eyes. He was talking to her, but looked straight through her, as if she wasn't there.

"The 1983 version was a poor remake," he continued. "Al Pacino's scar was pathetic in comparison."

Behind Leo's back Bonny's eyes lifted. She shook her head, mouthing the word "Go."

Alice turned her eyes away from Leo's to focus on Bonny. At that instant Leo blinked hard.

"Drink your espresso before it gets cold," he said.

Alice's trembling hand guided the cup to her lips. She sipped the bitter coffee. "I really must go." A few drops splashed across her fingers as she put the cup down. "Bye, Bonny."

Leo followed Alice to the front door. "Until we meet again," he purred in his deepest voice. He stroked her hair.

Alice rushed to the car, her head spinning. I need to talk to someone, she thought. I need to talk to Esther. She scraped the kerb with her back tyre as she screeched away.

On entering the clinic Alice rushed to her room and got out her mobile. She rang Esther's number. No reply. She rang again. No reply. She sent a text. 'Must speak urgently. Please ring asap'.

CHAPTER 27

Running always helped Alice think more clearly. If there was ever a day she needed her run, this was it. She changed into her gear, tied her hair back, and set off.

For the first time in weeks the sky was more grey than blue. As she jogged along the lakeside path Alice felt a cooling breeze. She glanced across the lake at a distant cumulonimbus formation. The top was white, rising into the heavens in the shape of a giant anvil. The bottom was slate grey, ominous. It'll be raining before I get back, she thought.

The cooler temperature meant that a personal best was on the cards. Concentrate. There were no birds or squirrels around to distract her.

As she changed direction to enter the woods Alice felt a twinge of pain in her ankle. She considered turning back, but increased her pace instead. She was soon dodging roots in the gloom of the woods and was forced to slow down. No personal best today. Another twinge from the ankle and Alice slowed her pace even more. She decided to walk until the ankle eased.

The events of the past week came flooding into Alice's mind. She tried to make sense of it all. Ten years ago, she thought, Paul Ireland raped Bonny Mason. Later, as Leo's partner, he was able to gain further contact with her. Bonny was too frightened of him to say anything. That continued until Ireland went to prison. He wasn't welcome after his release, having turned against Leo, so he began stalking Bonny. He couldn't get close enough to her, so he engineered an appointment with me, hoping he could trick me into helping him. That all makes sense.

The clouds thickened. There was drizzle in the air.

Ireland knows he can't have Bonny, thought Alice, unless he can get her away from Leo. In the hope of getting my support he decided to throw doubt on Leo's sanity by insisting his scar was self-inflicted. But the scar is irrelevant. What if Leo did cut his own face? At the time he was a troubled teenager with no father and an alcoholic mother. It's understandable that he's embarrassed about it now and doesn't want people to know.

The rustling of the leaves grew louder. Rain was falling.

Bonny refuses to tell the police about Ireland stalking her in case he ends up in prison and tries to kill himself. That's easy to understand. But there's one thing that makes no sense at all. Leo and Bonny both told me that he'd never set eyes on her before she was raped, and that he'd always regretted not seeing her perform. But Bonny gave me a photo of her at the circus with Leo in the crowd. Surely she must have spotted him in the photo, in which case why risk me seeing it?

The wind was rushing. Branches swayed.

So what do I do? Have it out with Leo and Bonny? Ask the police to sort it all out and put my reputation on the line? Pretend the whole thing never happened? I know what I should do...wait until I've spoken to Esther. For now, the best course of action is to stop thinking about it!

Alice stood still to survey the heavens. The sky was dark, rain falling out of it in lines. She closed her eyes and felt the drops hitting her face. Her mind cleared.

A branch snapped in the wind and crashed to the ground. Alice regained her concentration and scanned the area around her. She recalled being followed two days before, and realised she was standing near the spot where Ireland was hiding. She started to run.

It was harder than usual to avoid the branches as they swayed to and fro. Alice concentrated hard on the ground. A thin branch whipped across her forehead, knocking her off balance. "Ow!" She rubbed her head and carried on running.

The downhill section was next. The rain was heavy, the light poor. As she started down the slope Alice tried to focus on the thick roots snaking across the ground in front of her. Concentrate!

Alice screamed as she felt a searing pain in her ankle and flew headlong into the ground. There was a deafening thud, then nothing.

Alice came round to find herself face down. She tried to get up but shrieked with pain in her left wrist. The wrist was swollen, the little finger dislocated. Her nose was bleeding. She struggled to roll onto her right side and push herself up into a sitting position. She twisted to search for the offending root, but was unable to focus.

After blinking several times Alice was astonished to find a length of silver wire lying on the ground behind her. "What idiot left that there?" she groaned, trying to get up. Before she could stand her ponytail was jerked sideways, spinning her back down. She tried to speak, but a moaning sound was all that passed her lips. A wave of nausea overcame her. She felt her entire body tingling, then lost consciousness.

Alice dreamt she was in an earthquake. She half-woke, disorientated, in total darkness. The ground was rumbling, throwing her backwards and forwards. The wind and rain had stopped. She tried to get up but couldn't move any of her limbs. I must be badly injured, she thought.

As Alice came round further the pain took over. Her wrist felt like it was in a vice. She tried to move it, but the resulting agony was excruciating. Her nose was hot, throbbing. She couldn't feel the dislocated finger at all. Stay calm, she told herself, don't be frightened. A faint smell of rubber entered her single open nostril, and she knew where she was.

Alice realised that her arms and legs were fastened tightly, and knew that struggling would achieve nothing except more pain and reduced blood flow. A hood covered her head. Biting into the corners of her mouth was a gag which tasted of blood. She realised she was panting. Slow your breathing down, she advised herself, you can't afford to waste precious air.

A car horn blared and Alice was thrown to one side. She tensed every muscle in anticipation of a crash, picturing herself being dragged out of the wreck barely alive. Moments later she lurched forward as the car stopped abruptly. The engine idled.

To her surprise Alice heard the thadakh-thadakh of a train passing by. It comforted her to know there were people near. Maybe someone on the train will remember the car, she thought.

The engine revved. The car bumped over the crossing.

Alice's mobile rang in her shorts pocket. She instinctively moved to grasp it, giving a muted scream into her gag as a knife-like pain tore through her wrist. The mobile rang and rang, then stopped. The police can use the signal to trace my position, she thought. But it'll be ages before anyone knows I'm missing.

The car turned a corner then bumped around, throwing Alice from left to right. She was sobbing with pain, struggling to get any breath at all.

There was scraping along the side of the car. Seconds later all movement stopped.

The engine was silent. Her mobile rang.

The boot opened. Alice played dead. She felt a hand slide into her pocket to grasp the mobile. She recognised the sound of the battery being removed, followed by the phone thumping against the floor of the boot.

Two powerful arms surrounded Alice's body and lifted her out. She was heaved onto a shoulder which compressed her abdomen and chest, squeezing the air out of her lungs. The boot slammed shut.

Alice made no effort to resist or complain. Playing dead is my best option, she thought. I must save my energy for the one opportunity that might come my way. As she was carried along she bit into her gag to stifle her moans.

At last Alice was dumped onto her back and could breathe more easily. Her hands had gone dead. Almost immediately she heard the sound of repeated hammer blows, first to one side of her head, then the other, then around her feet.

The tether binding Alice's ankles was released. One leg was pulled to the side and tied down. Her legs were parted widely as the second was secured. She felt her shoulders being tightly gripped as she was pulled into a sitting position. Her wrists were untied and she was dropped back down, ready for them to be refastened, one out at each side.

A cold breeze blew across Alice's body. Her running clothes were still wet. She shivered.

Without warning the hood was yanked from her head. She instinctively opened her eyes, grimacing as the light burned into them. She forced them shut and lay still.

"I'll take the gag off, but if you make a sound it goes back on and stays on. Not that anyone will hear you out here."

Alice's body stiffened at the sound of Leo Mason's voice. She kept silent.

"Don't play games. I know you can hear me."

She squinted through her eyelashes, then blinked repeatedly, opening her lids a little more each time. Mason was behind her, just out of sight. Directly above was a lime tree, containing several giant balls of mistletoe. Bonny's nests, thought Alice.

"Romantic, aren't they?" he purred.

"Poisonous," replied Alice.

Mason laughed. He got up, stepped around her into view, and kneeled between her legs. Alice felt his knees touching her thighs.

"You worked it out, didn't you?" he grinned.

"I don't know what you're talking about."

"My scar. Though you didn't believe that wanker Ireland when he told you. It tickled me when you said you'd checked out Al Pacino. His scar was rubbish! When that remake came out they showed the original on telly. I recorded it by accident. What a stroke of luck that was. No, not luck, destiny. I watched it a hundred times while I was bunking off school." His face flushed, the grin giving way to a fierce stare. "Of course, she had no idea, useless bitch! She didn't give a toss. We'd have been better off with no mother at all. She treated me like a piece of shit. Then it all changed. For the first time I had control over my life. I was master of my own destiny. That's what everyone wants, isn't it?"

"I have no idea."

"Tony Camonte. A real man! Power, money...and girls. In the end, that's what all women are desperate for. A man to look up to, a man to respect, a man with power. Without power, I wouldn't have you."

"You don't have me."

"That's why I despise tossers like Paul Ireland, and that queen Harry Hart."

Alice gasped at the sound of Harry's name.

"Men like that think they can waltz in and take anything they want…" He snapped his fingers. "…just like that. Even if it belongs to another man. Now they know better."

"What are you talking about?"

"Ireland thought he could worm his way into my house, with his cute dogs, and sweet-talk my wife. One minute he's my loyal partner, the next he's stabbing me in the back. I soon sorted him out. As for Hart, who the hell does he think he is, writing letters to another man's wife? All I had to do was call in a favour from a dodgy mechanic and...crashbang!" Mason lifted his arms to the sky.

"What on earth have you done?"

"I meant Hart to get hurt, not his freak of a sidekick. But sometimes that's just how the cookie crumbles. Then, blow me, Hart gets done for manslaughter. Two birds with one stone. You couldn't make it up. The icing on the cake is that he actually blames himself for the crash. Priceless!" Mason threw his head back and cackled.

Alice struggled to absorb what she was hearing.

"The trouble these days," he continued, "is that all everyone talks about is freedom. Freedom to say what you like, freedom to do what you like, freedom to steal another man's wife! We need to get back to the old days. In the wild west, if you took another man's property you paid with your life. And you were left hanging from a tree as a warning to other would-be criminals. That was real justice."

"But you're a policeman, you can't-"

"Just ask Bonny, she'll tell you. With me protecting her, she hasn't got a care in the world. I take her everywhere, I keep prowlers away. What else could a girl possibly want?" He put his hands on Alice's thighs.

"Get your hands off me."

"And I'll do the same for you, Alice."

"Let me go, now!" She pulled against the ties, her face distorted by pain.

Mason stroked Alice's thighs. "You're starting to enjoy this, aren't you?"

"You can't possibly get away with this. I'll go straight to the police."

"I don't think so."

"If you kill me, they'll know it was you. There'll be forensic evidence in your car. If I disappear, Bonny will tell them everything."

"Of course she won't," howled Mason. "Bonny will tell them precisely nothing." The laughter stopped abruptly. "You should consider your position before you start making foolish threats. Anyway, who said anything about killing you?" He squeezed her thighs tightly.

"Ow! You're hurting me."

"Bonny won't back you up, not if she wants to see Tom again. They won't believe a word you say. They'll call you a liar and a fool. You'll end up on the streets, you and your poor dear mother."

"You bastard."

"Or maybe it'll be prison. You'll love it in there, a pretty girl like you. But enough of this silliness." He eased his grip. "I know what your true feelings are, the way you flirt with me, the way you kiss me. You've got a thing for older men, haven't you? Don't deny it."

"Some older men."

"I knew it! So why not give in to your desires? You know you want me. If you're worried about Bonny, you don't need to be. The two of you will get on just fine. Tom will have a new auntie, and before long he'll have a new brother or sister."

"You're insane."

"You'll have everything you need. You'll never have to work again. And if any man so much as looks at you." He moved his hands up to her waist. "I love you, Alice. You know you love me too." His hands slid under her running top, lifting it up over her bra.

"Leave me alone!" she screamed.

"Shut up!" He jerked forward to kneel across the tops of Alice's thighs. His hands pressed down on her shoulders. "I don't want to have to gag you again." His tone softened. "I want you to enjoy our kisses."

His face hovered directly above hers. He ran a hand through her hair, lowering his head slowly until their noses touched.

He forced his mouth against hers, devouring it with his lips and tongue. Alice squirmed from side to side with all her might. She felt a sickening crack in her wrist and gave a piercing shriek. Everything went black.

By the time Alice regained consciousness the clouds had disappeared, leaving a sheet of pure azure. Mason was standing at her feet.

"How long have I been out?" she asked.

"Long enough for me to slip you into something more comfortable." He ran his eyes down the length of her body, then back up to her face.

Alice lifted her head and peered across her chest and abdomen. She was no longer dressed in her running gear. She was wearing lilac lace bra and panties. "Where are my clothes?"

"The colour suits you. I knew it would."

"Have you touched me, you bastard?"

"Take advantage of a girl while she's asleep? What sort of man do you take me for? I did enjoy a sneak preview though. Very nice, very nice indeed."

"Let me go, Leo. Please."

"That's a bit better. You never know what you might get, if you ask nicely." He scanned her body again. "You remind me of Bonny, you know. That evening, here, was the best of my life. After today it'll be the second best."

A bulge appeared in Mason's trousers. Alice couldn't stop herself from looking at it.

"You can't wait, can you, you dirty bitch," he smirked. "How about a closer look?"

He pulled down his trouser zip.

CHAPTER 28

"That's enough!" burst a scream from the bushes behind Leo Mason.

He spun around. Alice stared between his legs at Bonny, standing motionless no more than twenty feet away. In Bonny's left hand were four knives, held by the blades, fanned-out. In her right hand, by the side of her head, was a fifth.

"What are you doing here?" thundered Mason. "I didn't give you permission to leave the house!"

Bonny didn't flinch. She was composed, her hands steady. Alice had never seen this Bonny before.

"Let her go."

"How dare you," snarled Mason.

"I said let her go!" yelled Bonny, her right hand easing backwards.

Without taking his eyes off Bonny for a second, Mason dropped in slow motion to kneel by Alice's right ankle. "How the hell did you find this place?" he asked. "You haven't been here since…"

"That's where you're wrong," replied Bonny. "I haven't been here since you forced me to marry you, that's true. How could I? No, it was before that, while I still had my freedom."

"Why come back?"

"To search for the bracelet Gran gave me. I lost it here, that day. I came three times. I suppose an animal or a magpie must've found it. You can't blame a primitive creature for taking what doesn't belong to it."

"How on earth did you find your way here on your own?"

"I used my brain. You know, the part of me that's been dormant for the last ten years. It wasn't difficult. The time it took to get here, the railway line, and this tree." She looked up at the lime. "There isn't another like it."

"But you couldn't have known I'd come here now."

"I know how your mind works. The way you reacted when Alice saw your god Tony Camonte, I knew you'd flipped." She turned to Alice. "I'm sorry it took me so long to get here."

"Don't worry," replied Alice.

Bonny glared at Mason. "I said let her go!"

Mason started to undo the ankle tether, still focusing on Bonny. "Come on, darling, there's no need for this."

"Don't waste your breath, you evil piece of shit."

Mason stiffened. "Don't call me that."

"Reminds you of your precious mother, does it?" jeered Bonny.

Mason jumped to his feet. "Don't you dare say that! You don't know what it was like, you with your perfect childhood. You didn't spend it covered in bruises, cleaning up the vomit and shit your mum left on the carpet."

"You're right, I did have a perfect childhood. I had a perfect life." Bonny began to tremble. "You took it away from me. You stole me from my family."

She nodded at Alice's ankle. Mason removed the tether. Alice brought her legs together.

"I should've told you the truth, Alice. If I had, none of this would've happened. It's all my fault."

"No, Bonny, it's okay."

"You have to realise what he's like. First of all he was all charm and sweetness. He came to every performance, stayed behind after the shows, gave me the Leo Mason eyes. We went for walks and held hands. I thought he was so nice, so kind. When it was nearly time for the circus to leave town he said I couldn't go. He said he loved me, couldn't bear to let me out of his sight. I told him my life was with the circus, but he wouldn't listen. That's when I met the real Leo Mason."

"There's no need to go over all this stuff," pleaded Mason, "is there, darling?"

"Shut up!" She raised the knife higher and nodded at the other ankle.

Mason moved across to it.

Bonny's trembling was more obvious. "He threatened me, said if I didn't do what he wanted he'd have me locked up. He meant it, I knew he did. It didn't matter what I said. I begged him, pleaded with him. You know what happened."

"Yes," whispered Alice.

"After that the threats got worse. He said the police would never believe me. Everyone would know I was a whore, even my family. Then he said he'd get a crook he knew to burn down the circus. I couldn't take that chance...I couldn't."

"No," replied Alice, her second ankle now free.

"I soon realised I was pregnant. I thought I'd be fine, my family would look after me. But he wouldn't leave me alone. I knew he'd never give up. He was obsessed, out of his mind. I had to marry him, I had no choice. You do understand?"

"Yes, Bonny, I understand."

"Now the arms!" cried Bonny.

Mason jumped forward to undo the left wrist tether.

"Everyone thought how wonderful he was, taking this poor girl under his wing, helping to bring up her baby as his own. Of course he couldn't tell people that Tom was really his son. That annoyed the hell out of him." She took a step forward. "They all think you're wonderful, don't they? Well, Leo Mason, the truth is you're a monster. An evil rapist who deserves to be locked away forever. I hate you."

"Bonny, please," he begged.

"I haven't finished!" she screamed. "There's something else I want you to know. You think you're such a great lover, don't you? Hah! I learned how to pretend. I haven't had the tiniest bit of satisfaction from you...not ever. You didn't just rape me that day ten years ago. You've raped me a thousand times since."

Mason gritted his teeth. His reddened face was inches away from Alice's as he undid the final tether. Free at last, she crawled away towards her clothes which lay in a pile nearby.

Mason stood to face Bonny. "I've had enough of this. If you're going to throw that thing, then throw it! Come on, what are you waiting for?" He held his hands out to Bonny, wafting his fingers towards his face. "You haven't got the bottle, have you?" He took a step towards her.

The knife flashed through the air like lightning, a spinning blur.

"Aargh!" screeched Mason as it flew past him and thudded into a tree trunk. He covered his left ear, then examined his blood-smeared palm.

Bonny took another knife. "One more step and you'll get this one between your legs."

"You can threaten me all you like," cried Mason. "I don't care how many times you cut me, I'll heal fast enough. But you won't kill me, will you? You won't kill Tom's daddy. He'd never forgive you. If you do kill me you'll go to prison, and what'll happen to Tom then? The best thing you can do now is kill yourself. Alice will make a far better mother."

Bonny's whole body shook. She drew back her hand.

"No, Bonny!" shouted Alice. "He's right. You'll never forgive yourself. Think of Tom. You must let the police sort this out."

Mason shrieked with laughter.

Bonny dropped both arms and started sobbing. The knives fell to earth.

"You're useless!" screamed Mason. He rushed at her, drawing back his fist. It smashed across her face, sending her flying through the air like a rag doll. He towered over her. "You couldn't even give me a daughter. The one thing I wanted more than anything in the world. Was that really too much to ask?"

Bonny glared up at him. "Of course I could've given you a daughter, you fool, but that was the last thing I wanted to do. A man like you shouldn't be allowed to have children. I've been taking the pill for the last ten years."

"No!" Mason buried his face in his hands. "How could you, after everything I've done for you? You knew how much it meant to me." He swung his arm back. Bonny turned her face away as his fist swept forward and thumped into the side of her head. She lay in a heap, motionless.

"Attack!" came a roar from amongst the trees.

Mason spun around to see two German Shepherds bounding towards him, teeth bared. One dog locked its jaws onto his ankle while the other leapt through the air, latching onto the left side of his face. In an instant they brought him down and tore at his flesh.

Mason wailed hysterically, struggling in vain to fight off the hounds. "Get them away from me!" he howled.

"Stand by!" came a further command from the trees. The dogs let go and withdrew by several feet. They sat on their haunches, monitoring Mason with burning eyes, awaiting further instructions.

Mason squealed in agony, both hands covering his face.

"Good girls," declared Paul Ireland as he strode towards his dogs. He ruffled their necks, then stepped forward to hover over Mason. "Try to get up and they'll finish the job."

"Is Bonny alright?" asked Alice.

Paul crouched down next to Bonny. She was lying on her side, moaning softly. He touched her cheek. "Are you okay?" She managed a tiny nod of her head.

Paul turned back to Mason who was eyeing the dogs. "Hands behind your back." He grabbed one of Mason's ropes and tied his wrists together. He took another and tied his ankles.

Alice could now see Mason's face. His scar was gone, replaced by an ugly wound oozing blood.

"Stand down!" called Paul. The dogs immediately bounded towards Bonny, tails wagging, and licked at her face.

"I've missed you," yelped Bonny, ruffling a dog with each hand before grabbing their necks.

Paul witnessed the scene with obvious pride.

"We need to ring 999, police and ambulance," insisted Alice, hobbling over to the others. She pointed at Mason's face.

"Oh my God, look at your wrist!" cried Bonny.

"Don't worry," replied Alice, "it'll be fine."

Paul made the call.

Bonny became restless. "I must go. Tom will be worried sick." She approached the tree from which her knife protruded. A peacock butterfly had settled on the handle.

"You should wait until the police arrive," advised Paul.

"No, I have to go." Bonny waited for the butterfly to flutter away. She pulled out the knife. "Alice, I'm so sorry."

"We'll speak soon," replied Alice.

Bonny disappeared into the woods.

"Don't let him out of your sight," Paul advised the dogs. He gently ushered Alice further away from Mason.

"How...why are you here?" whispered Alice.

"I was following Bonny as usual, despite your disapproval. The dogs tracked her into the woods, but we had to keep our distance to avoid being spotted. We lost her completely, and it took the dogs a while to regain her scent. Then I heard Bonny shouting in the distance. We got here just in time."

CHAPTER 29

Under normal circumstances Alice avoided ringing home for fear that Mum would panic, rush to the phone and fall over. These were not normal circumstances. The ringtone repeated louder and louder as Alice's heart pounded faster and faster. At last it stopped, and she heard an unexpected voice.

"Alice, is that you?"

"Esther, thank goodness you're there. But...what's happened? Is Mum alright?"

"She's fine. Well, sort of. What a relief to hear your voice. I was about to call the police. Where are you?"

"I'm in A&E. Don't worry, I'm fine. I fell and hurt my arm. Problem is, I've lost my phone."

"Ah, that explains it. I'm sorry I didn't respond to your text straightaway. I was stuck in a horrendous meeting. When I did try ringing I couldn't get through, so I came here to find Sofia with her nose against the window. I think you're in trouble. She says you never listen to her, and this is definitely the last time she'll let you go running on your own. She's convinced you've been kidnapped!"

"You've been there with Mum all this time? You're a darling."

"Never mind that. I'll come and pick you up."

"No, stay with Mum, I'll get a taxi. I've had the x-rays, and I'm waiting for the plaster. It's not too busy for a Friday night. I'll be with you in no time."

Two hours later Alice gave Esther a doorway hug and limped through to her mother.

"God help us," cried Sofia. "Your face is swollen, and what have you done to your arm?"

"It's nothing, Mum. I had a bit of a fall, that's all."

"Now perhaps you will listen to your poor mother. Maybe I'm not so stupid after all." Sofia held out her arms, one lower than the other. They hugged.

"What about you, Mum, are you alright?" Alice took a tissue and dabbed the saliva at the drooping corner of Sofia's mouth.

"Of course I am alright. I have my daughter with me. Promise me you will never go anywhere on your own again."

"Okay, Mum, I promise."

"Thank God, now I can rest. I know that my Aliki will never break a promise. Just like her father."

"The most important thing he taught me," Alice explained to Esther. "If Dad promised we would do something together, I knew he'd never let me down. I loved him so much for that."

Sofia smiled from one side of her mouth. "God bless you, Aliki," she mumbled, her eyelids closing.

Minutes later Alice was sitting with Esther at the kitchen table.

"This tea's disgusting," groaned Esther.

"Mum likes it. Speaking of which, has she had anything to eat or drink?"

"I heated her some soup. She had a few spoonfuls, and a mouthful of bread."

"I'm worried, Esther. I think she's had another mini-stroke, probably caused by the stress."

"Don't blame yourself, I'm sure she'll pick up. She was worse when I arrived. I wanted to call an ambulance but she begged me not to." Esther raised an eyebrow. "So, how did you hurt yourself?"

Alice took a sip of her tea.

"Come on," insisted Esther, "something's wrong. What happened?"

Alice gulped. "It was terrible!" she howled, bursting into tears. She told Esther the whole story. "I've been such a fool," she whimpered.

Esther squeezed Alice's hand, then reached into her handbag to fish out a KitKat. "You're not the first girl in the world to be taken in by a big smile and a stunning pair of eyes. No, this is my fault. Paul Ireland told me all about Mason, what he's capable of, but I refused to listen. I've been a complete idiot."

"It doesn't matter any more, does it? He'll be locked away for a very long time. Bonny and Tom will be better off without him. Paul can start to rebuild his life. And poor Harry...they have to release him, surely."

"They've got to."

"I'm glad it happened," insisted Alice. "In the end it was worth it."

"I wish I'd been there to see Mason arrested."

"He wasn't. One of the ambulances rushed him off to hospital just before the other crew took me. They must've arrested him there."

"I suppose so."

"Actually, I was surprised to be let home from A&E without being interviewed. I expect I'll be contacted tomorrow."

"Everything will be just fine," reassured Esther, "and I'll be back here first thing in the morning."

Once Esther had gone, Alice struggled to get Sofia into bed then dragged herself, shattered, to her own bedroom. She collapsed onto the bed fully-clothed, and drifted into a welcome sleep.

Her body jolted. She jumped up and hurried to her mother's room. Sofia was fast asleep, snoring gently.

Alice limped back to the landing, stood still, and listened. She heard the faint rushing of the breeze. Have I left a downstairs window open, she wondered? Too exhausted to check, she returned to the darkness of her bedroom, fell onto the bed and drifted off again.

What was that? Alice felt something touching her hair. There it was again, something...someone...touching her hair. Fingers, now running through her hair, stroking her scalp. She was desperate to get up, get away, but her entire body was paralysed. She peered through tiny gaps between her eyelids. Leo Mason's face. How did he get into the house? What's he going to do? Why can't I move?

A sudden noise. Alice woke, heart pounding, and stared from side to side into the darkness. She heard a moan, jumped up, and rushed to Sofia's room. The bed was empty. Sofia lay in a heap on her bedside rug, clutching at her duvet with one hand.

"Mum, are you alright?"

Sofia let go of the duvet and reached out to her daughter. "Help me, darling. Help me back into bed." Her speech was slurred.

"As soon as I've called the ambulance."

"No, Aliki, no ambulance. My time has come. I want to die in my own bed."

Alice fought to lift Sofia without the use of her broken wrist. Sofia couldn't help, her legs weak, her right arm limp by her side.

Having got her reasonably comfortable, sitting half-upright on a mass of pillows, Alice asked: "Can I get you anything? Would you like some water?"

"No, darling," mumbled Sofia, "bring two glasses of Tia Maria."

Alice was soon back with the liqueurs. Sofia held out her glass. "Stin iyia mas!" They chinked glasses and took a sip.

"I don't want to leave you, Aliki. It breaks my heart, but it is out of my hands. God knows that you are ready, otherwise he would not take me. He will protect you."

"Yes, Mum."

"Richard misses me so much. Now God has decided that we can be together again, forever."

Alice pictured Mum and Dad side by side, holding hands.

"So you see, darling, there is nothing to be afraid of. I can leave you with a happy heart."

"It must be wonderful," whispered Alice, "being certain that God is here for us." She flushed, covering her mouth.

"What do you mean, Aliki?"

"Nothing, Mum, nothing."

"You believe in God, don't you?"

"Yes, I think-"

"Of course you do! I may not have been a perfect mother, but I taught you everything I know about our faith."

"Yes, Mum, thank you."

Sofia peered into her daughter's eyes. "And yet, there is doubt in your heart."

Alice could not lie to her mother on her deathbed. "Some doubt."

"I knew this would happen," groaned Sofia. "I warned your father but he would not listen."

"What do you mean?"

"This is what I get for marrying a non-believer! I wanted to give you a proper religious education, like every good Greek mother. But Richard said you should be given all the facts and allowed to make up your own mind. Like a fool I agreed."

"Because you're wonderful."

"You must promise me that you will pray to God when I die. He will guide you."

"I will, Mum."

"Do you promise?"

"Yes, I promise." Alice leaned forward to kiss her mother's forehead. "You're the best."

"No, Aliki, not the best. I know that I worry too much." Sofia's eyelids closed.

Alice felt an urge to ask something but hesitated. She gazed at her mother's peaceful face.

The urge returned. "Mum?"

"Yes, darling?" murmured Sofia.

"There's something I need to ask you."

Sofia's eyes half-opened. "I know, Aliki. The photograph."

"The baby Dad was holding. It wasn't me, was it?"

"No, darling."

"It was a boy."

Sofia touched Alice's hand. "I should have told you, I know. But your father was so angry when I found out. I found the photograph like you, by accident. Everything was going so well. Richard was happy at work, we were in love, you were growing in my belly. Then I found the picture. When I showed it to him, he was so upset. He grabbed my arm and snatched it from me. It was the only time he ever hurt me. Straightaway I realised."

"That the baby was his."

"He would not talk about it, but I had to know. It was the middle of the night before he gave in. I can still see his face. He was crying like a child." A tear ran down Sofia's cheek. "He would not say much, only that his friend had stabbed him in the back and taken his wife."

"What? Dad was married before he met you?"

"Yes, Aliki. He said that he had no contact with her, or the baby, and promised me he never would. She went off with his friend, so he pretended that she never existed. I think it nearly killed him."

"Was this in Scotland?"

"He was working in the prison there. That was why he moved to Watertown prison, to start again."

"To meet his true love, eh?"

"It is a good thing he had shaved off that ridiculous moustache! Otherwise I would not have looked twice at him."

"Tell me again how you met. I love that story."

"It was at a dance. I was very shy then. I was sitting at the side, trying to look pretty."

"Mum, I've seen your wedding photos. You were gorgeous."

"My friend told me there was a man who would not take his eyes off me. She pointed to him, so of course I had to look. He was very handsome." Sofia gazed into the distance and nodded. "Yes, very handsome. I could not help myself. I smiled at him, and he came straight over. We danced for the rest of the night."

"How romantic. I don't suppose I'll ever be so lucky."

"Of course you will, darling. It is written in the stars, you wait and see." Sofia struggled to keep her eyes open.

"Mum?"

"Hmm?"

"What was the baby's name?"

"I am sorry, Aliki, I do not know. I asked your father but he would not say. And we never talked about it again. Now, let me sleep."

"I love you, Mum."

"I love you too, darling."

Sofia's eyes closed.

Alice prayed.

CHAPTER 30

The bedside clock told Angus it was 1.33am. He turned over to prevent himself from watching it. Its ticking got louder to compensate.

Angus couldn't sleep with his eyes open, but every time he shut them he saw Father Barrington's pleading face, mouthing at him like a silent movie actor. No sound, but the expressions spoke louder than words.

Angus felt sorry for Father Barrington. And he despised him.

There were moments of relief from this vision when his mother's face replaced the priest's.

Angus felt sorry for his mother. And he despised her.

"Aaargh!" He thumped the wall.

This is hopeless, he thought, as he sat up on the edge of the bed, rubbing his heavy eyes. He ran a hand through his lank greasy hair. His mouth tasted like the bottom of a birdcage.

Angus switched on the bedside light. His Fender lay on the floor, the G string broken. He recalled how Jess used to change his broken strings for him. Taking the guitar by the neck, he lifted it high and smashed it with all his might against the window sill. He tossed down the buckled instrument, threw on some clothes, and went downstairs.

There was an old tow rope in the basement. Angus grabbed it and headed for the car. He was going to Oxley Park. He knew which tree he would use.

Angus loved driving on country lanes at night. It was easier to spot the headlights of other cars. No headlights tonight. Angus put his foot down.

The Crossfire swung from edge to edge as it negotiated the bends. On the straights Angus jerked the wheel from left to right, glancing one verge then the other. He hurtled within inches of a giant oak and realised that the rope wouldn't be needed after all.

Angus flicked the headlights onto beam and searched ahead for the next big tree. There it was. He put his foot to the floor and headed straight for it.

At the last moment a wheel hit the bank, sending the car into an uncontrollable swerve. The tree scraped along the entire side, taking off the wing mirror, and showering broken glass into Angus's face. The car spun around and juddered to a halt.

Angus ran his fingers across his cheek and winced. He grabbed the steering wheel with his blood-stained hand, reversed into the middle of the lane, and sped off towards Oxley Park.

The car bumped over a level crossing. Angus hit the brakes. He got out and walked back to the railway. He stared down the line, into the black distance, and listened to the silence.

The kewick of a tawny owl pierced the darkness. For a moment Angus didn't feel alone.

He walked along the line and lay down, exhausted, between the tracks. Peace.

Angus was woken by something touching his cheek. He opened his eyes to find the snout of a red fox sniffing at his face. The fox darted away. Angus struggled to his feet. Every muscle in his body ached. He dragged himself back to the car and drove off in the direction of the park.

As he was halfway up the locked main gate Angus detected movement at the corner of his vision. He turned his head to find a pleather-clad figure approaching. She wore the tightest of mini-skirts and was gliding along on shiny red stilettos, her slim hips swaying. She stopped at the gate and gazed up at Angus.

"Ah wouldn't risk it if ah wur you," she warned, pointing at the spikes along the top of the gate. "There's a gap int' 'edge round t'other side o' the park. That's the best way ta get in at night."

Angus climbed down.

She took a stick of gum from her red plastic handbag and popped it into her mouth. "Cum on, ah'll show you."

Angus let her take his hand.

"What 'appened ta your face?" she asked as they circled the park perimeter.

"Broken glass," he replied. "It's nothing."

"What's wi' the rope? Plannin' ta 'ang yourself, are you?" She chuckled for a second then stopped. "Jesus, you are goin' ta 'ang yourself!"

"Not while you're here."

"Ah can't stay wi' you arl night, ah'm workin'."

"Stay with me for a bit."

They reached a tiny gap in the hedge. The girl squeezed through without difficulty. Angus grimaced as a blackthorn twig scratched across his cheek. She pulled him through.

"Ah've 'eard they swim naked int' lake 'ere. Fancy a swim?"

"No thanks."

"Cum on! Or you can watch me if you like."

"Let's just sit."

"Arl right, suit yourself," she shrugged, chewing her gum open-mouthed. "What's your name?"

"Angus."

"Ah'm Kylie. Pleased ta meet you."

They sat together on the grass.

She tapped at the rope. "So, things 've bin bad, 'ave they?"

"You could say that."

"If you're goin' ta top yourself, you won't mind givin' me your money, will you?"

"I've come out with nothing." He pulled out his car keys. "Just these, and the rope."

She took Angus's keys and put them in her handbag. "You'll be needin' the rope, won't you?" She smiled the most delightful smile Angus had ever seen.

"That can wait," he replied, lifting the rope from his shoulder and tossing it onto the grass. He reached out for her hand.

"Christ," she cried, "you've got rough fingers. Are you a builder or summat?"

"That's from playing guitar."

"You can play guitar? Will you play fur me?"

"I don't have one with me."

"Shame. Never mind, sum other time." She pointed at the rope. "Oops! There won't be anuther time, will there?"

They both smiled.

"Let's lie down 'n watch the stars," she suggested, dropping backwards onto the grass.

Angus followed suit. He was still holding her hand.

The stars twinkled.

"Kylie?" asked Angus. "Why are you…?"

"Ont' game? Ah wish ah 'ad a pound fur every time a fella asked me that."

"I'd like to know."

"It's a long story, 'n you don't 'ave much time."

"Give me the short version."

"Ah grew up in Bradford, in a children's 'ome."

"I'm sorry."

"It wurn't that bad. Sum o' the staff wur nice. When ah wur fourteen ah met Adam. 'E wur twenty-five. 'E 'ad a sports car 'n wur really cool. Ah thought ah loved 'im."

"What happened?"

"Ah used ta boast about 'im ta t'other girls. Two o' 'em started goin' out wi' a couple o' 'is mates. You know the rest. Wi'd get taken ta parties. Men's parties."

"Oh."

"Int' end ah ran away. First ta Carlisle, then 'ere."

"You're working your way north?"

"Not any more. Ah like Inverness. Ah'm goin' ta settle down."

"Where do you live?"

"Ah'm stayin' in a motel, a mile from 'ere. Ah won't 'ave ta pay rent. Ah'm friendly wi' the owner. Would you like ta see it?"

"I'm busy," replied Angus, tugging at the end of the rope.

Kylie jumped up. "Tha' can wait." She held out her hand. "Cum on."

As they reached the car, Kylie yelped, "You didn't tell me you 'ad a sports car!" She took the keys from her bag. "Ah'll drive."

Angus didn't bother to do up his seat belt.

"It's not much, ah suppose," she said as they entered her motel room. "Ah've got me own shower though." She drew the curtains, and started to undress.

"I told you," said Angus, "I've got no money."

"Cum on, don't be daft," she replied, slipping off her bra and panties. "Look at the state o' you. You need a wash."

Angus stood silently as she undressed him. She led him to the shower and started the water running.

"Perfect," she advised, holding her hand in the flow. "In wi get."

Angus followed Kylie into the shower like a lamb. She washed his hair, then his face, his arms, his body, his genitals.

"Crikey, there's no life down 'ere at all," she chuckled. "Hello, is there anybody 'ome?"

After she'd washed Angus she began to soap herself. Angus watched the suds sliding down across her perfect small breasts. He admired her as an art lover might.

She put him to bed. Within seconds he was fast asleep. He dreamt they made love.

The light of the morning woke Angus. Kylie lay naked by his side, sleeping peacefully. He slipped out of bed, pulled on his grubby clothes, and found his car keys. He crept into the shower room and picked up a lipstick. On the mirror he wrote the words 'Thank You' followed by a smiley face.

Angus returned to the bedside, leaned down to kiss Kylie gently on the cheek, and left.

CHAPTER 31

Esther arrived as the undertaker was leaving with Sofia's body. She gave Alice a long hug.

"Do you think Sofia would be offended if we went for coffee?" asked Esther.

"She'd be upset if we didn't," replied Alice. "Shouldn't I be staying here though? What if the police turn up wanting to speak to me?"

"Don't worry about them. You've done nothing wrong, so you're free to come and go as you please. They'll be in touch soon enough."

As they pulled into Teggins Farm it began to shower. Sunlight gleamed through millions of liquid spheres, creating a brilliant arch of light across the heavens.

"Richard of York gave battle in vain," said Esther, indicating the rainbow with a sweep of her hand.

"We had another version at school," replied Alice. "Run off you girls, boys in view!"

They stood side by side admiring the colours until they realised they were getting soaked.

"Cinnamon cake?" asked Esther.

"If you insist," grinned Alice.

They were soon served.

"I've got some news," said Esther, in a tone that made Alice nervous. "Don't worry, it's not as bad as it sounds."

"What is it?"

"Paul Ireland has been arrested. He's in custody."

"What?" cried Alice, prompting several customers to look round. "That man is a hero," she muttered, leaning forward. "How dare they arrest him?"

"It's not surprising if you think about it. His dogs attacked a police officer and made quite a mess of him."

"We've got to do something," insisted Alice in a forced whisper.

Esther motioned Alice to calm down. "They're not going to release him until they've spoken to everyone involved. Bonny Mason's statement will be key."

"Damn!" Alice covered her mouth with one hand, holding the other up around the room. "They'll have a job speaking to Bonny," she murmured, taking a letter from her pocket. "She put this through my door during the night."

Esther read the letter.

> Dear Alice,
>
> I'm so sorry that I lied to you and put you in such danger. Can you ever forgive me? At least now you know what he's really like. You can see why I was too frightened to say anything.
>
> I don't know where Leo is, and I don't care. I've packed a case and as soon as I've written this I'll wake Tom. The circus is in Trowbridge at the moment. My family and friends will look after us.
>
> Please ask the police to leave us alone. You and Paul can explain what happened. I've left a note for Leo telling him to forget about me.
>
> I hope you feel better soon. I'm so sorry.
> Bonny

Esther handed back the letter. "She wanted to tell you everything but was terrified of what he might do."

"The circus flyer was a clue though."

"Indeed. Part of her was desperate for you to discover the truth."

"I suppose she'll have to make a statement," sighed Alice, "whether she wants to or not."

"If they can find her. The circus will do a good job of hiding her."

"She won't be able to resist performing forever. I hope I get to see her in the ring one day."

"That would be something," smiled Esther. "I'll come with you."

They each took a nibble of cake.

"There's something seriously wrong with me," groaned Alice. "I really fancied him!"

"There's nothing wrong with you."

"There is, Esther. I still get in a flap when I think about him, even now that I know he's a monster."

"Don't worry about it," chuckled Esther.

"But he's insane."

"Not insane. Obsessed."

"We're all obsessional to one degree or another. He's bonkers."

"Who's to say where obsession ends and madness starts? But honestly, I don't think he's mad. He's a psychopath. The only way to cope with psychopaths like Leo Mason is to humour them, agree with everything they say, never contradict. These people have nothing you could call a conscience. Who knows what they're capable of if they're crossed, or think they have been. To survive with someone like that, you'd have to appeal constantly to his ego, agree with him at all times, even worship him."

"That's exactly what Bonny had to do all these years," sighed Alice. "It was the only way to survive."

"Well, I for one don't blame her. Men like Mason, given the right circumstances, become Adolf Hitler."

Alice shuddered. "He's not going to plead guilty, is he? He's going to deny everything."

"Probably."

"But there'll be DNA evidence, once they find Bonny and Tom. That will surely prove his guilt beyond doubt."

"I hope so."

They sipped their coffees.

"Esther," said Alice, "I need your advice."

"Makes a change," teased Esther.

"I think I'm in the wrong profession."

"I beg your pardon?"

"I've told you how my interest in psychology started. It was Dad's influence...and Columbo's."

"And thank goodness for that."

"When I was a kid I used to dream of being a private investigator. Recently I've been wondering why that dream can't come true. I think I'd make a better detective than I ever will a psychologist. I'm like the teacher who realises she was born to be a writer. I took a wrong turning somewhere, and it's not too late to put that right."

"That seems fair enough, if you're serious. But don't forget, this is a traumatic time. You may feel differently in a few weeks. Whatever happens, I'll be here if you want to talk."

"Especially as we'll be living together," smiled Alice. "You haven't forgotten, have you?"

"You can move in as soon as you like."

Esther drove Alice home. "Do you want me to come in with you?" she asked, as they pulled up outside the house.

"I don't think so. The sooner I get used to being home alone the better. Don't worry about poor little orphan Alice, she'll be okay."

Alice couldn't remember the last time she'd been in the house on her own. A shiver passed through her body as she slid the key into the front door lock. She paused for a few moments, turned the key and entered the hall.

The door at the end of the hall was slightly ajar. A thin shaft of light fell across one corner of the carpet. I must've left the kitchen light on, thought Alice.

She imagined Mum's voice. 'We do not have money to burn, Aliki!'

Alice closed the front door and limped towards the light. She held out a hand ready to push against the kitchen door. The instant she touched it she was halted in her tracks by a noise. The unmistakable noise of a cork popping. Alice froze, fingers against the door, heart thumping.

"It's a little early in the day," mused Leo Mason, "but any time is the perfect time to drink champagne."

Into Alice's mind jumped a picture of two deep brown eyes and a crucifix scar. A tingling sensation started in her stomach, passed through her chest, and settled in her throat. She gulped.

Alice took a deep breath, pushed against the kitchen door, and entered the room.

"What a mess!" she blurted as Leo's face came into view. His forehead was wrapped in a bandage, an area of which was soaked through with blood.

"As blunt as ever. It's a mess, but wait until I've had plastic surgery. For the right price I'll have my scar back, just how you liked it." He gazed deep into Alice's eyes.

"How come you're not in hospital?"

"They advised me to wait for a surgeon to look at it, but I told them I had something more important to attend to."

"Oh, and what's that?"

"A proposal." Leo picked up a champagne glass, his eyes refusing to leave hers for an instant. He started to pour.

"Sounds interesting," breathed Alice. "But I thought you might have some more pressing business to deal with."

"That's all in hand. I've spoken to a couple of my close colleagues." Leo placed the full glass on the table and picked up the empty one, his gaze unwavering. "They've arrested Ireland."

Alice was beginning to feel mesmerised as Leo's eyes burned deeper into hers.

"As I said," he continued, "everything's in hand. That loser will go down for a very long time." He filled the second glass and handed it to Alice. "All that's left is for us to...harmonise our accounts of what he did to you."

"Yes, I see," smiled Alice, holding up her glass.

They chinked glasses and drank their bubbly.

"There are one or two difficulties to be ironed out," she nodded.

"Minor difficulties. Nothing we can't get around."

"We'll need to stick close...very close. Which reminds me, I'll need my phone so we can keep in touch."

Leo beamed with delight. He took Alice's mobile from his pocket. "Some interesting photos."

"What? How did you-"

"Four zeros is not a particularly tough code to crack."

"Right."

"I've changed it to four two four two." He handed the phone to Alice.

"Four two four two," winked Alice, tapping in the numbers. "Yes, it's working fine." She put the mobile down on the kitchen table and drank more champagne. "My glass is empty."

"There's a second bottle," said Leo, topping up both glasses. "It's in the fridge."

"So, what about these minor difficulties?" asked Alice. "First of all, how are we going to explain what happened yesterday, and why you were there?"

"Simple. Ireland tricks you into meeting him in a secluded place. I happen to be in the area and spot you. He sends his dogs after me, but against all the odds Leo saves the day."

"What if the dogs talk?" grinned Alice.

"They won't be saying much once the vet's given them each a little injection."

"What about Bonny? We'll need an explanation for why she was there."

"There's no evidence that she was there. Ireland will say so, but he won't be taken seriously. When they ask Bonny, she'll say nothing at all. She knows better than to contradict me."

"How can you be so sure?"

"She knows what's good for her," growled Leo, "and she'll keep quiet to protect Tom."

"Perfect. One more thing. Ireland is bound to say that you're Tom's natural father. The court may insist on DNA evidence."

"If it comes to that," he shrugged, "I'll admit I was a bad boy and had sex with Bonny after taking her case. She was crazy about me. I should've resisted, but I'm a man after all."

"Brilliant."

"I get no more than a slap on the wrist, while Ireland gets to make lots of new friends. Everybody's happy."

"Ecstatic!" cried Alice.

"You haven't said anything to your friend, I hope."

"Esther? Of course not. Anyway, you don't have to worry about her. She'll do anything I ask. The stupid cow worships me."

"I knew it," chuckled Leo. "We're very much alike, you and I." He raised his glass. "To us."

They chinked glasses and drank.

"Oh, dear," giggled Alice. "This champagne's making me giddy." She gazed into his eyes. "I'm tingling all over. I think I may need to...lie down."

"I'll bring the champagne."

"One bottle won't be enough," cooed Alice. "We may be up there for some time." She handed Leo her glass, opened the fridge door, and wrapped her uninjured hand around the neck of the second bottle. "Follow me."

"Anywhere."

Alice walked slowly to the foot of the staircase, then even more slowly up the stairs, swaying her bottom from side to side in front of Leo's face.

"Lovely view," he breathed.

"Glad you like it," replied Alice. When she reached the top of the stairs she took one step onto the landing, swivelled around on her good foot, and swung the bottle in an upward arc through the air.

"Aaaagh!" screamed Leo Mason as the bottle thumped into the bloodstained area of his bandage. He somersaulted backwards, his head jerking violently as it thudded down onto the staircase. He landed in a heap at the bottom.

"Gotcha!"

Alice hobbled down the stairs and over the unconscious Mason. She returned to the kitchen, picked up her mobile, and stopped the video recording. "Try and explain this, you bastard!"

PART TWO

CHAPTER 32

"Thank you all so much," said Alice into the microphone, "for being here today to celebrate the life of Sofia Maria Alexander...Mum." Alice smiled as she wiped away a tear with her fingertips. "We will remember her always. For her beauty, for her wisdom, for her sense of humour...but most of all, for her meatballs!"

Everyone laughed.

"I expect we've all got our favourite Greek proverb," Alice continued. "Yours might be, 'Wonder is the beginning of wisdom'. Or maybe, 'It is not what you profess but what you practise that makes you good'. The Greeks may be a bunch of rascals, but they certainly know one or two things about life. My personal favourite is, 'I don't need a friend who changes when I change, and nods when I nod, my shadow does that much better'."

Another ripple of laughter.

"Mum's favourite Greek proverb was, 'The young wish to be old, and the old wish to be young again'. But, as the Greeks also say, 'The heart that loves is always young'."

A round of applause.

"Which explains why Mum never grew old. She was the most loving person I've ever known, or ever will know. Which makes me all the more sad that I've always been such a disappointment to her." Alice surveyed the frowns and shaking heads before her. "I'm afraid it's true. I can't cook, I can't sew, I'm allergic to housework. You see, I was always a bit of a tomboy. Not a proper Greek girl at all."

"You're perfect!" called a Greek female voice.

"She had hoped I'd redeem myself by marrying a Greek stallion and producing a houseful of babies."

"You have plenty of time," from the same voice.

"Thank you, Auntie Coula."

"You're welcome, Alice my darling."

"Of course you're right, I do have plenty of time. I will experience many things, hopefully some wonderful things. But my beautiful mother will not be here to share them with me." Alice wiped away another tear and beamed. "But don't worry, she'll be here in my heart, and in my mind, always ready to give advice." Alice mimicked Sofia's voice. "You can't go out dressed like that, Aliki, what if you meet a nice rich boy?"

A roar of laughter.

"Thanks for everything, Mum. I love you."

The mourners enjoyed a meal of bread, fish, olives and retsina. After the food came Greek coffee. As Alice took a sip she realised how much she was going to miss watching Mum making coffee using her special briki pot.

"Alice," said a voice behind her.

Alice turned with a grin. "Auntie Coula." They kissed each other on both cheeks. "It's wonderful to see you."

"There is someone here I think you should meet," said Coula, pointing indiscreetly at a tall, dark, bearded figure on the other side of the room. "His name is Anthony. Adonis in Greek," she winked.

Alice glanced across at the god, then leaned towards Coula with eyebrows raised. "Auntie Coula, I don't think this is the most appropriate time to-"

"His family is rich."

"And I bet we're related."

"Perhaps he is a distant cousin," shrugged Coula, "but that doesn't count, does it?"

Alice shook her head and gave Coula a big hug.

"Well, darling, you can't blame me for trying."

By early evening everyone had gone and it was time for Esther to drive Alice home.

"You can sleep at mine tonight if you like," said Esther as they pulled up outside Alice's house.

"Thanks for the offer, but I need to be alone tonight. Are you coming in for a minute?"

"Not for coffee if you don't mind. After three Greek coffees I won't sleep for a week."

"A weak tea then? I can make two cups with one bag."

"A glass of water for me, thanks."

They sat at the kitchen table with two glasses of water and a box of Maltesers.

"I've got some news," said Esther. "They've released Paul Ireland."

Alice choked on a Malteser. "Thank goodness! I must speak to him, to say thank you. And to apologise for being such a fool."

"Join the queue."

"No news about Harry, I suppose."

"Not yet. The wheels of justice turn slowly. He should be out in a matter of weeks. The good news is that he's been moved to a single cell and is finally getting some protection."

As soon as Esther had left, Alice went to bed exhausted. She slept far better than she'd expected, undisturbed by nightmares. She was however concerned as she heard Mum being informed that there was no record of a Richard Alexander in Heaven. She knew it had to be an administrative error, and was delighted when Mum found him watching the highlights of his beloved Macclesfield Town beating Manchester United 6-0 in the FA Cup final.

In the morning Alice was woken by a knock at the door. She threw on one of Jamie's old shirts and hobbled downstairs. There, on the doorstep, was the last person she'd expected to see.

"Bonny!" she screamed. "What...how…?"

"Hello, Alice," murmured Bonny. "I need your help."

Alice glanced past Bonny at the car parked in front of the house. In the driver's seat was a man she didn't recognise. In the back sat young Tom.

"When we left home I was in such a hurry," explained Bonny, "that I lost my house key. We can't get in."

Alice threw her arms around Bonny. "Come in, all of you. Who's the driver?"

"That's Charlie, my brother. He brought us back. He's going to stay for a while."

"It's good to meet you," said Charlie as they were introduced.

Alice admired his chiselled jaw and luxurious locks.

"I've heard so much about you," he continued. "Thanks for everything you've done for Bonny. I don't know how I can ever repay you."

Maybe I'll come up with something, thought Alice.

Once Tom had finished a bowl of Coco Pops, Bonny asked Charlie to take him through to the lounge to see what was on television.

"How's Tom coping?" asked Alice as soon as she was alone with Bonny.

"He isn't. When I told him we were going to the circus he was excited. The first couple of days were fine, but then I made the mistake of telling him that his dad was in trouble because he'd done something wrong. From that moment Tom crazed me to come home. All he could think about was seeing Leo. He's been a good father...in many ways."

"Poor little man."

"And he's missing his friends."

"Of course."

"Alice, would you talk to Tom for me? I don't mean now, but..."

"He'll need a great deal of psychological support. You both will. I'm here for you, Bonny, you can count on that."

Bonny put an arm around Alice's neck and kissed her cheek.

"You didn't mention you had a brother," rebuked Alice.

"I've got three. Charlie's the oldest."

"He looks about...forty?"

"You're good."

"He's got powerful arms. Is he an acrobat?"

"Charlie's a juggler. He can keep anything up in the air, including chainsaws."

"Wow!" Alice paused. "Won't he be missing his family while he's here with you?"

"Charlie's single."

"You're joking. He's so..." Alice blushed, covering her mouth. "You won't tell him I said anything?"

"You can tell him yourself. He'll be around for a few weeks. Tom needs a father-figure now that…" Bonny squeezed her hands together. "How's Paul getting on? Is he alright?"

"He's been released, that's all I know."

"I must talk to him. Will you come with me?"

"Whenever you're ready."

The following morning Alice went with Bonny to Paul Ireland's house. There was no sign of life as they approached the front door. Alice knocked. Silence. She knocked again.

"He must be out," she said, "otherwise we'd hear the dogs barking."

The door inched open. There, resembling a vagrant, and reeking of cigarettes, was the weary figure of Paul Ireland. His jaw dropped and his eyes widened as if he was seeing a ghost.

"Bonny," he said in a choked voice. He stared at her, seemingly unaware of Alice's presence.

"Hello, Paul," murmured Bonny. "Can we come in?"

"I'd rather you didn't. This dump isn't fit for visitors."

"Is there somewhere we can talk?" she asked.

He gave a tired shrug.

"There's a cafe around the corner," suggested Alice.

The girls sat quietly as Paul ate buttered toast. "Thought you wanted to talk," he said at last.

"We want to thank you," said Bonny.

"And to apologise," added Alice, "for misjudging you."

"You," replied Paul, "and most of my so-called friends and colleagues."

"What are you going to do?" asked Bonny.

"I can't plan ahead until I know the dogs are safe."

Alarm swept across Bonny's face. "What d'you mean?"

"They attacked a police officer, put him in hospital. How would you rate their chances?"

"That's not fair! If it wasn't for them…"

Alice's body jerked upright. "We'll go to the newspapers. We can organise a petition. They'll have to listen, won't they?"

A wave of hope lifted Paul. "It would mean so much." His body sank. "It's no good, it'll never work."

Alice stood up. "I'll be outside, making some calls." She left Bonny and Paul together.

CHAPTER 33

"What the fuck am I doing here?" muttered Angus under his breath.

The barmaid came over. "Did you say something?"

"Another beer."

"Are you sure? Isn't that your two-seater in the car park?"

"Like to come for a ride?" offered Angus.

"No thanks," she replied, holding out her hand to indicate her engagement ring. "I'll get you that beer."

Angus knew perfectly well what he was doing in the White Horse.

Kylie had saved his life, brought him back from the edge. He was just as tired, just as despondent, just as hopeless as before. Death was still the only way out. But he couldn't bring himself to let Kylie down.

It was easier, thought Angus, when I'd made up my mind. For a short time I knew exactly where I was going. Now, thanks to Kylie, I'm back where I started. Nowhere.

Angus was surviving, nothing more. His broken Fender lay on his bedroom floor where he'd tossed it. His acoustic sat on its stand gathering dust. Every day was like every other. Pointless.

This day was different. It was Jess's birthday. Angus had considered writing a birthday message on Facebook. He'd changed his mind, but not before noticing a comment written there by Jess. She was looking forward to her birthday dinner at the White Horse.

So here was Angus, on a bar stool, finishing his third pint of Guinness in fifteen minutes, waiting for Jess to turn up.

He had no idea what he was doing.

The barmaid brought his next pint and took away the empty glass. Angus took a swig.

A foursome approached the bar. Angus heard Jess's voice and jerked his face away. He listened as they ordered their meals. He knew Jess would ask for a Caesar salad.

The group returned to their table. Angus gulped his beer, his mind blank.

"Everything alright?" asked the barmaid.

Angus nodded. He paid for his drinks and was ready to leave.

"What are you doing here, Angus?"

He turned to peer into Jess's eyes. "I'm celebrating your birthday."

Her eyes widened. "Oh my God, you knew we were coming here, didn't you?"

"Don't be daft," mumbled Angus, "how could I possibly-"

"You can't do this, Angus. It's not fair. It's not right!"

"What's the matter, darling?"

Jess turned to the approaching Colin and forced a smile. "Colin...this is Angus."

"I was just leaving," slurred Angus, making for the door. His legs failed to carry him in a straight line and he thumped his shoulder into Colin's chest before spinning down to the floor.

"I don't think so," insisted Colin.

Angus climbed to his feet and headed for the exit. He managed to reach his Crossfire before Colin caught up with him.

"You're not going anywhere!" shouted Colin.

Angus turned and flew at Colin with his head down and both palms forward. The moment Colin hit the ground Angus jumped to his car and swung the door open.

"No you don't!" yelled Colin, grabbing Angus's wrist and wrenching it behind his back.

"Aaaargh!" screamed Angus.

Colin yanked the keys from Angus's grasp, released his hold and took a step back.

Angus dropped to his knees and threw up on the driver's seat.

"Why are you doing this?" cried the approaching Jess.

Angus tried to focus on her face. "I'm sorry," he whined. "I'm so sorry."

"Why can't you just leave me alone?"

Angus wiped his sleeve across his mouth, dragged himself to his feet and scrambled away into darkness.

CHAPTER 34

"This is the best view in the world!"

Having paused for breath on a grassy slope near the summit of Blencathra, Alice was gazing westward through the haze towards Derwent Water and the peaks of the north-western Lakeland fells. She closed her eyes and turned her face to the sky, inviting the late summer breeze to caress her skin.

"I'm hungry," said Harry. "Will this spot do for our picnic?"

"Perfect," replied Alice, taking off her back-pack. "We can sit on that boulder."

They tucked into egg sandwiches and cheese crackers, followed by flapjacks and a flask of coffee.

"I've been waiting for an opportunity," said Harry, "to thank you properly for saving my life." He took a small gift box from his pocket and gave it to Alice.

"Are you proposing?" chuckled Alice.

"Open it and see," teased Harry.

Inside the box was a miniature leather satchel. Alice undid the buckle and pulled out a circular brass tin. She twisted off the lid.

"Oh my goodness," she cried, "a compass. It's beautiful!"

Alice threw an arm around Harry's neck and squeezed tight until he began to choke. She let go and examined the compass.

"Turn the lid over," he suggested.

Alice flipped the lid to find a poem etched in miniscule letters on the inside. It was The Road Not Taken, by Robert Frost.

"Do you know it?" asked Harry.

"No," she replied.

Harry read the poem to Alice.

"Two roads diverged in a yellow wood,
And sorry I could not travel both
And be one traveller, long I stood
And looked down one as far as I could
To where it bent in the undergrowth;

Then took the other, as just as fair,
And having perhaps the better claim,
Because it was grassy and wanted wear;
Though as for that the passing there
Had worn them really about the same,

And both that morning equally lay
In leaves no step had trodden black.
Oh, I kept the first for another day!
Yet knowing how way leads on to way,
I doubted if I should ever come back.

I shall be telling this with a sigh
Somewhere ages and ages hence:
Two roads diverged in a wood, and I-
I took the one less travelled by,
And that has made all the difference."

"I...I don't know what to say," stuttered Alice.

"You don't have to say anything, sweetie."

They hugged.

"You know, Harry, I'm the one who should be thanking you. If it wasn't for you, I don't think I'd be here now."

"I don't understand."

"That evening, before you called to me from the rooftop, I was ready to give up. Losing Jamie and Dad nearly destroyed me, and I knew Mum would soon be leaving me too. I had nothing left to live for. Then you came into my life. When you called out to me, it was as if Jamie was calling, as if he was begging me to help you, so that somehow his death wouldn't be in vain. Does that make sense?"

"Thank you, Alice. It's a consolation to know that something positive has come out of my prison hell. If I needed to be there on that roof to help you, then I'm glad I was there. I'll never forget the pain, and nothing will bring Grant back, but it helps to know there's a silver lining. And you're the best silver lining I could ever wish for."

They sat for a while, arm in arm, enjoying the majestic view and listening to the croaking of a pair of soaring ravens.

"So," said Harry, pouring the last of the coffee, "does this mean we're friends?"

"For life," grinned Alice.

Harry held out his mug. "Here's to a long life."

Their mugs met.

After finishing their picnic they resumed their walk to the top of Blencathra.

They each threw a rock onto the summit cairn before taking the stony downhill path to Scales Tarn.

"Are you alright?" asked Alice as they approached the tarn. "You haven't said anything for at least five minutes. That must be a record."

"Why do you think he did it?" asked Harry. "He must have known I was no threat to his marriage. Bonny and I were just pen friends after all."

"It's hard for people like us to get inside the mind of a Leo Mason. He was obsessed with Bonny. He owned her, treasured her like a priceless work of art. Every man was a threat in his eyes, gay or straight, young or old. That's why he wouldn't let her go anywhere on her own. Any man showing the slightest interest in his prized possession risked paying a high price."

"I can vouch for that," sighed Harry.

"He had complete control over every facet of Bonny's existence. He kidnapped her for ten years."

"But he wasn't prepared for a reckoning with Alice Alexander!" cheered Harry.

"I didn't do anything," insisted Alice. "Well, not on my own. It was teamwork that got the better of Leo Mason."

"That reminds me," said Harry. "I've had a postcard from Bonny. She's on holiday with Tom and Paul."

"Where are they?"

"On the Kennet and Avon canal near Bath. Tom wears the captain's hat, Paul is his first mate, and Bonny's in charge of the cabin."

"Sounds delightful," mused Alice. For the boys, she thought.

"Hopefully they can look forward to many delightful times together."

"Fingers crossed. What about you, Harry? Any plans for the future?"

"My agent's negotiating with the TV company. They're desperate to get me back, after all the publicity. And I've started writing my autobiography. How about you?"

"I expect everyone will try to talk me out of it, but I've decided to quit my job. I need a new start, a new direction. Watch this space."

"The important thing is to move forward, Alice, not concentrate on the past."

"The past is going to trouble me for some time yet." Alice stopped walking and turned to Harry. "Can I share a secret with you?"

"Are you kidding? I love secrets!"

"I've got a half-brother, one I've never met."

Alice got out the photograph of Dad holding the baby and showed it to Harry. She told him about her conversations with Mum.

"What a story," gasped Harry.

"There's more. After Mum died I had to contact everyone she knew, and all the banks and businesses she'd had dealings with. Her papers were everywhere. Some of her stuff was in the loft, and while I was up there I found a tin with a picture on the lid, of a piper playing on the bank of a beautiful loch."

"A Royal Scotch shortbread tin!" cried Harry.

"How did you know that?" asked Alice. "Oh, stupid question."

"Aam a wee Caledonian, dornt ye ken. So what was in the tin? Presumably not biscuits."

"Letters mainly, plus a few documents. I checked through them and realised there was no reference to Mum anywhere. It was Dad's old stuff, from before they met."

"How fascinating."

"Right at the bottom, under the papers, was a plastic photo album."

Alice got out some more photographs and handed one to Harry. It showed two tiny figures. One was a baby, rattle in hand, beaming from ear to ear. The other was identical in size, but not smiling at all. It was a pale blue teddy bear.

"Turn it over," urged Alice.

Harry read the writing on the back. "Angus and Tedder. I'm guessing Tedder is the bear," he grinned.

"My brother's called Angus. It isn't much to go on, but…"

"Will you try to find him?"

"I don't know, Harry. I'm not sure what to do."

"What's your heart telling you?"

"I think I want to meet him. But the chances of tracing him must be so slim. I don't know if I could cope with the disappointment."

"Angus is a common name in Scotland. If only you had a surname." Harry's face lit up. "What about Angus Alexander?"

"I thought of that. I tried Google, Facebook and all the other social network sites. Nothing."

"I see."

"What d'you reckon, Harry?"

"Well, the population of Scotland is only five million or so, assuming he's still there, but you're still looking for a needle in a haystack. Have you thought of asking a private investigator to trace him?"

"I wouldn't know where to start, or who I could trust."

"Why don't you ask Paul? I'm sure he could point you in the right direction."

"Thanks, Harry, I will."

Harry browsed through the photos. "These are so sweet. Can I keep one?"

CHAPTER 35

Alice sat by the riverbank on a rusting wrought-iron bench. She listened to the rustling of thousands of leaves, many of which, displaying hues of ochre and brown in sympathy with the bench, were gently floating to the ground around her. She snatched at one or two without luck.

The river was clear enough for Alice to follow the trout gliding effortlessly past, until the sun escaped from behind the clouds to transform the surface into a glittering sheet.

For twenty minutes Alice had enjoyed watching the ducks parading up and down. Suddenly they scattered in all directions as a pair of German Shepherds came bounding into the water in the hope of catching one. Following behind, but remaining on the riverside path, were two Collies, their noses elevated with an air of dignity suggesting that they wouldn't dream of following the two thugs into the river.

"Come out of there!" called Paul.

The German Shepherds leapt onto the bank and proceeded to shake themselves, showering Alice with spray after spray.

"Thanks a bunch," cried Alice, turning herself away in the vain hope of keeping at least her face dry.

"Paul," shouted Bonny, "can't you control them?"

"She's not made of candy floss," laughed Paul.

"Just as well," replied Bonny.

"I'd prefer not to smell of wet dog for the rest of day," groaned Alice.

"Sit still!" ordered Paul.

Alice froze, statue-like.

"I don't think that was meant for you, Alice," chuckled Bonny. She held out her arms ready for a damp hug.

The three of them sat for a while chatting, Alice in the centre, the dogs either side of the bench, gnawing at their dog chews.

"They're so obedient," said Alice.

"A lifetime of training," explained Bonny. "I've had my two since they were pups."

"Same here," added Paul.

"That reminds me, Paul," said Alice, "of something I've been meaning to ask you. How on earth did you persuade the police to let you have your dogs back when you were first released from prison?"

"I didn't. They were discharged from the force and taken in by an elderly couple. After my release I tracked them down. The old couple couldn't really manage them and were relieved to see me. The police knew nothing about it."

"Tut-tut," joked Alice, "you really are quite the villain."

"A reformed villain," replied Paul, taking an e-cigarette from his pocket and waving it in the air.

"Well done." Alice put an arm around each of her companions. "You've put on weight, Bonny. You look incredible."

"Thank you."

"And your hands have almost healed." Alice noticed, on Bonny's wrist, a hinged silver bracelet with engraved floral panels. She stroked it. "That's gorgeous."

"It's Victorian," said Bonny. "It belonged to my Gran. I lost it ten years ago when... you remember."

Alice covered her mouth.

"It's okay," smiled Bonny. "I was intending to show it to you. I knew you'd like it."

"How on earth did you get it back? You're not going to tell me it was in the house all along?"

"No," said Bonny. "Paul gave it to me on my birthday last week."

"Sorry, I'm confused. You mean it's not the original one?"

Bonny leaned forward to look past Alice at Paul. "This wonderful man went and bought himself a metal detector, would you believe."

"I went three times," explained Paul. "Spent hours and hours. I found it in a patch of brambles."

"Wow!" responded Alice. "Still there after ten years."

"I'm thinking of becoming a detectorist. Tom's keen to come out with me."

"Sounds like fun," lied Alice. "How is Tom?"

"He's getting there," said Bonny. "Talking to you helped a lot. He's being teased by some of the kids at school, so Paul's teaching him self-defence, just in case."

"I suppose what happened is common knowledge?"

"Even more so now," said Paul, "because a lot of Leo Mason's old convictions have been thrown into doubt. I suspect there'll be dozens of reopened cases, which will mean more publicity."

"If it gets bad," sighed Bonny, "Tom and I will have to move away."

Paul closed his eyes.

"Let's hope it doesn't come to that," said Alice. She changed the subject. "Paul, can I ask your advice about something?"

"Of course, fire away."

Alice told Paul and Bonny about the photographs of Dad, Angus and Tedder. "I'll need some help if I'm going to find my half-brother."

"I know an investigator who'd fit the bill perfectly," said Paul. "Sammy Rice. We go back years. Sammy's one of the few people who stood by me, believed I was innocent. This sort of thing's right up Sammy's street. I'll have a word with him if you like?"

"Would you?"

Later that day Alice received a text from Paul. She had an appointment with Sammy Rice at his office in Carlisle at 10am the following day.

The lift to Sammy's office was out of order. Paul led Alice up the narrow staircase. What little air there was tasted musty. The walls were cracked and discoloured by patches of damp. Alice started to wonder if the expedition would prove a waste of time.

They arrived at the top floor. Paul tapped his knuckles against Sammy's name on the office door. No reply. He turned the handle and pushed the door slowly open. Alice glanced past him at an empty desk on which sat an ageing computer, an anglepoise lamp and a 1970s mustard-yellow telephone. She followed Paul into the dimly lit room, the single window obscured by a closed plastic venetian blind. She scanned the room, taking in a row of pinboards covered in photos and handwritten notes, before focusing on a second desk, identical to the first, but even more bare. On it sat a half-empty whisky tumbler next to a completely empty bottle of Tullamore Dew. Behind these was the slumped figure of a balding fat man, snoring. Alice screwed up her face as she breathed in the stench of body odour and vomit.

"I see business hasn't picked up," said Paul.

Sammy moaned but didn't move.

"Where's Suzie?" asked Paul.

"Gone," croaked Sammy. "Got a better offer."

Paul helped him to sit up.

"Aaargh!" cried Sammy, clutching his abdomen.

"What's up," asked Paul, "too much whisky?"

"Not enough," groaned Sammy. "Been throwing up blood again." He downed the remaining whisky in one gulp.

Paul asked Alice to go to a nearby shop for milk. By the time she returned, the blind was drawn and the window wide open. She poured some of the milk into the empty whisky glass and put it into Sammy's hand. He took a mouthful and instantly screamed out with another bout of stomach pain.

"We should ring 999," advised Alice. She walked over to the mustard-yellow phone and lifted the receiver. The line was dead. She made the call on her mobile.

"Is there anything I can do?" asked Paul while they waited for the ambulance.

"Don't bother about me," muttered Sammy, "I'm finished."

After the ambulance had taken Sammy to hospital, Alice and Paul stayed behind to clean the place up.

"He isn't always like this," said Paul. "He's usually razor sharp, memory like an elephant, and he can read people better than anyone I know. You can't con Sammy, he has his own built-in lie detector."

"How did he end up like this?" asked Alice, running her finger along the blind and examining the sticky dust between her thumb and fingertips.

"Sammy's too soft. He's a master at tracking down lost friends and family, but he charges next to nothing. He's running a registered bloody charity."

"Is there no one to look after him?"

"No family that I know of. Just a long line of ex-wives and girlfriends. Believe it or not, he's never had any trouble attracting the ladies. Suzie was his latest secretary. I thought he'd struck gold this time, but it seems like he's blown it."

"Poor man," sighed Alice. "If only we could do something."

Paul locked the office door, and the pair made their way down the stairs. Near the bottom they found themselves face-to-face with a young woman.

"Can we help you?" asked Paul.

"I've come to see Sammy Rice," she replied.

"He's not available. He's been taken ill."

She was horror-struck. "Oh my God, was that Sammy in the ambulance?"

"I'm afraid so."

"What am I going to do?" Her eyes welled up.

"We're...colleagues of Sammy," said Alice. "Maybe we can help."

Paul gave Alice a wide-eyed stare.

"It's my brother!" cried the young woman, bursting into tears.

"Let's go up to the office," said Alice, taking her arm.

Paul squeezed past the pair to unlock the door, and sat down at Sammy's desk. He pulled open a couple of drawers looking for a notepad. He found a tatty one, together with a blunt pencil, and handed them across the desk to Alice. "Take notes please, Miss Alexander."

Alice glared at him through half-closed eyes. "Yes...sir!"

"What's your name?" asked Paul.

"Zoe," replied the young woman. "Zoe Guest."

"Tell us about your brother, Zoe."

"I've already told Sammy all about him."

"It won't hurt to go through it again," reassured Alice.

"His name is Robbie...Robbie Johnson. We have the same mother. Different fathers."

Alice leaned forward.

"He's a good boy really. He's full of energy, so you can't blame him for getting into a few scrapes. He's never been in any serious trouble though. Not like his dad."

It was Paul's turn to lean forward. "His dad's name wouldn't happen to be Jimmy Johnson?"

Zoe shuddered at the name. "I suppose you must've come across him, in your line of work."

"Oh yes," growled Paul. "I've come across him alright, too often for my own good. Before he was convicted, and since." Paul rose from his chair. "I'm sorry, Miss Guest. We can't help you."

"Please, I beg you."

Alice glowered at Paul with a look powerful enough to force him back onto his chair.

Zoe glanced at Alice, then back at Paul. "Please," she whispered.

"Okay," sighed Paul, "tell us everything you know."

"My dad and Jimmy Johnson were business partners. After Dad's accident, Jimmy started coming round our house a lot. Dad never came home from hospital. I don't remember much, I was only five. I do know that Jimmy paid for the funeral. Mum always reminded me of that when she wanted me to be polite."

"You don't like Jimmy?" asked Paul.

"He's disgusting. When he started touching me I had to get out. I felt bad leaving Robbie, but what else could I do? After I left, Robbie started getting into more trouble. We used to meet secretly and he'd tell me all the things he'd been up to, as if he was proud of them. I tried telling him off but he wouldn't listen. Then a few months ago he got a job and I thought he was settling down. Two weeks later he disappeared."

"What was the job?" asked Alice.

"I'm not sure. Robbie wouldn't tell me. He just said he was working for MI5."

"Probably working for his dad," said Paul, "or one of his dodgy business partners."

"I know what you're thinking," said Zoe, "but you're wrong! Robbie's nothing like his dad." She started to sob. "If only I could talk to him, I know everything would be alright. I'm the only one he'll listen to. I should never have left." Tears ran down her cheeks.

Alice placed the notepad and pencil on the desk and comforted Zoe. She gave Paul her sternest look.

"I'm sorry," said Paul, "but it's not much to go on, is it?"

"Zoe," said Alice, "it sounds as if Robbie's disappearance might be related in some way to this job. Is there nothing else you can tell us?"

"No," replied Zoe. "When I asked him about it, he just grinned and said his codename was Simba, and he was working for his uncle. Then he roared."

"He did what?" asked Paul.

"You know, like a lion." Zoe shaped her fingers into claws and gave a half-hearted roar.

"You're having a laugh!" snapped Paul. "I've had enough of this."

Alice walked Zoe down. "I'm sorry," she said as they reached the street door.

"Please help me," implored Zoe. "You're my last chance."

Alice peered up the staircase. "I'll speak to him. We'll help you find your brother, I promise."

"Thank you," gasped Zoe, giving Alice a hug. "Will it be expensive, only I haven't got any money."

"Forget the cost. We can worry about that after we've found Robbie."

Alice persuaded Paul to have a coffee in the diner across the road. She took a sip of her double macchiato, closing her eyes to intensify the hit. She put her cup down firmly on the table and started her appeal. "That girl needs our help! At least we should try."

"It's a wild goose chase," countered Paul. "He's probably run off to the big city in search of fame and fortune. If he needs help, he knows how to contact his sister, doesn't he?"

"I don't buy that. He loves his sister. He would've been in touch by now, if he could."

"I'm sorry, Alice, but you're not seeing this clearly. Looking for a lost sibling...it's a bit close to home, don't you think?"

"Yes, I know, I've thought of that."

"Let it go."

"I promised Zoe we would help her."

"You did what?"

"I'm sorry, but-"

"You'll just have to unpromise."

"I can't do that," yelped Alice. "The poor girl is trying to find her brother, for God's sake. And I don't break promises. Not ever. I can't let her down. I'd rather we worked as a team, Paul, but I'll understand if-"

"Okay, okay." Paul held up his hands in resignation. "I suppose we'll be doing this for nothing?"

"Probably. But aren't you intrigued, just a little bit?"

"Intrigued isn't the word I would use. Uneasy."

"Why?"

"I always worry when I hear Jimmy Johnson's name."

"You said you've had dealings with him?"

"He's an evil bastard. Drugs, trafficking, you name it. Whenever we thought we'd nailed him, he'd get off on some false alibi or a technicality. He was untouchable. We used to think he had a guardian angel. We got him in the end though. He was shagging some married woman when her husband came home and surprised them. What a mess. The husband's been in a coma ever since."

"I take it you came across him while you were in prison."

"He was on a mission to make my life hell. Let's leave it at that, shall we?"

"Sorry."

"Shit!" Paul looked as if he'd seen a ghost. "Why the hell didn't I think of it before? He had a guardian angel alright. Leo bloody Mason!"

That night Alice slept fitfully. She dreamt that she'd sneaked into the prison and was hiding behind a door, trying to hear a conversation between Jimmy Johnson and Leo Mason. She could hear their voices but couldn't make out what they were saying. She peered between the hinges, trying to lip read. To her surprise the two men fell silent and turned their heads slowly towards her. The door vanished into thin air. Alice held her breath as both men stared straight into her eyes. They started to smile. Both mouths widened more and more, until they reached unnatural freakish proportions. From each mouth came a giggle, getting louder and louder until it developed into insane cackling. The two faces were changing shape. They morphed steadily until, laughing hysterically at Alice, appeared the faces of Banzai the hyena, and Scar, evil uncle of Simba, from The Lion King.

Alice screamed. She sat bolt upright, her heart pounding. As her eyes acclimatised to the semi-darkness of Esther's spare bedroom, the realisation dawned that she'd been dreaming. The Lion King has always been one of my favourite films, she thought, but that was strange, even by my standards.

She remembered the conversation with Zoe in Sammy's office. "Oh my God!" Alice held her head. "I know who Robbie was working for."

She threw on her clothes and was outside Paul's front door in ten minutes.

"Do you know what time it is?" he groaned through the letterbox.

The door opened to reveal a bleary-eyed Paul dressed in nothing more than a pair of boxer shorts. He glanced past Alice into the empty street. "Are you coming in or what?"

Alice put the kettle on while Paul got dressed.

"I hope," he said, "you haven't come round in the middle of the night to nag me about that Zoe girl. I told you, I'm on board. But I don't fancy our chances if I can't get any sleep."

"Sorry, Paul, but I had to talk to you. I know the identity of Robbie Johnson's boss!"

"What?"

"You must have started my subconscious working when you said Leo Mason was Jimmy Johnson's guardian angel. Add to that what Robbie told Zoe about working for his uncle, codename Simba. It's staring us in the face."

"Speak for yourself."

"You have seen The Lion King?"

"No."

"What? Everyone's seen The Lion King."

Paul yawned and rubbed his eyes.

"Never mind. There's a character, a lion, called Simba. He has an uncle, a nasty piece of work, called Scar!"

Paul stopped rubbing. He thumped his fists on the table, sending his coffee flying. "Is there no limit to that scumbag's destructive influence?"

"Let's assume that Robbie was working, in some capacity, for Leo Mason. He disappeared months ago, when Mason was still a free man. Mason might know something that can help us find Robbie. He must've had opportunities to talk to Jimmy Johnson in prison. If he didn't know anything before, he has to know something now. We've got to find out."

"I hope you're not suggesting that I ask him."

"Someone's got to."

"No way! This is madness."

"Okay," said Alice. "I'll talk to him myself."

CHAPTER 36

"I knew you'd come sooner or later," smirked Leo Mason.

Alice did her best to maintain a confident facade. She sat down, eyeing him through the glass panel, trying not to focus on the ugly scarring across his left cheek. She couldn't resist.

"What d'you think?" he asked. "I quite like it myself. I might even keep it as it is."

Alice rubbed her wrist.

"Still painful, is it?"

"It's getting better."

"I always knew you were a tough cookie."

"Leo, I've come to ask for your help."

He threw his head back and cackled, his face almost out of view. The laughter stopped abruptly. His eyes rolled downward to peer across his cheeks at Alice. A grin appeared on the lower half of his face.

Alice shivered.

"You know I'd do anything for you," he simpered, lowering his head.

"Do you mean that?"

"Your wish is my command."

"I'm trying to trace someone. A missing person."

Mason leaned forward. "Someone I know?"

"His name is Robbie Johnson."

He dropped back. "Never heard of him."

"I'm offering you a chance to do something right," snapped Alice, "just for once!"

"Now, now."

She collected herself. "I promised his sister I'd help her find him."

"And you never break a promise, do you?" Mason paused, stroking his jaw with thumb and forefinger. "I might be able to help you. But what's in this for me?"

"The satisfaction of doing the right thing."

"Satisfaction? Hassle more like. Young Robbie's bound to open his mouth. He's as thick as two short planks, and he knows enough to-"

"So he's alive?"

No reply.

"What difference could it possibly make? Your situation can't get any worse."

"I've got my reputation to think of."

Alice brought her hands together. "Please."

Mason studied her hands. "Okay, here's the deal. I help you find the boy, and in return you visit me here, once a week, for the rest of my sentence."

Alice gasped.

"And Bonny," he added. "I want to see Bonny."

"That's impossible."

"Too bad," he shrugged. "Sorry I can't help." He stood up.

"Okay! I'll come once a week. But not Bonny. She couldn't cope with…"

Mason sat down, bringing his hands together under his chin. "I suppose you're right, the poor delicate flower. She only has to come once. I'll help you after I've spoken to Bonny, not before."

"Leo, please."

"That's the deal, take it or leave it."

She shut her eyes and nodded agreement.

"Do you promise?"

Her eyes snapped open.

"Say it! You promise to bring Bonny to see me, and to visit me every week for the duration of my sentence."

"I promise," murmured Alice, "to bring Bonny to see you, and to visit you every week…"

"For the duration of my sentence."

"For the duration of your sentence."

"There, that wasn't so hard, was it? I'll have a word with Jimmy Johnson. He'll know where his lad is. I'll see you here same time next week. Both of you!"

One week later Alice was looking through the same glass panel at an empty chair. She felt sick. Her heart leapt as Mason made his entrance.

He sat down with a sinister grin. "Hello, Alice. I'll speak to Bonny first, you after."

"Bonny's not here," replied Alice, glancing at her lap. She forced herself to make eye contact. "I'm sorry, I meant to ask her, but-"

"What? We had a deal!"

"I know, but I need time to work out how to approach her."

"I've got all the time in the world. I thought you needed my help. You said it was urgent."

"It is." Alice took a deep breath. "Leo, do you trust me?"

"Absolutely," he grinned.

"Then help me find Robbie. His sister is beside herself with worry. I can't ask her to wait any longer. I'll bring Bonny next week."

Alice expected Mason to jump out of his chair. Instead he sat like a statue, in perfect silence, for what seemed an eternity.

"Will you wait for me?" he asked finally.

"What?"

"Will you promise to stay faithful until I'm released?"

Alice was stunned. Her head started to swim.

"Not to be with any other man," he growled.

"What are you talking about?"

"You know exactly what I'm talking about. Promise!"

She knew she had to agree. "I promise to stay faithful to you, and not to be with any other man, until you're released."

"Good girl," he smirked. "You learn fast."

Alice shut her eyes.

"07594 524668."

She grabbed a pen from her bag.

He repeated the number.

As soon as she got back to her car Alice dialled the number, touched the speaker button, and handed her mobile to Zoe. They listened to the dialling tone.

"Hi," said a male voice. "If I know you, leave a message after the beep. If I don't, piss off!"

"It's Robbie!" yelped Zoe. The phone beeped. "Hi, Robbie, it's me."

They heard a click. "Zoe, is that really you?"

Alice left Zoe alone to speak to her brother.

A week later Alice sat once more looking through the glass panel at Leo Mason.

"Lovely to see you again," he breathed. "You look great, as always."

She didn't reply.

"Did you manage to track down young Robbie?"

"Yes. Thank you for that, you've done a very good deed."

"Don't worry, you'll have plenty of chances to repay me. Anyway, we can talk about that later. Right now I want to speak to Bonny."

"Bonny's not here," replied Alice coolly.

A look of surprise swept across Mason's face, followed by a quizzical stare. He threw his head back and howled with laughter. "You cheeky minx. You deserve a good spanking! Something for me to look forward to. Now send Bonny in please."

"Bonny's not here," repeated Alice. "There's no way I'm going to put her through the trauma of seeing you."

"You can't do that. You promised."

Alice shrugged.

"What about your dad? He'll be turning in his grave."

"There's something I forgot to tell you. My dad did teach me never to break a promise..."

"I know that."

"...except in extreme circumstances."

"What?"

Alice continued, now in a Scottish accent, "Follaw yer conscience, mah wee lassie, an' ye willnae ga far wrang."

"No!" he screamed, thumping the glass.

A guard moved forward. Alice held up her hand. The guard hesitated.

"I have to do what's right," she declared.

Mason leapt out of his chair. "You'll pay for this!" he roared. "I'd think very carefully if I were you. I won't be in here forever."

"I can't worry about that," replied Alice.

"Aaargh!" screamed Mason, lunging forward at Alice. His face and hands crashed into the glass. Two more guards appeared and rushed towards him. He lashed out at them but was wrestled to the floor and handcuffed.

Alice left.

CHAPTER 37

Angus downed a mouthful of beer and put the empty bottle down on the It's a Wonderful Life disc.

I don't watch films, he thought. Stix reckons it'll help me understand. Understand what?

Angus picked up his laptop and Googled 'It's a Wonderful Life plot summary'.

'George Bailey is the in-debt manager of the Building and Loan bank in Bedford Falls. It is Christmas Eve, and George, who has long considered himself a failure, faces financial ruin. He is standing on a bridge, high above the river, contemplating suicide. In the skies above, two celestial voices discuss George's dilemma and decide to send down guardian angel Clarence to help George out.

Before meeting George, Clarence is told about the multitude of selfless acts he has performed, such as rescuing his younger brother from drowning, preventing a grieving pharmacist from dispensing poison by mistake to a sick child, foregoing his plans of college and travel to keep the Building and Loan from letting its struggling customers down, and preventing the despotic Mr Potter from taking over the town and reducing its inhabitants to penury.

George has married his childhood sweetheart Mary, who has stuck with him through thick and thin. He does his best to forget how circumstances have conspired to thwart his life's ambitions, forcing him to live out a comparatively tedious life. But even the love of Mary and their four children is insufficient when George, faced with a large shortfall in his books, is likely to go to prison thanks to the vengeful Potter.

Standing on the bridge, George declares that he wishes he had never been born. Guardian angel Clarence jumps into the water himself, knowing that George will save him. Clarence then shows George how different life would have been, had he in fact never been born. After a nightmarish walk through a George Bailey-less Bedford Falls (now a miserable hole called Potterville), where none of his friends or family recognise him, George is made to realise how many lives he has touched, and helped, through his existence. Thanks to Clarence, George awakens to the fact that, despite all its deprivations, he has truly had a wonderful life.'

What on earth was Stix thinking, wondered Angus, suggesting I should watch this tearjerker crap?

Angus did have some sympathy for George. He too had great ambitions which had been thwarted. But that's where the similarity ended. He had no Mary to love him. He was not in the habit of performing selfless acts. He hadn't touched the lives of other people in any meaningful way.

Angus wished that he'd never been born.

He went into the kitchen to get another beer, but instead found himself breaking an entire loaf of bread into crumbs and putting them back into the bag.

Fifteen minutes later Angus was walking through the main gate of Oxley Park. He made a beeline for the oak tree near the duck pond.

The bench was in its place, as always, under the oak. An elderly pair sat there, throwing crumbs to the ducks. Angus waited.

In the nearby play area a father was pushing his giggling daughter on a swing. A young couple lay together on the grass, watching the swifts circling high above.

The elderly pair ran out of crumbs. They helped each other up and shuffled away. Angus walked over and sat down, scaring most of the ducks onto the pond. He ran his hand across the back of the bench until his fingers found three words carved there. He didn't have to read them to know what they said. 'Angus loves Jess'.

He opened his bag of breadcrumbs and tossed a few handfuls onto the ground. Dozens of ducks scrambled towards him to devour the feast. Others were on their way across the water to join the group.

"Hi, guys," said Angus. "How's it going?"

The ducks were too busy squabbling to reply. He observed their antics.

"You know, I really envy you lot. All you've got to worry about is food, sleep and sex. You go swimming every day, and you can fly! What a life. No philosophical dilemmas about the existence of the great duck-god, eh?"

One of the ducks quacked what sounded to Angus like 'Hallelujah'!

"I bet you never feel the need to search for anything more. Just as well really, you'd be on a wild duck chase. It's better to see the world as it really is, don't you think?"

A duck shook its head from side to side.

"I've just read a book called How To Be Happy. There's a chapter about an experience machine. Once you're plugged into this machine you can live a life which feels just like normal life, except everything you experience is created by a computer. In this machine you're guaranteed a happy life. The question is, would you rather live outside the machine and take a chance on being happy, or live in it and be certain?"

None of the ducks expressed an opinion. Angus shook the bag to release the rest of the crumbs.

"I didn't have to think about it. I want to live in the real world, like you guys, achieving things with my own ability and effort. That's why I became a guitarist. And I was determined to be the best guitarist in the world. Then I met Jess. For those of you who weren't around, Jess and I met here, in the park. This is our bench, our tree." Angus gave the trunk a slap, startling the ducks. "We're not together any more. I screwed up."

Having hoovered up the remaining crumbs, the ducks waddled away.

Angus turned to the oak. "She's got someone else now. Still, any fool can fall in love and live happily ever after. It's just me now, me and my music. Only one problem. Another girl! This one's called Stella. She's nicked my drummer. One minute we're on the verge of the big time, the next my life's going down the pan. And that's it, end of story."

Angus turned back towards the pond. Most of the ducks were now swimming around on its surface. "Have any of you seen It's a Wonderful Life?" he asked. "Nor have I. It's about a man who thinks the world would be better off without him."

"Do you think the world would be better off without you?" asked a trembly voice.

Angus turned to find his white-haired old lady standing a few feet away. "I'm certain of it."

"I take it you haven't found another one in a million young lady yet?"

"I haven't been looking."

"That's a shame," she sighed. "But you're not alone. You have friends to look after you?"

Angus shook his head.

"How about family? Do you have brothers or sisters?"

"No."

"What about your parents?"

"I have a mother."

"Then go to her," advised the old lady. "Your existence and hers are intertwined. You must speak to your mother." Without another word she turned and waddled away.

Angus returned to his car and set off for Inverness. He knew he was nearing the end of his journey into darkness, but the old lady's words had sent him on a detour. Seeing his mother had been the last thing in his mind. But the old lady was right. However much he hated his mother, Angus couldn't deny that he was the most important person left in her life. And she was the only person left in his. She had the right to see him once more, before he died. So, whether she was truly wise or not, Angus was following the old lady's advice.

The car knew the way, which was just as well, as Angus paid little attention to anything going on around it. He parked in front of his mother's house.

Angus sat for several minutes, his mind blank. His mobile rang. He pulled it from his pocket and, without checking the screen, touched the receive button.

It was his mother's hysterical voice. "Is that you, Angus? Are you there?"

"You know exactly where I am," he groaned, looking for a gap in her front curtain.

"What did you say?" she whined. "Angus, please come, as soon as you can!"

"I'm already here, as you perfectly well know."

"What do you mean you're here?"

"Don't play your games with me, Mother."

A deafening clunk hit Angus's ear. Moments later her face appeared at the window.

Angus got out of the car. The front door flew open, and his mother ran down the path at him, hands in the air.

"Thank God, thank God!" she cried, throwing her arms around her son's neck. Her knees buckled.

Angus struggled to prevent her from pulling him to the ground. He managed to get a decent hold and dragged her inside.

"How did you know?" she screeched. "I only heard a few minutes ago."

Angus sat her down on a kitchen chair. "Mother, I've had enough of your games."

She buried her face in her hands and began to wail.

Her words started to sink in. "What do you mean, how did I know?"

She continued to howl.

Angus shook her shoulders. "Mother, what's happened?"

"It's your father," she screamed, "he's dead!"

"No!" Holding his breath, Angus sank onto a chair. "Wait a minute. You haven't heard from Callum for twenty years. You couldn't possibly know anything-"

"No, Angus, not Callum. I don't mean Callum!"

Angus groaned with relief.

"It's Father Barrington. Iain has hanged himself!"

She was now hysterical, wailing inconsolably. A full minute passed before Angus could calm her down enough to take in his words.

"You're not making sense. First you say my father's dead, then you say it's Father Barrington."

She gripped his arm. "I wanted to tell you, as soon as you were old enough. But he wouldn't let me. I'm so sorry, Angus!"

"Tell me what? Tell me what, for Christ's sake?!"

"He said he'd prayed for guidance. He said that God had instructed us not to tell you...not ever."

"What are you talking about? Are you...are you saying that Father Barrington is my father?"

She nodded several times, her face twisted with anguish.

Angus jumped up. "You're insane!"

"Lord, forgive me."

"You're a liar," he cried. "I'm leaving."

Before he could move she threw her arms around his waist.

"It's not possible!" screamed Angus.

She sank to the floor, clutching his legs. "It's not my fault," she shrieked. "It's not my fault!"

His ankles were now manacled by her adrenaline-fuelled grip. He didn't struggle. He stared straight ahead, wondering what sort of hell he'd now entered. Worse than the previous hell.

Angus needed to get away. But more than that, he needed to know the truth. He lifted his mother back into her chair, sat next to her, and waited for her to start talking.

"Iain and I were friends at school," she sobbed. "Not sweethearts, but close friends. We talked about religion mostly. Well, he did most of the talking, I listened. He had some fascinating ideas. He was charismatic, even in those days. After leaving school he went away to study for the priesthood. We lost touch, and I met Richard. When Richard proposed I thought my life was perfect. It was a lovely surprise to learn that Iain Barrington was to officiate at our ceremony. But then, on the morning of the wedding, Iain tried to talk me out of it. He said he'd always loved me, but the priesthood had been his priority. Now he realised he'd made a mistake. I was shocked and confused. I couldn't cancel the wedding at the last minute, so I married Richard."

Her tears dripped one by one onto the table.

"I wanted the marriage to work, but I couldn't stop thinking about Iain. So one day I decided to confess. I thought Father Evans was taking confessions that day, but it was Iain. I should've left there and then, but he begged me to wait. He reminded me that God works in mysterious ways. He told me how he felt about me, that he couldn't live without me. When I left that confession box I was in love with Iain Barrington. I couldn't help it." Her eyes pleaded for Angus's sympathy.

"Go on."

"By the following month I was pregnant. I knew it was...I knew you were Iain's baby. When I told him, he was appalled. He made me promise never to tell anyone. He said his career would be ruined, completely ruined. What could I do?

After you were born Richard was wonderful. He loved you from the moment he set eyes on you. But the happier Richard was, the greater the pain in my heart. I had to tell him, I had no choice. I had to tell him."

Angus shook his head.

"Richard took it badly. He was still wonderful with you, but he wouldn't talk to me at all. I pleaded with him, explained that it wasn't my fault, but it was no good. In the end I had to ask him to go. But he wouldn't leave you. Even after he knew he wasn't your real father, Angus, he loved you more than anything in the world."

A glimmer of hope entered Angus's heart. He knew at that moment that he must find Richard, must meet him, get to know him.

"We lived in silence. I thought I could cope, but eventually I fell apart. Then I met Callum. He stopped me in the street one day to ask if there was a cafe nearby. I showed him the way, and we drank a pot of tea together. He told me he worked at the prison. When we realised that he and Richard were friends I should've run a mile. But he was a wonderful listener. I talked and talked, it was such a relief. We met many times in that cafe. I didn't lie to him. He knew everything, the whole truth. When he told me he loved me, it was the answer to my prayers. You see, I couldn't have Iain, and I'd lost Richard. Callum arrived, like a knight in shining armour, to save me. He was a fine man. It didn't really matter that I wasn't in love with him. You do understand?"

"I'm trying to."

"At first Richard wouldn't even consider divorce. Then he said he would only leave if he could take you with him. He went to a solicitor, but there was no chance of him getting custody. He wasn't your real father. So he moved to England, and I've never seen him since."

"What about Callum? I never understood why he had to leave."

"It happened gradually, but over the years I became more and more involved with the church. I told myself it was God's will, but the truth is I wanted to be close to Iain. He was the only man I ever truly loved. Iain and I spent more and more time together. On church matters, you understand, nothing intimate. I wasn't going to make that mistake again. Callum was a fine man, and a good father to you, but it was never going to last. I'll never forget the day he asked me if I still loved him. I didn't know what to say. After that it wasn't long before he left. I broke that poor man's heart." She covered her face.

"Callum knew everything," said Angus, "the whole truth. He went into the relationship with his eyes open. He took a calculated risk and lost. No, Mother, it's not Callum you should feel sorry for, it's Richard. He's the real victim in all of this." Angus grabbed her hand. "I must see him! You have to tell me where he lives."

"No, Angus, that's not a good idea. At least, give it some time, until you've had a chance to think things through. After all, you've just lost your father."

"That devil wasn't my father!" yelled Angus. "Richard was my father. Where is he?"

She brought her palms together and looked up. "Oh God, help me, please."

"Where is he, damn you?!"

"Richard died, a year ago," she howled. "He drowned."

"No!" roared Angus, his hands covering his ears. He jumped up, kicked his chair across the kitchen, and ran out of the house.

CHAPTER 38

Ten minutes after leaving his mother's house Angus was parked in a lay-by, a quarter of a mile from Kessock bridge. Leaving the keys in the ignition, he got out and walked the rest of the way.

Angus reached the centre of the bridge and leaned over the barrier. The tide was out. Good, he thought, the drop to the water is much greater today. The wind was brisk, the waves choppy.

Angus gazed across the firth at the mouth of the Ness. He imagined what it would feel like to fly low across the water like a shag, skimming along the river towards St Mary's Church.

He had no idea where Father Barrington had killed himself, but pictured him hanging above the St Mary's pulpit. Angus knew that his rejection of the priest may have prompted his suicide. He didn't care.

A car slowed down as it passed, almost coming to a halt before accelerating away. What if someone stops, thought Angus? Better get on with it. He lifted one foot onto the top of the barrier and held the position for a moment, allowing one last thought to enter his mind. He thought of Richard. Richard drowned, his mother had told him. It was fitting that he was about to die in the same way.

"The water's rough," said a voice behind him. "I'd rather not have to go in after you, Angus, if it's all the same."

Angus turned to find a man wearing a tartan shirt. "Who the hell are you? And how do you know my name?"

"It's a long story," replied the stranger.

"You're not my guardian angel, are you?"

"What?"

"That's a relief. For a moment I thought I was going mad."

"No, Angus, you're not going mad."

"Anyway, it was nice knowing you." Angus turned back to face the water.

"I'm here on behalf of your sister."

"I don't have a sister."

"She's your half-sister. Her name is Alice. She'd like to meet you."

Angus froze. What sort of trickery is this, he thought. Surely Mother doesn't have any other children. An appalling idea flashed into his mind. How many illegitimate children has that swine Barrington been responsible for? They would all be my half-brothers and sisters. "I don't want to know," he replied.

"Her dad was Richard Alexander, your mother's first husband. Your father."

Angus's supporting leg weakened. He toppled backwards onto the ground. The stranger helped him up.

Angus thought he recognised the man's face. "You're that magician, aren't you?"

"That's right. My name's Harry Hart. And I've just pulled off my greatest ever trick!"

Harry walked Angus back to the lay-by. "I'll drive," he said. "I'm going to show you one of my favourite places."

He took Angus to Inverness Castle. They sat on a steep grass bank overlooking the Ness. Harry told Angus all about Alice. He took from his pocket a photograph of a man carrying a baby.

"It's me," declared Angus, "and Richard."

"Yes."

"My mother said he drowned. Do you know what happened?"

"It was an accident. He was raising money for his wife Sofia's cancer treatment."

"Did she get better?"

"I'm afraid not. Alice is an orphan."

"That's a shame."

"It is. She's lost both parents. But she's found a brother."

"I'm not her brother," insisted Angus. He told Harry about his mother's liaison with Barrington.

"That's astonishing," said Harry, "but it won't make any difference to Alice. She's in love with the baby in that picture. She's desperate to meet you."

Angus considered this. "No, it won't work. Alice sounds special. I'm not the kind of person she'd want to know."

"What on earth do you mean by that?"

"I'm a waste of space, Harry, and a fool. The world would be a better place if I'd never been born."

"I doubt that."

"I have no purpose, I have no friends. I hurt everyone who cares for me. I hate myself."

Harry put a hand on Angus's shoulder. "I've been around long enough to know if someone's a waste of space. You don't even come close."

"You don't know me, Harry."

"That's true, but..." Harry paused. "Did you ever watch Rainbow Moon?"

"What, the children's programme?"

"That's right."

"Never seen it."

"Oh," replied Harry, clearly disappointed. "I was on the show for over a year."

"Sorry."

"No matter. I did this thing called Harry's Golden Rules. Each week I'd tell the kids one of my rules about life. You know, how to treat other people, that sort of thing."

"Was it a religious programme?"

"God no! Why do you ask?"

"No reason."

"Anyway," continued Harry, "what I'm trying to say is, I'm not a bad judge of character. My first impressions are usually right."

"Usually?"

"Okay, let's see how you match up. Rule number one. 'Be honest'. Are you always honest, Angus?"

"Even when I shouldn't be."

"Fair enough. Rule number two. 'Do your best'. Do you always do your best?"

"I try to. But my best isn't usually good enough."

"Hmm. Rule number three. 'Be true to yourself'. Do you live your life according to who you are, and what you believe?"

"I'm sorry, Harry, I don't really know who I am. And what I believe keeps changing."

"We're not doing too well, are we? Okay, number four. 'Make the most of each day'."

Angus shook his head. "Let's skip that one."

"Number five. 'Be kind to others'."

Angus remembered with anguish his recent encounters with Stix, Stella and his mother. He stared silently at the river, tears welling up.

"Let's jump to number ten," suggested Harry, "the most important rule of all. 'Recognise the value of love'. That's something you understand, isn't it? Something you feel inside."

Angus threw his arms around Harry's neck and cried into his tartan shirt. "Help me," he bawled. "Please, help me."

Harry drove them to his hotel. "You're staying here tonight where I can keep an eye on you. As long as you don't mind sharing a double bed."

"You do know I'm straight?"

Harry screamed with laughter. "Of course I do, you silly boy! Anyway, you're not my type."

Harry rang for room-service. They sat on the balcony drinking Sauvignon Blanc.

"Tell me your life's story," ordered Harry.

"Not much to tell."

"Never mind that, I want to hear it all."

Angus talked for hours. Finally he said: "That's it, a mess from start to finish."

"You're not finished," replied Harry, sharing the last few drops of their third bottle of wine. "There's a long way to go, and a lot to learn."

"But what's the point? When it comes down to it, Harry, what's the point of anything?"

"If you're asking me about the meaning of life, I don't understand."

"There you go. Even my guardian angel doesn't have the answer. What hope have I got?"

"No, Angus, what I'm trying to say is, I don't understand the question. What is the meaning of life? You might as well ask, what is the colour of life? It's a question that doesn't make sense."

"It's you that's not making sense."

"There are gurus out there who'd like us to believe that understanding the secret of life's meaning requires great wisdom. The truth is there is no secret. We all have the power to discover meaning for ourselves. The power to build our lives as we see fit."

"Where's the handbook?" asked Angus.

"There isn't one. Well, that's not strictly true. There are hundreds of good philosophical guides. The trick is to learn from other people's mistakes so you don't have to make the same ones yourself."

"There are too many mistakes waiting to be made."

"That's no reason to give up. We just have to keep learning, and keep helping each other along as best we can."

"You make it sound so simple, Harry."

"That's because it is."

"No it's not. If it wasn't for you I wouldn't even be alive now."

A look of pain crossed Harry's face. "Let me tell you something. I was locked away in prison for over a year, for something that wasn't my fault. It was a living hell in there. I thought I was going to die. Then Alice came along. She saved me, saved my life." Harry wiped away a tear. "Now it's my turn, to help you. And so it goes on. One day you'll get the chance to do something amazing for someone. Possibly someone you haven't even met."

"I hope so."

"Life's a struggle, Angus, of that there is no doubt. But it's worth the effort, as long as we all follow the rules."

"Harry's Golden Rules?"

"Exactly!" They clinked glasses.

"Trouble is," admitted Angus, "my life consists of my music and not much else. I was aiming for stardom. Now I don't care if I never pick up a guitar again as long as I live."

"Dreams, Angus, dreams. They're a nightmare. We have a vision that after years of hard work we'll enter a paradise of our own making and live happily ever after. I should know, that was me for the first part of my career. Sacrificing the best years of my life for a future that wasn't guaranteed. It never entered my head that I could find happiness in the present. Until I met Grant. Then I couldn't imagine how the future could be better than what we had." Harry paused. "I also learned not to trust the future."

"What happened?"

"Car crash. I lost the only man in the world I will ever truly love. At least I was with him when he died."

"I'm sorry."

"Don't count on the future, Angus. Live now while you have the chance."

"I'll try."

"Take it from me, it's the special relationships in our lives that really matter. The rest is just distraction. Only fools neglect the ones they love because they're too focused on their dreams. I fell into that trap once. I nearly lost Grant because I wasn't paying him any attention. Work was taking up all my energy. He left me. That day my life changed." Harry smiled. "He played hard to get for a while, to teach me a lesson, but I deserved it. I never made the same mistake again."

"Shit."

"What's the matter?"

"Identical story," groaned Angus.

"What's her name?"

"Jess."

"Go after her, you idiot. Win her back!"

"She's engaged," sighed Angus, "I've left it too late."

"Never mind. You'll find someone else."

"No, Harry, I lost the only girl in the world I will ever truly love."

"That's ridiculous." Harry closed one eye. "I see what you've done there. Very clever. We've both made up our minds that we're going to spend the rest of our lives alone. That is ridiculous, isn't it?"

Angus nodded.

"Are you sure you're not gay?" teased Harry.

They both slept like logs on the double bed.

Harry woke Angus with a cup of tea. "Rise and shine! It's time to start the first day of the rest of your life."

"Sod off," growled Angus. "Just leave me here to die."

"Oh dear. Looks like someone drank most of the wine. Fancy a slice of cold pizza?"

Angus gave Harry the middle finger.

"Come on, drink some of this tea."

Angus dragged himself into a sitting position, blinked a few times, and took the cup. "It's your fault I'm still alive, you tosser."

"Think nothing of it. Actually, I'm glad I saved you. I'd like to thank you, Angus. I've been mulling over what we said. There must be someone else out there, someone special. There's got to be. I fell into the trap of believing I was a victim of fate, that I'd lost control of my life. Fate is a seductive concept. The truth is, I did lose control of my life, but I can get it back if I choose to. Then anything's possible. Thanks to you, my destiny is back where it belongs...in my own hands."

"My pleasure," murmured Angus.

"And I realise now that I've been blaming Grant's murderer for my sadness. Sooner or later I've got to take responsibility for that sadness and do something about it. It's within my power to change my attitude, and I must do it, or spend the rest of my life feeling sorry for myself."

"And you learned all this from me?"

"I've been approached by my TV company. They want to resurrect the show, but I've been too frightened to make a decision. The way my luck's been going, what if it all goes wrong? I told myself my career had been murdered as well as Grant."

"You're gonna say yes to the show?"

"You're damn right I am!"

"That's great. Now there's only one of us without a future."

"You've got a future, Angus, trust me. You're a guitarist, that's where your future lies."

"That was all a stupid dream."

"There's nothing wrong with dreams. But why not use your talent now to do something worthwhile. How about teaching music to disadvantaged kids? Imagine the difference you could make to their lives. Set yourself a future goal by all means, but living in the future's not enough. Live now, Angus. Make every day count."

"Will do, Oracle."

"So...what am I going to say to Alice? Will you meet her?"

Angus twisted up his face. "I don't know, Harry. I need to think about it."

CHAPTER 39

"Get in there!" screamed Tom, as his spirited shot sent the football flying into the top corner of the goal despite Charlie's heroic dive.

"I bet you can't do that again," smiled Charlie, picking himself up from the grass and rolling the ball back to Tom.

"Did you see that, Mummy?" yelled Tom at Bonny, who was sitting with Alice at a wicker table which supported a large jug of liquid matching the colour of its woven willow.

"Great shot," replied Bonny, despite not having seen the ball fly in.

"I'll do it again, watch!"

Tom carefully placed the football, took four measured steps back, then rushed forward, wellying the ball miles over Charlie's head. It flew down the steep garden and over the fence, landing in the stream which trickled across at the bottom of the slope. The goalkeeper set off to retrieve the ball.

"Ready for a top-up?" asked Bonny. Without waiting for a reply, she poured Alice more Pimm's, along with several chunks of strawberry, orange and cucumber.

"I love your garden," purred Alice, admiring the manicured lawn, the weed-free flower beds, and Bonny's collection of stone ornaments. "He's ugly!" she grimaced, pointing at a hideous gargoyle which was squatting in front of a stunning mass of purple and white dahlias.

"That's Griff," advised Bonny. "Tom couldn't stop laughing when he spotted him at the garden centre, so Leo…went back and…"

Time to change the subject, thought Alice. "Charlie's brilliant with Tom, isn't he?"

"He's been so wonderful. I couldn't ask for a better brother. But then he's always been great with children. He's a natural."

"Charlie's so quiet most of the time, but he comes to life with Tom."

"He's like that with all the kids. He's going to make a wonderful father one day."
Bonny paused. "Charlie's been even quieter than usual recently…and I suspect
I know the reason." She touched Alice's hand. "I think Charlie might be falling in
love."

Alice blushed.

"I suppose I shouldn't say anything," continued Bonny, "but it's no good waiting
for Charlie to tell you. He's so shy, he's never asked a girl out in his life!"

"I find that hard to believe. Any girl would be lucky to have such a lovely man.
The fact that he's gorgeous doesn't do any harm either."

"I've told him he's got to say something soon, otherwise he'll miss his chance.
He's going back to the circus in a week or so."

"As soon as that?"

"The thing is, Alice, Charlie's hoping that you might go with him, for a while at
least, to see how you-"

"Goal!" shouted Tom. "Come on, Mummy, are you playing?"

"Not me," replied Bonny, rising from her chair. "I've got to get lunch ready, unless
you want to starve." She turned to her companion. "You'll play, won't you, Alice?"

"It's a long time since I kicked a football," mused Alice. "I used to have a mean
shot though, when I was in the school team."

"We'll take turns," instructed Tom. "Charlie prefers being in goal."

"If you say so," grinned Charlie.

Tom placed the football in position and moved aside. Alice got up, took a step
back, then tore towards the ball, belting it at the centre of the goal.

"Aargh!" screamed Charlie, as the ball thumped into his face before looping
down the garden, clearing both fence and stream with a single bounce. Blood
ran from both sides of his nose.

"Sorry!" yelled Alice, covering her mouth with both hands. "Are you alright?"

Bonny, who had witnessed the accident through the kitchen window, ran out with
a box of tissues. She handed the box to Alice with a wink, waving her towards
her stricken brother. "Come on, Tom," she said, "time for a glass of lemonade."

Alice nursed Charlie until the bleeding stopped, then gently dabbed his face until
most of the blood had been removed. "No more footy for now," she suggested.

"I think you're right," muttered Charlie, examining the blood stains down the front of his shirt. "I'll pop in and get changed."

"Bring out the dinosaurs!" pleaded Tom as Charlie went past him.

Alice gave Tom a quizzical look.

"Charlie's teaching me how to juggle," explained the boy. "I can juggle three dinosaurs, all at the same time," he added proudly.

Charlie soon returned carrying a set of six multicoloured bean bags, each in the shape of a miniature stegosaurus.

"Me first," chimed Tom, grabbing three of the dinosaurs. After a series of false starts, he managed to keep all three up in the air for all of twenty seconds.

"Well done," said Charlie, "you're improving."

"I've been practising," beamed Tom. "Are you going to show Alice some of your tricks?" He handed the three dinosaurs back to his teacher.

"Maybe later," replied Charlie, glancing towards Alice with the shyest of smiles.

You're so cute, thought Alice, managing for once not to verbalise her opinion. No…you're adorable.

After lunch there was no way that Charlie was going to escape from displaying his skills. Picking up all six dinosaurs, he moved to the centre of the lawn to commence his demonstration. Alice watched, mesmerised, as Charlie sent the creatures cascading through the air for a full minute before catching them all with his hands behind his back.

"That was amazing!" she thrilled, clapping her hands.

"You should see him juggle nine at the same time," said Tom.

"Maybe later," responded Charlie.

"Are you going to have a go, Alice?" asked the boy.

Alice screwed up her face a little, tilting her head to one side. "It looks very difficult."

"You start with two dinosaurs," explained Tom, grabbing Alice's hand and pulling her out of her chair.

"Okay," she replied, smiling at Charlie, "I'll give it a go."

"Show Alice the same way you showed me," suggested Tom.

Charlie's face reddened.

"Turn round," said the boy, pulling one of Alice's arms until she was standing with her back to Charlie, then pushing her so that her back rested against his chest.

Charlie held his arms forward, one either side of Alice's body, a dinosaur in each hand. "You start like this," he advised, tossing one bean bag into the air with his right hand, then lobbing the second from left hand to right, before catching the first one in his left palm.

"Can you show me that again?" asked Alice, who was finding it difficult to concentrate with Charlie's stubbly jaw brushing her ear.

After Alice's first juggling lesson was over, Bonny led Tom inside to help her with the washing-up.

"We'd better fetch that ball," said Alice, taking Charlie's hand and leading him down the garden.

"The water's deeper than I thought," she observed after they'd climbed over the fence and reached the stream.

Alice leaned forward to slip off her shoes, but before she could do so she was whisked into the air by a pair of powerful arms. She sat sideways, leaning against Charlie's chest as he carried her across the stream and placed her gently down on the opposite bank.

Alice gave Charlie a hug before kissing him softly on the lips. "Charlie?" she asked. "Would you take me with you to see the circus?"

CHAPTER 40

The last of the stack of 78s dropped down the spindle onto its neighbour with a slap. The arm swung across and plonked the stylus into the groove. Billie Holiday sang Stormy Weather.

Sammy took a swig of whisky. He held the bottle up to the light to examine the last precious drops in the base. Putting the mouth of the bottle to his own, he twisted his wrist to invert it, and waited for the drops to find his tongue. He counted them, an increasing interval elapsing between each one and the next. After twelve he gave up, tossed the bottle over his shoulder, and waited for the sound of shattering glass. The bottle bounced off the wall without breaking.

Stormy Weather ended. The Dansette had long been temperamental and the arm failed to lift automatically from the shellac disc. Sammy nodded his head in time with the clicks. He hugged the fluffy white toy bunny he'd bought for Emily but hadn't given her.

I need another drink, he thought. With superhuman effort he hauled himself up from the chair. The room whirled around his head. He gripped the bunny tight and waited for the spinning to stop. It didn't.

The next thing Sammy knew he was coming round on the floor. His forehead throbbed. He rubbed his hand across the painful area and examined the smears of blood on his fingers. He instinctively grabbed the bunny and held it tight against the wound.

The room started to spin again. Sammy screwed up his eyes.

After some time he reopened them. The red and white bunny was lying forlorn on the carpet. Sammy touched his forehead. The bleeding had almost stopped.

I'm sure I had another bottle, he thought. Where the hell did I put it?

He crawled around the flat on his hands and knees, searching for the lost bottle, leaving a red trail wherever he went.

"I must've thrown it out by mistake," he groaned to himself. He crawled towards the front door. It was his last hope.

Sammy kept a walking stick by the door. He managed to hook the door handle and pull it down. He heaved himself backwards to allow the door room to open. After several deep breaths he dragged himself into the courtyard where his wheelie bin lived. He hooked the bin with the walking stick and brought it crashing down next to his head. The lid flew open, the contents erupting onto the pavement. Sammy commenced his search.

"'Ave you lost summat, Sammy?"

He was too drunk to recognise the voice.

"D'you need any 'elp?"

Sammy gazed up at the visitor's face which eclipsed perfectly the morning sun. A corona of light surrounded her head. "Have you come to carry me to Heaven?" he murmured.

"You what?"

"Don't bother," he sighed. "I don't believe in Heaven, so I doubt they'll let me in."

"Hah! You think ah'm an angel, do you? A fallen angel, maybe."

"There's a bottle in here somewhere," groaned Sammy. "Help me find it, will you? I need a drink."

"Ah think that's the last thing you need, by the looks o' you. Cum on!"

She steered him back inside and onto his bed.

Sammy's head lay heavy on the pillow. "Stay with me," he pleaded.

"Ah'm not goin' anywhere, Sammy."

He fell into oblivion.

Early next morning Sammy regained consciousness. "That's disgusting," he whined, sticking out his furred tongue.

"You've bin sick int' night," explained Kylie.

"Not again. Any blood?"

"Everywhere!" she cried.

"I mean blood in the vomit."

"Ah don't think so."

"Thank God for that," gasped Sammy.

"'Ow's your 'ead?"

"Don't ask. Have you got any vodka?"

"No, Sammy. But ah found 'alf a bottle o' whisky in your cupboard." She got up and went into the kitchen.

"Hallelujah, there is a God. Bring it here, will you?"

"You're too late," she called. "Ah poured it down t' sink."

"No!"

She reappeared with a glass of milk and a plate of sliced bread. Sammy retched.

"Cum on, Sammy, you've got t' 'ave summat. If you don't, ah'm callin' the ambulance."

"No way, I've had enough of hospitals."

"Cum on then." She picked up a slice of bread.

"I'll try, in a minute." He gazed at her face as she put the plate and glass down. "What on earth are you doing here, Kylie?"

"Ah've missed you!"

"I'm serious. You should be in Scotland, starting a new life."

"Ah don't think Scotland's all it's cracked up ta be."

"Why?"

"The men may 'ave a sexy accent, but they're not very nice. Well, not the ones ah met anyway."

"That's hardly surprising. You don't exactly meet an average cross section of the population in your job."

"It's not me job, Sammy. Ah've always met the wrong kind o' fellas, ever since ah wur a kid. It's my fault...it must be."

"Don't be silly, Kylie, you-"

"Ah thought it might be different if ah made a fresh start. But..." Her eyes were moist.

"Come here," he said, offering an arm.

She kneeled by the bed and wrapped her slim hand around his thumb. "Ta tell you the truth, Sammy, the only time in me 'ole life ah felt safe, wur the short time ah spent wi' you. You're a luvly man." She kissed his cheek. "An' you're a laff!"

"You really are an angel, Kylie. Thank goodness you've come."

"Just in time, if y'ask me. What the 'ell's 'appened ta you, Sammy?"

"After Suzie threw me out, I started drinking more than was good for me. Before long it was out of control."

"Lyin' ont' ground, sortin' through the rubbish lookin' fur your last drop o' booze!"

"I really have hit rock bottom, haven't I? But it doesn't matter. I've got nothing left to live for."

"'Ang on, what about your daughter?"

"Emily? I have to forget about her. Look at the state of me. I can't stand the thought of Emily being ashamed of her father."

"But she luvs you! She'll understand. You said the two of you wur gettin' close."

"I've stopped replying to her calls and texts."

"No, Sammy, you can't just give up."

"I told you, there's nothing left to live for. Emily will be better off without a big fat waste of space in her life. And nobody else cares about me."

"Ah care about you," she urged, squeezing his thumb. "You've bin good ta me. An' ah feel safe when ah'm wi' you. It's a nice feelin'. Ah'd like ta feel like that all the time."

"I don't think I can-"

She pressed her index finger to his lips. "You're like a dad ta me, Sammy. You're the dad ah never 'ad." She hugged him. "Now cum on 'n 'ave sum o' this bread."

He managed a nibble.

"You might've lost your way, Sammy, but at least you 'ad one ta lose." She handed him the glass of milk. "Until you're back on your feet, ah'm gonna watch you like an 'awk. You 'aint touchin' anuther drop o' booze while ah'm around."

"Forget about me, Kylie. You've got your own life."

"You call this a life! Ah'm a prostitute. Ah'm a nobody."

"Then give it up."

"What?"

"Give it up," he pleaded. "Please."

She hesitated. "Tell you what, ah'll do a deal wi' you. Ah'll stay off the streets as long as you stay off the booze. 'Ow d'you like that?"

"I'd like that very much. But I can't promise-"

"Ah mean it!" she snapped. "One drop an' ah'm back at work."

"Okay," he agreed, "I'll do my best."

"That's more like it. An' when you're back on your feet ah can work for you, in your office. It'll be me first proper job."

"Don't get your hopes too high. I've never made much money."

"You're jokin'," she cried. "You should be makin' a packet in your line o' work."

"I feel embarrassed charging people who are desperate for help."

"Embarrassed? Fur Christ's sake! My customers are desperate, but ah charge 'em the goin' rate. They get a bloody good service. Ah bet your customers do an' orl."

"I always do my best," shrugged Sammy.

"Exactly." Her face lit up. "Tell you what. Ah'll be in charge o' the books. Ah'll make sure you get paid all right." She shook his hand.

Sammy remembered something. His face turned grey.

"What's the matter?" she asked, withdrawing her hand. "Don't you want me ta work fur you?"

"Of course I do. But it's not that simple. Emily's found herself a new job…"

"Good for 'er."

"…in Norfolk."

"Crumbs, that's the middle o' nowhere!"

"At first she decided not to take the job," explained Sammy. "She told me she didn't want to risk us losing touch."

"That girl must think the world o' you."

"It's a brilliant opportunity for her. I told her she'll regret it if she lets it go."

"Are you goin' ta follow 'er then? Move ta Norfolk?"

"I don't know," he sighed.

"Ah'll cum with you."

"What? Are you serious?"

"Ah'm not lettin' you out o' me sight, Sammy. Anyway, I could do wi' a fresh start!"

CHAPTER 41

Tom Jones was in fine voice as ever.

Alice sang along. "My, my, my, Delilah, na na na na na na na na na. Why, why, why, Delilah, na na na na na na na na na. So, before, they come to break down the door, forgive me Delilah I just couldn't take any more." The trumpet solo started as she pulled into the car park.

Alice entered the Lakeside Clinic for the last time. She glared at Diana Foster's photograph and stuck out her tongue. I don't suppose you'll miss me, she thought. I certainly won't miss you.

She was halted in her tracks by the realisation that one of the photos was missing from the board. "You bitch!" she spluttered before covering her mouth. "You could've waited," she muttered, "'til I've actually gone."

Alice had no appointments. It was a morning for clearing her desk and saying goodbye to some people who'd become special friends.

At noon Alice was in the main office, a small glass of Chardonnay in one hand, a large sausage roll in the other. Her colleagues were spread around the room, chatting away to each other. She gazed from one face to another, realising for the first time how much she was going to miss them.

A solemn Diana Foster entered. One by one the staff became aware of her presence until silence reigned.

"Hello, Miss Foster," said Alice. "How are you?"

Miss Foster nodded at Alice, then cleared her throat to address the room. "On an occasion such as this, it falls to me to say a few words."

This should be interesting, thought Alice.

"I think it's true to say that Miss Alexander's time with us has been...eventful."

"It certainly has!" blurted Alice. She covered her mouth. "Sorry."

One corner of Diana Foster's mouth twitched. "There were a few...teething problems at first." She coughed. "But it's fair to say that...the Lakeside Clinic is losing a...a valued member of the team."

A round of applause broke out. Miss Foster nodded once more at Alice, stepped forward to shake her by the fingers, and retreated to her own room.

"Short and sweet," said Alice.

"Not short enough," said one of the girls.

After the party Alice said her goodbyes and was soon out in the car park dressed in her running gear. For the very last time she trotted through the gap in the hedge.

Since the injuries she hadn't bothered timing her runs. That meant she was better able to enjoy the scenery, and less likely to trip over natural or man-made obstacles.

After the run it was back to the house to spend the afternoon doing housework for Esther.

The doorbell rang. Alice burnt the tip of her finger on the iron. She plonked it down, licked her finger, and ran to open the front door. She threw her arms around Harry's neck and squeezed tight.

"Woah!" croaked Harry. "Pleased to see me?"

Alice relaxed her grip and ushered Harry into the house. "I've been on tenterhooks since you phoned. You said you've got news about Angus?"

"Settle down and put the kettle on," he teased, waving her away.

Alice managed to get two mugs of tea and a plate of tartan biscuits on the table within a couple of minutes. "Come on, Harry, what've you discovered?"

Harry picked up a biscuit, took a nibble, and beamed. "I'm a clever so-and-so."

Alice trembled with anticipation. "Well?" she begged, with a series of tiny nods.

"After you told me that your dad worked in a prison up in Scotland, I started thinking. This fellow who went off with his wife, what if he was a colleague of your dad at the prison? It seemed a good shout to me. People in those sorts of jobs tend to socialise together, don't they?"

"I suppose so."

"So I thought I'd do a bit of detective work. I had a tough time in Watertown prison, but I did get on with one of the officers. His name's Graham. We sort of clicked straight away." Harry blushed.

"Oh yes?"

"If it hadn't been for Graham I wouldn't have survived."

"You nearly didn't."

"He's a gem. Anyway, Graham and I got together for a drink a couple of weeks ago, and I told him about Angus. He offered to talk to some of the older officers, the ones who knew your dad, to see what he could find out."

"That's great."

"I told you, he's a gem. He got back to me a few days later. It turns out that, before moving to Watertown, your dad worked at Porterfield prison, in Inverness."

"Thank you so much, Harry. I must go there."

"No need, I've already been."

"What?!"

"I've performed in Inverness dozens of times. I've got a lot of friends there."

Alice smiled. "Of course you have."

"It took a few days, but I managed to track down an old colleague of your father. A fellow called Wojciech Ostrowski."

"Are you pulling my leg, Harry?"

"He's Polish, ex-RAF. He flew Hurricanes in the Battle of Britain."

"Wow."

"Retired years ago. He's getting on a bit now, but he remembers your dad. They were great friends."

"What did he say?"

"He remembers the whole thing. Richard's first wife was called Isla."

"Isla?"

"She was quite a catch, according to Wojciech. All the guys fancied her. The man who took her from your father was called Callum MacMicking."

"MacMicking? Are you sure that's a real name?"

"Yes, and it's rare. Very rare."

"Callum and Isla MacMicking," said Alice. "If I can find them, surely they'll tell me where Angus is."

"No need."

"Oh my God, I see. Angus's surname is MacMicking."

"Exactly. I've been on the net. Your brother's a guitarist. He's in a band called Spear Thistle."

"You're kidding!"

Harry handed Alice a piece of paper. On it was written www.spearthistle.com.

"I can't wait to go online and see what he looks like."

"He's a fine-looking man," grinned Harry, "especially face to face."

Alice was gobsmacked. "You've met my brother!" she screamed. "Tell me all about him."

CHAPTER 42

"Thanks to all you wonderful folks for joining us here at the Rainbow Theatre for the final Spear Thistle gig." Angus grinned as a mixture of enthusiastic cries and disappointed groans met his ears. "Okay," he yelled, "let's have some fun!"

Cheers filled the hall. Stix tapped a stick against the rim of his snare drum to set a tempo, then cried, "One, two, three…" as the duo launched into their rendition of the Z.Z. Top classic Sharp Dressed Man. The final gig was underway. The Rainbow rocked.

A few numbers into the set Angus noticed a girl with burnt orange hair in the audience. Unlike the rest of the fans she wasn't dancing or jumping around. She stood serene, watching him perform, betraying no sign of emotion other than the hint of a grin. Angus was distracted. He tried to ignore her during the next few numbers but his gaze was drawn to her more and more. He thought he detected a broadening of her grin each time they made eye contact. Maybe, he thought, she's just enjoying the show. Or maybe…maybe she's pleased to have my attention.

During the interval Angus peeked around the curtain to get a better look at the girl. There she stood, on the same spot, gazing in his direction. Their eyes met. She smiled. A definite smile this time. Angus pulled his head back behind the curtain.

The second half got going with B.B. King's Better Not Look Down. Angus found himself singing to the girl, as if the rest of the crowd had faded away. "Better not look down, if you want to keep on flying, put the hammer down, keep it full speed ahead. Better not look back, or you might just wind up crying, you can keep it moving if you don't look down." He sang with a flutter in his heart, conscious more and more of a strange connection with this enigmatic lass.

After three encores the show ended. Angus and Stix came down from the stage to hug and shake hands with their loyal followers. Angus watched the mystery girl from the corner of his eye. She studied him as he moved amongst the fans. He was too nervous to go near her.

In time, almost everyone had left the hall. Stix was chatting with Stella. The girl was rooted to her spot. Angus jumped onto the stage and grabbed a towel to wipe his brow. He threw the towel down and turned to find her standing in front of the stage, just a few feet away.

"Hello," said Angus. "Do I know you?"

"I hear you're looking for a new drummer," replied Alice.

"Can you play?"

"No, but I'm a quick learner!"

Angus grinned. He sat down on the edge of the stage. "Is there something I can do for you?"

"You can take me for a walk if you like."

During the next few weeks they went for many walks together. There was a lot to discuss, a lot to discover. At first Alice did most of the talking, but she gradually coaxed Angus out of his shell.

One day they were passing a boatyard on the far side of Watertown Lake. Three geriatric rowing boats sat neglected at the water's edge.

"They used to keep several boats here when I was a girl," said Alice. "These days kids are too busy playing computer games to bother with having fun."

"That's our good fortune," declared Angus. "What d'you think?"

They paid for half an hour, choosing the boat with the least water in its bottom. Alice rowed first.

"Careful!" cried Angus as a splash flew from one of the oar blades into his face. "You did that on purpose."

"Ha, ha! Don't worry, it's water, not acid."

When it was Angus's turn he lulled Alice into a false sense of security with some faultless strokes before chopping an oar at the surface, showering her from head to knees.

"I'll get you for that!" Alice leaned out of the boat with a cupped hand and sent several sprays in his direction.

Angus let go of the oars to shield his face. The water kept coming, so he threw his weight from side to side to give Alice something else to think about.

"Hey," she screamed, "stop it!"

Within moments the inevitable happened and she was in the lake.

"Hooray!" yelled Angus as he threw himself in after her.

They splashed around until Alice started to shiver. She swam back to shore while Angus clambered into the boat and rowed it home.

The boatyard man had a supply of beach towels. The pair sat on a bench, towels over their shoulders, gazing out across the lake.

"I'm gonna miss you when you go back to Scotland," protested Alice.

Angus stared silently across the water.

"Have you decided when you're leaving?" she asked.

"Soon," he replied, leaning forward to rest his face on his palms.

"What's wrong?"

"Nothing," he murmured.

"Come on, what is it?"

Angus turned to look into Alice's eyes. "The last few weeks with you have been…"

She put an arm around him.

"Before we met I'd forgotten how to laugh. When I'm with you I want to laugh all the time. I'm in a wonderful dream, but soon it'll be time to wake up. I'm not sure if there's anything to wake up for."

"You've got a lot to look forward to, Angus. You're a talented musician with a great future ahead of you."

"Nothing good will ever happen to me. I don't deserve it."

"What on earth does that mean?"

"You don't know me, Alice. Not the real me. I'm thoughtless, selfish."

"We're all selfish creatures at heart."

"You don't understand. I'm a bad person."

"If you really believe that, then do something about it. Become a good person."

"I don't know how," whimpered Angus. He buried his face in his hands.

Alice didn't know what to say. She gave him a long hug.

The following day they walked with linked arms through the gates of Watertown cemetery. For the first time Alice approached her parents' graves without feeling lost, without feeling alone.

Angus looked on as Alice tended the graves, following her every move. Once she'd finished they stood quietly together. A robin landed on Richard's gravestone and eyed them both.

"Dad adored birds," she said. "One of my earliest memories is of him in the garden, coaxing a robin onto his hand."

"He was lovely man," sighed Angus, "I'm sure of it."

"He was special. Not just to me. The world was a better place with him in it."

"That's something you've inherited," he whispered.

"I don't think so," blushed Alice.

"All I know is, for the first time in my life, I've found someone I feel comfortable with." He squeezed her hand.

The robin jumped down from the gravestone and tugged at a worm.

"My money's on the robin," quipped Alice.

They watched as the robin won the contest and flew off with its prize.

"You know," said Angus, "in my heart, Richard is my real father. I never met him, but I do love him."

"He loved you too, didn't he?"

"I hope so. I wish I could ask him."

"I think you know the answer."

Angus brightened up. "Never mind, I've got an adorable new sister." He tickled her ribs.

"We'll see about that," giggled Alice, punching him in the side.

"Ouch!" He grabbed her wrist with one hand and encircled her waist with the other, wrestling her into submission.

"Bully!" she cried.

Angus rested his head on Alice's shoulder for a moment, eyes closed. He released his hold and took a step back.

"Do you mind if we walk over to see Jamie?" asked Alice.

Angus held back as she approached the grave. He waited quietly while she chatted to Jamie, filling him in on the latest news.

"Bye for now, Jamie," she concluded. "See you soon."

They walked arm in arm towards the gates.

"Jamie must've been a great guy," said Angus.

"He was the love of my life."

Angus remembered his conversation with Harry on the subject. "Do you think there's only one person in the world for each of us?"

"I used to think so, but now I'm not so sure. What do you reckon?"

"After I lost Jess I was certain I'd never find love again. Then a wise man advised me to keep an open mind."

"Very wise."

"Yes, he is."

CHAPTER 43

"I can't believe I've got all my favourite people with me," said Alice, "in the same place, at the same time." She gazed with delight around the circular table tucked into a quiet corner of the Old Siam restaurant.

Alice held out a hand to each side. One was taken by Angus, the other by Charlie. Bonny, looking gorgeous in a red low-cut dress, sat directly opposite, between Paul and Harry.

"Well, I will have," continued Alice, nodding at the only empty chair, "once Esther escapes from her meeting."

A traditionally dressed Thai waitress appeared from behind an elegant teak dividing screen carved with lattices of lotus flowers and elephants. With poise she lit the candle and took the orders before floating away.

Alice picked up her glass of sparkling wine. "I'd like to propose a toast." The others raised their glasses. "To the newly engaged couple, to Bonny and Paul."

"Bonny and Paul!" came the replies from around the table.

"You'll be next," declared Bonny, grinning across at Alice with raised eyebrows.

Alice's face and neck became hot.

"I knew it," chuckled Bonny, "she's blushing." They all laughed. Bonny lifted her glass. "Alice and Charlie."

"Alice and Charlie!" responded the others.

"So, Alice," teased Harry, "will you be joining the circus?"

"I don't think so," grinned Alice. "What could I possibly do? I can't juggle, I can't tumble, and I certainly don't fancy the trapeze."

"You could learn to eat fire," suggested Paul.

"No thanks," replied Alice, "I've played with enough fire for one lifetime."

Everyone nodded.

"I'm staying put," she continued. "However, I do have some exciting news for you all. I've done it. I've quit my job."

"Fantastic," said Harry. "Now I can train you up to be my new assistant."

"I'll be too busy," chuckled Alice. "As planned I'm going to open my own detective agency. It's what I've dreamed of, ever since I was a child."

"Well," said Paul, "they say that women make the best detectives."

"Of course they do," confirmed Bonny, slapping the back of Paul's hand.

"I'm not just talking about missing persons and cheating partners," stressed Alice. "I want to get my teeth into the juicy stuff as well. The forensic side."

"How do you know it'll suit you?" asked Harry. "Are you sure you have all the right skills?"

"I think so. I'm determined to find out."

"Good for you," declared Paul.

"I'm not foolish enough," continued Alice, "to dive in without a life jacket. If there's one thing we've all realised, it's that we can't always look after ourselves, solve our problems, without help. We've certainly learned the value of teamwork. It took teamwork to get the better of...you-know-who..."

Paul took Bonny's hand.

"...and I can honestly say that, without you guys, I wouldn't have survived the last few months."

"Thank goodness you did, sweetie," said Harry.

Alice leaned across to pinch Harry's cheek. He winced.

"Sorry, Harry," she giggled, "I think I'm turning into my Auntie Coula."

Harry rubbed his cheek.

"So what I'm leading up to, is that I'm asking you all for your help."

"Anything," replied Bonny and Paul in unison.

"I don't mean that I want you all to give up what you're doing and work for me. It's just that I'd like your advice and support, and sometimes your practical help, whenever you're available to give it. We all have our own particular skills. I've got my psychology training. Paul, you have your police background with all the knowledge that's brought you. Bonny, you've got so many talents, and I'm sure you could get any man to tell you his darkest secrets."

"That's true," said Paul, glancing at Bonny.

"What about me?" asked Harry.

"You'll be invaluable," said Alice, "since you know so many influential people. Especially now you're back on television. Likewise you, Angus. Now that you're rehearsing with your new drummer, the sky's the limit."

"We'll see," said Angus.

"And as for you, Charlie, your job will be to keep me grounded, keep me on an even keel."

"I'll do my best," he replied.

"You've decided to leave the circus?" asked Bonny.

Charlie shrugged, nodding.

"So, what do you say people?" asked Alice. "Are we a team?"

From all around the table came replies of, "Absolutely!" and "Of course!"

Alice raised her glass. "Here's to a long and rewarding partnership. Here's to teamwork."

"Teamwork!"

The following morning Alice and Angus were on the road to Scotland.

"Excited?" asked Angus as he drove the Crossfire across the border at Gretna Green.

"Very much," said Alice. "And nervous. I've never been to Inverness. It'll be weird seeing the places where Dad used to live and work."

"Are you sure you want to meet my mother? I told you, she's not the easiest. Maybe it's not such a great idea."

"You're my brother, Angus. I want to meet your mother whatever she may have done to my dad. I don't blame her for what happened. Anyway, if she'd stayed with him I'd never have been born."

"I'm not actually your brother though, am I?"

Alice slapped him on the arm. "Of course you are! You're the only brother I've got, so I'm not letting you off on a technicality."

They took the scenic route via Loch Lomond, Glencoe and Fort William. When they reached the southern tip of Loch Ness, Angus stopped the car to put the soft top down.

"There's no rain in sight," he said. "It's less than forty miles to Inverness, and most of that is along the banks of Loch Ness. I'll drive slowly so you can watch out for Nessie."

Alice gazed across the deep blue loch, occasionally closing her eyes to enjoy the breeze caressing her face. Her first time in Scotland and she was already in love with the country.

They arrived at Inverness. Angus took Alice on a tour past the castle, the prison, and the football ground. He pulled the car into his lay-by.

"Why are we stopping?" asked Alice.

Angus pointed ahead. "There's a lovely view from the centre of the bridge."

They stood together on Kessock Bridge, arm in arm, enjoying the majestic views in every direction.

"This is heaven," purred Alice.

Angus kissed her cheek.

"The fresh air's making me hungry," she said.

"Fancy some haggis?"

"Errr...no offence, but I'd prefer a pasta."

They drove to a small trattoria for spaghetti pomodoro followed by gelato.

They got to Angus's place at midnight.

"Are you sure you'll be okay sleeping in the basement," asked Alice.

"It won't be the first time. Come on, I'll show you up to the bedroom."

"Thank you so much, Brother," said Alice as she reached the top of the stairs, "for a wonderful day." She turned to face Angus who was standing one step below her. She put her arms around his neck and hugged him tightly.

Angus couldn't sleep. He played his acoustic, softly so as not to disturb Alice.

The morning sun found a gap in Alice's curtains. It cast a bright line across her eyelids to wake her up. She wandered downstairs to find Angus slumped in a corner of the basement, guitar on lap. She crept back to the kitchen to see if there was any food in the house. She found some bread in the freezer and a tin of baked beans on the shelf.

Angus appeared at the instant breakfast was ready. "Let's go out into the garden," he mumbled. "I could do with some air."

They sat on the grass, under an apple tree, eating their beans on toast.

"Did you sleep well?" he asked.

"Like a log. How about you?" She could see the answer in his heavy eyes.

"It wasn't a wasted night. I've written a new song."

"How wonderful! Will you play it for me?"

Angus's face turned red. "I'm not sure that-"

"Please."

Alice grabbed Angus's hand and led him down to the basement. She picked up his guitar, kissing him on the cheek as she lifted the strap over his head.

Angus strummed a chord, coughed gently, and began to sing.

> I was crying in my lonely world,
> Lost in misery and so afraid,
> In stepped you,
> To take my pain away.
> I was dying in my lonely world,
> My morality I had betrayed,
> In stepped you,
> To chase my shame away.
> Only you could show me the light,
> Only you could help me to fight,
> And I thank you.
> Only you could show me the way,
> Only you could turn night to day,
> So I ask you,
> Lady will you be my friend?
>
> Now my world has turned since you arrived,
> Thanks to you that I'm still alive,
> So I know,
> I should not hope for more,
> But there's a brand-new ache I feel inside,
> That I fear can only be denied,
> Cause I know,
> You'd surely show me the door.
> Only you could show me the light,

Only you could help me to fight,
And I thank you.
Only you could show me the way,
Only you could turn night to day,
So I ask you,
Lady will you be my friend,
Lady will you be my friend,
Baby will you be my friend.

Alice held her breath as the final echoes of the melody drifted away. Finally she gasped for air. "That was beautiful." She stepped forward to kiss Angus's cheek.

He stood silent, motionless.

She kissed the other cheek.

He kept perfectly still.

Alice moaned as she threw her arms around Angus's neck and kissed his lips.

He responded, arms around her body, pulling her towards him.

They jerked apart.

"This is wrong," cried Alice.

"We should never have met," moaned Angus. "I have to take you home."

CHAPTER 44

"I knew you'd like them," said Alice as she decorated Jamie's grave with salmon pink begonias. "Sorry I haven't seen you for a while, but I've had a lot on my plate recently."

A jet passed overhead, leaving condensation trails in its wake. Alice paused, following it with her eyes until the drone of its engines faded. She wanted to make sure that Jamie could hear what she was saying.

"Things are going fine between Charlie and me. I hope you're not too jealous. You'd definitely like him, Jamie. He's a good man, without a single fault. Well, I haven't discovered any yet. Actually, he reminds me a lot of you. Not as handsome maybe, and not quite as tall. But just as gentle as you, just as kind. I think he's going to propose soon. Two engagements in two years, eh? I must be quite a catch."

After a long chat with Jamie, Alice said goodbye and drove home to get dinner ready for Esther and herself.

"How's Charlie getting on with his new job?" asked Esther, pouring two glasses of Pinot Grigio.

"Not too bad," replied Alice, taking a sip of the chilled wine.

"Give him time. He'll be fine."

"I hope so. It's just that…"

"What is it?"

"He misses the circus so much. He talks about it a lot. His new life is so different, Esther. I don't know if he'll get used to it."

"As I said, give him time. Look at Bonny, she's perfectly happy with town life."

"That's different. She's had a long time to adapt. And she's got Tom."

"That's it," chuckled Esther, "you need a baby! Come to think of it, that's not such a bad idea. It would help settle Charlie down. He's definitely the paternal type."

A profound sadness overcame Alice.

"I know that look," said Esther. "What's wrong?" She put her glass down. "Are you in love with Charlie, Alice?"

A tear emerged in Alice's eye. "I want to be. I really want to be, but…"

"There's something missing?"

"I just don't know."

"If you ask me, you haven't been right since your little trip to Scotland."

"No, Esther, nothing happened in Scotland. Nothing."

"Are you absolutely sure about that?"

"It's impossible," moaned Alice, her tears now flowing. "We're not meant to be together."

"Tell me why it's impossible. Angus is not your genetic brother." Esther paused. "Oh, I see. You've got no actual proof that he isn't your half-brother. You only have his mother's word, and she's a bit screwy from what you've told me." Esther straightened. "I've got it. Why don't you ask him to have a DNA test? That would prove it, one way or another."

The hint of a smile passed Alice's lips.

"You've already done one, haven't you?" spluttered Esther. "You rascal! How did you get a sample?"

"I managed to collect a few strands of his hair, before the Scotland trip."

"You sneak. I take it the DNA was negative?"

Alice nodded.

"There you are then. It's not impossible at all, is it?"

"What about Charlie?" sighed Alice.

"It sounds harsh, but Charlie will get over it. And you said yourself he's not happy away from the circus."

"Even if I was free, Esther, that doesn't mean…"

"Don't be daft. I'd be surprised if Angus isn't already crazy about you. If he isn't he soon will be."

"It's two weeks since we went to Inverness and he hasn't contacted me."

"Then contact him, you fool."

"It's too complicated." Alice covered her eyes.

"There's something else, isn't there?"

"I don't want to talk about it."

"Don't be ridiculous, Alice! I'm your mentor, remember?"

Alice hesitated. "I was in Carlisle two days ago, for a meeting with Sammy Rice."

"The chap who's handing over his detective agency to you?"

"That's right. I was walking past a cafe, around the corner from Sammy's building, and…there they were, sitting in the window."

"Who?"

"Angus, and a girl."

"What? Did you recognise her?"

"No. Seeing them put me in a spin, Esther. I didn't know what to do. I walked around like a headless chicken for a while, then…"

"What happened?"

"I had to speak to him. I couldn't help myself, so I went in. Angus turned white when he saw me. I knew straight away I'd made a mistake, but it was too late. I sat with them and had a coffee."

"Who was the girl?"

"Her name's Kylie. I think they've known each other for some time."

"There you are, she's just an old friend."

"But he's never mentioned her. Not once."

"She's not that important then, is she?"

Alice's shoulders sagged. "She's very important, I know it. You should've seen them together, before I disturbed them. Laughing and joking, holding hands. They're in love, I'm sure of it."

"Oh."

"I told you, Esther, we're not meant to be together. My future is with Charlie. And you're right…I need to get pregnant, as soon as possible."

CHAPTER 45

The phone rang. Alice peered across the desk at Sammy. He nodded at the phone.

Alice cleared her throat and picked it up. "Mr Rice's office, Alice speaking. Errr... how can I help you?"

"I'm being followed," said a female voice. "It's been going on for months. I've told the police, but they won't listen."

"Who do you...errr...who do you think is following you?"

"If I knew that I wouldn't need your help, would I?"

Alice took down the caller's details and made her an appointment. She put the phone down. "How did I do?"

"Not bad," replied Sammy. "But remember what I said about keeping your cool. You've got to sound confident on the phone, otherwise you'll never get any work."

"I don't feel confident."

"That's not the point! The customer needs to believe that you're in control, that you can handle anything that's thrown at you."

"Okay, Sammy, I'll get there eventually. As long as you're here to show me the ropes."

"You've got me for another couple of weeks max," he said, lifting both arms and gesturing around the room, "then all this is yours."

"Do you think I'll be ready?" she sighed.

"You'll have to be. The sign writer's been booked to do the door next week. I had to pay in advance. Alice Alexander, Private Investigator. Cost a fortune."

"Aaargh!"

"Not having second thoughts, are we?"

"No, Sammy, I'll be fine. I'm sure I will."

"You'll be in good company. There are more and more female PIs around these days. Mind you, it wouldn't suit every woman. Most of them are more interested in finding themselves a man and having kids."

"Not me, Sammy. The men in my life have given me nothing but grief. I'm single, and I plan to stay that way."

"What, no fella?"

"Not any more."

"Well, sweetheart, if you ever get lonely at night, just give me a call."

"Cheeky bugger!"

"I'm serious."

"I bet you are. No, Sammy, it's too risky. What if I fall for you? You'll be off in a week or two, leaving me broken-hearted."

"I suppose you're right," he smirked. "Which reminds me. One or two of our neighbourhood villains are not exactly chuffed with life at the moment. Have you heard of Micky Sullivan?"

"No."

"Local gangster. He's been rearrested on a murder rap. Leo Mason was in charge of the original investigation. He almost certainly suppressed evidence so that Sullivan could escape justice. I reckon there'll be other similar cases."

"Leo Mason is an evil man," shuddered Alice.

"You don't know the half of it. I'm told he had a network of unofficial underworld contacts and informants that he'd built up over several years."

"Like Robbie Johnson?"

"Right, though he was small fry. I asked Robbie why he stayed undercover even after Mason was jailed. He replied that he'd been ordered to keep his head low, and Leo Mason wasn't a man to disobey."

"Can we change the subject?" groaned Alice.

"Good idea."

"So," she said, "you'll soon be off to Norfolk. Sounds lovely. A bit flat though."

"Perfect for me. No hills."

"Have you found somewhere to live yet?"

"Kylie's down there as we speak, looking at a few places."

Alice's heart missed a beat. "Who's Kylie?"

"I forgot, you haven't met her. Kylie's a Yorkshire lass who's coming to Norfolk with me to help set up the new business."

"I...I see," stuttered Alice. "How long will she be down there with you?"

"It's a long-term venture for both of us. That's the plan anyway."

"Won't her boyfriend have something to say about that?"

Sammy chuckled. "Kylie's having a break from men at the moment."

"Sensible girl," sighed Alice. "You say she's in Norfolk looking for a place?"

"We won't need much to start with. Just a couple of bedrooms and an office. As long as it's not too far from Emily's house." Sammy grimaced and rubbed his belly.

"Are you okay?"

"It's nothing, just my indigestion. I'll pop down to the shop and get some milk."

"Yes, Sammy, if you can get past the Queen's Head without going in."

"No way! My drinking days are over, Kylie's made sure of that. She's changed my life completely. I've never felt better."

Sammy disappeared down the stairs.

The phone rang.

"Cool," said Alice to herself, "confident." She picked up the receiver. "Mr Rice's office, Alice speaking. How can I help you?"

Silence on the line.

"Hello," said Alice.

"Hello," returned a Scottish voice.

Alice almost dropped the phone. Cool, she thought, confident. "How can I help you?"

"I have a personal problem I'd like to discuss," said the voice. "Do you have any free time today?"

"One moment please, I'll check my diary...yes, I do appear to have some availability today. Are you able to come to the office? I prefer to discuss problems face to face, if that's agreeable."

"I see." He rang off.

"Shit!" spluttered Alice. She thumped the desk.

She thought she heard a noise downstairs, but it was masked by the banging of her heart. She listened. The lift was on its way up. Sammy's back, she thought. He didn't go into the Queen's Head.

She heard the lift door open.

"Face to face is better for me too," said Angus, standing in the doorway, acoustic guitar in hand.

"Do come in, Mr..."

"Please, call me Angus."

Alice got up and floated round to the front of the desk. "Okay, Angus. Would you like to tell me about your problem?" She sat back against the desk.

"It's like this, Miss..."

"Please, call me Alice."

"It's like this, Alice. I'm in love with a girl. I've been in love with this girl since the very first moment I set eyes on her. I didn't know how to tell her, so I wrote her a song. But the song didn't have the desired effect."

Alice was desperate to disagree, but was struck dumb.

"So I decided to add some extra lines. If I play you the song, would you be kind enough to give me your opinion?"

"Yes please," Alice whispered.

> I was crying in my lonely world,
> Lost in misery and so afraid,
> In stepped you,
> To take my pain away.
> I was dying in my lonely world,
> My morality I had betrayed,
> In stepped you,
> To chase my shame away.

Only you could show me the light,
Only you could help me to fight,
And I thank you.
Only you could show me the way,
Only you could turn night to day,
So I ask you,
Lady will you be my friend?

Now my world has turned since you arrived,
Thanks to you that I'm still alive,
So I know,
I should not hope for more,
But there's a brand-new ache I feel inside,
That I fear can only be denied,
Cause I know,
You'd surely show me the door.
Only you could show me the light,
Only you could help me to fight,
And I thank you.
Only you could show me the way,
Only you could turn night to day,
So I ask you,
Lady will you be my friend,
Lady will you be my friend,
Baby, will you be my…
One more thing my heart has to say,
Darling please please show me the way,
Cause I love you,
Tell me how this story ends?

Angus peered longingly into Alice's eyes.

"The song is perfect," she murmured. "There's only one thing missing."

"What's that?"

Alice rushed at Angus, jumped up onto her toes, and kissed him for all she was worth.

WATERTOWN POST

Wedding With a Difference

I'd be surprised if any of our readers have ever attended a wedding ceremony complete with serenading groom, a knife-throwing bridesmaid and a performance by a nationally acclaimed magician. If that all sounds intriguing, read on!

Miss Alice Alexander from Watertown and Mr Angus MacMicking from Inverness were married at noon on 14th October on the plush lawn behind the private residence of Mr Harry Hart, much loved magician and one of Watertown's most celebrated residents. The bride and groom tied the knot in front of Mr Hart's giant statue of Michelangelo's David, overlooking the garden lake. David was wearing a kilt for reasons of modesty.

The bride, dressed in a stunning satin and lace wedding gown, entered on the arm of the kilted Mr Hart, to the melody of Spring by Vivaldi. Matron of Honour was Mrs Bonny Ireland, wearing a sky blue ruched bodice midi dress. Bonny's eleven-year-old son Tom, dressed in a dapper cobalt blue suit, ably performed the role of page boy.

During the ceremony Angus, on bended knee, accompanied himself on guitar as he sang a heartfelt song of love to his bride. There was not a dry eye present.

The wedding breakfast was served on the lawn under the hazy glow of an Indian summer sun. To the delight of the party Harry Hart performed a range of magic tricks, one of which climaxed with page boy Tom disappearing into thin air. Bonny Ireland then stunned everyone with an awe-inspiring exhibition of knife throwing.

The entire party was in stitches during the speeches given by Mr Hart and best man Mr Paul Ireland, husband of Bonny. In a break with tradition the bride made a short speech in which she expressed her sadness at the absence of her late parents, Mr Richard Alexander and Mrs Sofia Alexander. Angus's father, Mr Callum MacMicking, was present at the ceremony. His mother Isla was unable to attend due to ill health. The bride and groom are planning to visit her soon with a delivery of wedding cake.

The bouquet toss provided a moment of hilarity. The bouquet sailed over the heads of the young maids present, into the unprepared grasp of the bride's old friend and mentor Miss Esther Williamson.

The happy couple will enjoy their honeymoon on the idyllic Isle of Skye. On their return they will set up home here in Watertown, from where Alice will commute to her office in Carlisle where she has established her own private investigation agency. I understand that Paul Ireland, who is an ex-policeman, will be employed by the agency. Angus will continue to front the up-and-coming duo Spear Thistle, having secured the services of talented drummer Neil Murton.

After the wedding I was fortunate enough to obtain an exclusive interview with Harry Hart who confirmed that, in true Scottish tradition, both he and David had 'gone commando' for the wedding. He talked about the renewed success of his television show, and revealed his plans to give Spear Thistle their television debut early next year.

Remember, you heard it here first.